PRAISE FOR *SE*

"*See You at the Finish Line* sparkles with romantic tension and humor. Somehow managing to be both hopeful and wry, this book is opposites-attract at its most rewarding. One of the best romances I've read in a long, long time!"

—CARA BASTONE,
national bestselling author of *Promise Me Sunshine*

"*See You at the Finish Line* is the kind of sporty romance that will leave readers swooning. As Hammett's characters test the romantic waters with one another, the 'will they or won't they' vibes make the book impossible to put down. Sexy, surprising, and sharp-witted in all the best ways. Once you cross the finish line, you might just be tempted to start all over again."

—CHAD BEGUELIN,
author of *Showmance*

"Filled to the brim with smart wit and delicious tension, *See You at the Finish Line* is a must-read!"

—HANNAH BONAM-YOUNG,
USA Today bestselling author of *Out on a Limb*

"A fast, fun and cinematic crowd-pleaser that had me smiling—and my heart racing—until the very last sentence!"

—CALE DIETRICH,
internationally bestselling author of
The Rules of Royalty and coauthor of *If This Gets Out*

"*See You at the Finish Line* is a charming, sexy rom-com with a relatably spiky short king and a himbo you'll fall in love with. I raced through it (if you'll pardon the pun)."

—PJ ELLIS,
author of *We Could Be Heroes* and *Love & Other Scams*

"I loved this book! A sizzling, funny, and sweet read set in the ultracompetitive world of the Oxbridge Boat Race. I was completely engrossed in George and Lucas's journey from enemies to lovers. Zac Hammett has crafted a truly smashing rom-com and I can't recommend it enough. Bravo!"

—ELIZABETH DRUMMOND,
author of *The House Sitter*

"If you thought the only thing *Red, White & Royal Blue* was missing was some strenuous activity, Zac Hammett's delicious debut is your new favorite romance—sharp wit and crackling sensuality, propelled forward in the competitive world of juicy Oxbridge rivalries."

—JUSTINIAN HUANG,
author of *Lucky Seed* (and former Oxford exchange student)

"I had so much fun with *See You at the Finish Line*—Zac Hammett is officially brilliant. It had all my favorite rom-com tropes, as well as being funny, clever, and so epically readable. I loved everything about it and can't wait to see what Zac writes next."

—LUCY VINE,
author of *Hot Mess* and *Book Boyfriend*

"Equal parts riotous humor and delicious chemistry, *See You at the Finish Line* is a charmingly good time. From the page-turning slow-burn romance to the brilliant moments of self-discovery and self-confidence, George and Lucas's triumphant love story will have readers cheering until the very end."

—JULIAN WINTERS,
award-winning author of *I Think They Love You*

"Hammett makes an effervescent debut with this enemies-to-lovers sports romance. With amusing banter between the leads and sexual tension aplenty, this diverting contemporary is a triumph."

—*Publishers Weekly*, starred review

SEE YOU AT THE FINISH LINE

SEE YOU AT THE FINISH LINE

ZAC HAMMETT

SLOWBURN

A zando IMPRINT

NEW YORK

zando

The characters and events in this book are fictitious. Any similarity to real persons, living or dead, is coincidental and not intended by the author.

Copyright © 2025 by Zac Hammett

Zando supports the right to free expression and the value of copyright. The purpose of copyright is to encourage writers and artists to produce the creative works that enrich our culture. Thank you for buying an authorized edition of this book and for complying with copyright laws by not reproducing, scanning, uploading, or distributing this book or any part of it without permission. If you would like permission to use material from the book (other than for brief quotations embodied in reviews), please contact connect@zandoprojects.com.

Slowburn is an imprint of Zando.
zandoprojects.com

First Edition: September 2025

Design by Neuwirth & Associates, Inc.
Cover design by Christopher Brian King and Ash Tsai

Cover illustration by Ricardo Bessa

Oars art by iconfield from Noun Project

The publisher does not have control over and is not responsible for author or other third-party websites (or their content).

Library of Congress Control Number: 2025936718

978-1-63893-331-1 (Paperback)
978-1-63893-359-5 (ebook)

10 9 8 7 6 5 4 3 2 1
Manufactured in the United States of America
LBK

FOR VINCENT

As the two oldest and most prestigious universities in the UK, Oxford and Cambridge have a rivalry that stretches back centuries. In 1829, a Cambridge student challenged his friend who was studying at Oxford to a rowing race. Almost two hundred years later, the tradition is still going strong . . .

1

LUCAS

DON'T LOOK OUTSIDE THE BOAT. That's all I can think right now. Don't look outside the boat. It's a shame, since I must have the best view in the house. To the left of me, the Oxford crew are poised in menacing silence. Behind them, a small flotilla of boats containing the umpire, TV crew, and various VIPs. On the banks of the Thames, a crowd of people ten or twelve deep. At least, I assume there is. I can't look, but I can hear them, chanting out rival slogans as they sip on their plastic pint glasses and shuffle impatiently in the crisp March air. It still feels crazy to me that a student rowing race can attract this much attention. But I mustn't start thinking like that. If I don't look, none of it's real. Don't look outside the boat. Don't look. Don't look. Don't look.

There's only one problem with not looking outside the boat. I'm the Cambridge cox, which means I sit in front of our eight rowers, shouting orders and steering with my rudder. Directly opposite me is George, our all-American boat club president, setting the pace in what's known as the stroke seat. I once read that if you look someone in the eye for four minutes straight, you risk falling in love with them. George and I have conclusively disproved that theory. It's mad to think how many hours the two of us have spent sitting opposite each other in the boat like this over the past year. I know every inch of George's face; the sweep of his neat blond side parting that melts mothers' hearts, the masculine brow and perfectly proportioned cheekbones that remain tanned year-round, the stoic expression behind his gray-blue eyes. He looks like a model—mainly because he is one. In his underpants no less, plastered on billboards around the world. You'd think that would make him arrogant beyond belief, but it's much worse: George is a people pleaser, desperate to be liked by everyone he meets.

"Starting positions," booms the umpire over his megaphone.

Shit. George and the rest of the team slide forward on their seats and grip their oars. The crowd falls quiet. This is it. I look down the length of the boat to check that it's straight. The current is pulling us dangerously off course. I raise my hand.

"Waiting on Cambridge," the umpire announces.

George glances up and checks our position.

"We're good," he whispers.

What's his problem? Steering is my job. I look back down the line. "No we're not."

Every single person lining the course or watching on TV is waiting for me to get on with it. But we need to start perfectly straight or we'll risk crashing into Oxford.

"We're good," George says again.

"Wait," I insist.

I look down the boat one more time, but now I'm doubting myself. Are we straight or not? Why doesn't George trust me?

"When you're ready, Cambridge," the umpire says pointedly.

"Trust me, we're good," says George, giving the umpire a big goofy thumbs-up.

I stare at him. "What the hell are you doing?"

"Just letting him know we're all good."

"But we're not! What's wrong with you?"

George glances fretfully back at the umpire. I don't believe it. He doesn't want to annoy him.

"He's not going to give us extra points for starting on time, George. He's not going to pat you on the back."

"Lucas—"

"Let me get the boat straight."

"It is straight."

"No it's not."

"Yes it is!" George flashes me a kilowatt smile. "You got this."

I'm going to explode if he doesn't shut up. Now is not the time for a pep talk. Before I know what I'm doing, I lower my hand. Just like that, the umpire sounds his starting klaxon. The rowers start pulling on their oars, the crowd cheers like mad, and commands come tumbling out of my mouth. What I'm saying, I have no idea. I'm having some kind of out-of-body experience.

"Back off, Cambridge!" the umpire screams.

I snap out of it and glance to my left. The boat is off course. It's heading straight toward Oxford. I yank hard on my rudder.

"Fucking hell, George. I told you!"

George pulls on his oar and says nothing. Once the race gets going, the rowers are like pistons in a machine, sliding backward and forward with mechanical precision, not an ounce of energy to spare, let alone brain power. It's me who has to do the thinking. I glance over at Oxford. They're already half a boat length ahead. How is this happening? How is this the race we've prepared all year for? I have to act fast. The course is four miles long, but the advantage switches hands depending on who's closest to the fastest river current at any given point. I've memorized the course's fluctuations. If we aren't ahead by the halfway point at Hammersmith, we never will be. And Oxford's lead is increasing.

"We need to do a push," I say to George. "Ready?"

A push means cranking up the stroke rate so high that the rowers might not have anything left for the rest of the race. As George slides forward on his seat, I can see the beads of sweat on his forehead, the capillaries bursting in the whites of his eyes.

"It's too early," he splutters.

I stare back at him, rage pulsing through my veins. What's he worried about now? Upsetting our coach by deviating from the race plan? I'm not an idiot. Doing a push this early is a hell of a risk. But it's now or never.

"It's not too early," I scream. "Now push! Push! Push!"

I hear a ripple of excitement pass through the crowd as the boat speeds past Thames Rowing Club. A lot of the real fans gather here, on the first half of the course, not at the finish line, by which point the race has almost always been won or lost.

As I shout at the rowers to crank up the stroke rate, I feel the boat begin to glide through the water. We're edging closer to Oxford. Is this the moment the tables turn? I glance to my side. Oxford have hit back with a push of their own. They've re-established their lead without a struggle. If anything, it's bigger than before.

I can already feel our rowers tiring. I can see it on George's face. I bring the crew back down to their regular stroke rate and glance at the Oxford boat. There's clear water between us. My gamble failed. Worse, our spirit has been broken.

Nothing is more demotivating than a bad push.

I try to rally the team, knowing there are still nearly ten minutes left of this torture. But I can see the Hammersmith Bridge approaching, the point at which we conclusively lose our advantage.

The race is over, and everyone knows it.

. . .

I close my eyes and feel the water hit me. The shower is too hot, painfully hot, but that suits my mood. I've been warned many times how bad it feels to lose the Boat Race, but it's done nothing to prepare me for the sheer sense of waste. All that training, all that anticipation, for nothing. At the end of the race, the rowers were physically spent to the point of collapse. I felt equally depleted, but I knew it was my job to get the team away from the cameras and back into the boat house. I couldn't bear to look George in the eye as we rowed over to the shore. Neither of us said a word. Arriving at the boat house, we received a pitying round of applause from our friends and family, which only made the humiliation worse. Compared to that, this shower is heaven, and I feel like everything will be all right if I can just stay underneath it forever.

"Guys," says George, "gather round."

I open my eyes and scowl. George is standing in the middle of the changing room, a towel around his waist. We move toward him in various states of undress. When I first started rowing, I was self-conscious about all the casual nudity. But now I know these guys so well that I barely notice who's fully dressed and who's butt naked.

"Before we do the press conference," says George, "we need a team talk."

Everyone trades glances. Waiting for us upstairs is an annoyingly large number of journalists. Evidently, George wants to get our story straight before anyone goes off message.

"Firstly," he says, "A for effort."

The rest of the team ignore him. We're all still too raw for a positive take.

"Listen, we gave everything, and you can't ask for more. At the end of the day, there can only be one winner. It's as simple as that."

The crew nod vaguely. Wait, don't start agreeing with him. I might be the one who shouts orders, but George is the president, and people tend to follow his lead. I can feel the anger brewing inside me. Are we really not going to talk about what went wrong out there?

"So don't be too hard on yourselves," says George. "In fact, give yourselves a pat on the back. Next year, we can come back stronger—"

"Let's hope not," I snap.

Sometimes I just can't help myself. Everyone turns in my direction.

"What's that?" says George, his genial expression buckling.

"Let's hope we're not all back next year. Not if you're planning to fuck up the start again."

George blinks as if he literally can't comprehend that someone's criticizing him.

"You told me we were straight when we weren't," I insist.

"Come on, Lucas," says Johannes, "what's done is done."

Johannes is a six-foot-seven Swiss guy who does his country proud by remaining steadfastly neutral whenever there's a conflict.

"I gave my opinion," George says calmly. "That's all."

"I'm the cox. It's my call."

"You were freaking out! I was trying to help."

"No you weren't. You were desperate to start because the umpire was getting impatient, and nothing is worse to you than the idea of pissing someone off."

George is momentarily winded.

"He's right," says a glacially posh voice.

I look over at Tristan Barnes, who has turned from his usual pasty white to a bright shade of red. Tristan is a politician's son with a thick neck and beady eyes who inspires no love in any of the crew, but he's the only one who shares my dislike of our president.

"You don't question the cox, George. Not at the start of a race."

George can't handle being attacked from two sides.

"Look, Tristan, you're entitled to your opinion—"

Without warning, Tristan flings a shoe across the room and lets out a grunt of rage. We're all familiar with Tristan's mood swings, but George looks concerned to see that his strategy isn't working. I need to go in for the kill.

"Maybe your judgment was off," I say. "You got in pretty late last night."

George is wrong-footed but recovers quickly. "There were a lot of people at that dinner. I have responsibilities as president."

"Do they include that girl you left with?"

The rest of the crew breathe in sharply. Now the gloves are really off. But George remains calm.

"She asked me to walk her home."

"And shag her when you got there?"

"She'd had a long day."

"Oh, so now your shags are a charitable service?"

George glances down at the contents of his towel, then smiles at me breezily. "Don't knock it till you've tried it."

The rest of the crew ooh in delight. George has them in the palm of his hand.

I look him in the eye without flinching. "I'd rather kill myself."

I'm not sure that's strictly true. The first time I ever saw George, I had the same thoughts most people do when they meet him. I'm only human. But then we started working together, and believe me, those thoughts are in the past.

"Seriously," says George, "what's the big deal? If you were getting some, I'd be congratulating you."

That's a low blow and he knows it. My love life is a barren desert. As I glare back at him, I feel a surge of humiliation. Only now we're not in the middle of a race. Now there are no cameras. I look at George, take a deep breath, and charge straight at him.

. . .

Ten minutes later, we emerge for the press conference in our boat club blazers, cheeks flushed, hair wet but combed. George makes us wait until everyone is dressed so we can go upstairs as a united front, conscious as ever of the image he's presenting. It didn't take much effort for the team to stop me from beating George to a pulp. In fact, it was embarrassingly easy. That's the problem when you're almost a foot shorter than most of your teammates. Since coxes are technically dead weight, we tend not to be giants. As I stand sulking, Johannes tidies my hair and I want to cry. I'm trying not to look at George, but every time I do, I'm convinced he looks pleased. Me losing my shit appears to confirm the narrative that the race was all my fault. Presumably, George's only disappointment is that I haven't given him a black eye he can parade to the media.

The press conference is being held in the club room of the boat house where our squad has been based for the past week. As London is sixty miles from Cambridge, we're renting our boat house from King's College Wimbledon, one of London's most exclusive private schools. It still blows my mind that teenagers can have an entire facility like this on the banks of the Thames. At my school, we shared a football pitch with the local donkey.

The club room is a large, wood-paneled room whose walls are mounted with oars commemorating various famous victories, and numerous team photos commemorating the art of manspreading. As we step into the room, a dozen cameras flash. Our coach, Dame Deborah Hobbs, gives us a wooden nod. Despite the occasion, Deb looks the same as she always does: regulation tracksuit, hair sitting halfway between a mullet and a bob, and ruddy chapped skin that has never known the sweet caress of moisturizer. A quadruple Olympic gold medalist, Deb made waves in the rowing world when she was appointed coach of the Cambridge men's team. The pressure on her to succeed is immense, and she must be finding this just as painful as we are. Unfortunately for the assembled media, she's unlikely to elaborate on those feelings. As anyone knows who watched her infamous acceptance speech at the ironically titled *Sports Personality of the Year* award ceremony, Deb tends toward the monosyllabic.

A table has been set up in front of the rows of reporters with a cluster of microphones and only two chairs. Deb takes one of the seats reluctantly, while George dives in next to her. The rest of us line up behind them, our main function to stand there and look dignified in defeat. In charge of proceedings is an officious-looking moderator with a clipboard and a poorly executed comb-over. As he opens the floor to questions, an eager woman on the front row shoots her hand up.

"Deb—Helen Wheeler from *The Daily Telegraph*. Tough result for you today."

"Yes," says Deb.

Helen Wheeler stares at her. "Sorry, do you want to—"

"Only one question allowed," the moderator says briskly.

"But I didn't ask a question!"

The moderator is unbothered. This is a guy who lives for the rule book. He gestures at the next reporter.

"Neil Ronaldson from *The Times*. Can you tell us what the race strategy was today?"

Deb looks at him blankly.

"No."

There's a murmur among the reporters. This is ridiculous even by Deb's standards. She must really be hurting. The next reporter thinks long and hard before asking his question.

"Deb, what do you think Cambridge could have done differently?"

Deb pauses for an equally long time before answering.

"Lots."

The reporters are on the verge of mutiny.

"If I may," George says.

The reporters turn their attention toward George. As the cameras flash in his direction, he blossoms like a flower.

"We don't comment on specific tactics," says George, "but I can say that we prepared for every eventuality and executed our strategy to the best of our ability."

The reporters nod gratefully, which gives George the approval he's craving.

"George, can you tell us what was going on at the start of the race there?" asks the next reporter. "Looked like there was some disagreement between you and your cox."

It's taking everything in me not to pipe up and make some headlines.

"No disagreement," says George. "We were making sure the boat was straight."

"But it wasn't," says the reporter. "We could see that. Was that the cox's fault?"

Everyone holds their breath. Not even the moderator is objecting to the follow-up question. I brace myself. If George had any dignity, he'd admit to his mistake. Instead, he's about to throw me under the bus and end my rowing career.

"Absolutely not," says George. "Lucas had a flawless race. The start wasn't the issue. Oxford beat us because they had more power than us. It's as simple as that."

. . .

Our friends and family are still gathered on the terrace they watched the race from—a large, first-floor balcony that has been decorated with sponsors' banners and balloons in Cambridge's official shade of light blue. The boat club struggled so hard to find a sponsor who wasn't tangentially complicit in global warming or arms dealing that we've ended up being sponsored by a brand of toothpaste. As we appear at the terrace, the guests stop their chatter and offer another half-hearted round of applause. There's only one thing that's going to make any of this remotely bearable, and it's the free bar. As I head toward it, I feel a tap on my shoulder and spin around.

"Hi, Lucas. Helen Wheeler from *The Daily Telegraph*."

"What are you doing here? Press conference is over."

"I didn't get a chance to get your comments on the race. Could I just—"

"No. No comment."

I push past Helen Wheeler and look out across the crowd. It's events like this which remind me that rowing is not a sport for people who grew up like I did. It's for people who've been competing at regattas since boarding school. People whose fathers and grandfathers rowed for Cambridge. People who actively enjoy wearing blazers. I can see several former Cambridge rowers, or Old Blues, as they're so brutally called. One bloated man in his fifties is sounding off to some poor woman about the famous dead heat of 1877, while another appears to be demonstrating his rowing technique to a trio of baffled undergraduates by squatting on the floor. I can't decide what's more tragic—if these men in their ill-fitting blazers are former winners or losers.

Beyond them, there's Tristan and his father, a government minister who was sacked after an unfortunate hot mic incident involving a breastfeeding journalist. He looks positively delighted that it's his son who bears the stench of failure today. Tristan's father is much shorter than him, while his mother is a slim little apology of a woman, which suggests that Tristan is either a genetic abnormality or the result of an affair. Tristan is venting while his mother and girlfriend, Eleanor, work overtime to placate him and assure him that everything would have gone differently if he'd been in George's place.

As my gaze reaches the far side of the terrace, I see a familiar pair of big brown eyes and long dark eyelashes and my heart almost stops. Amir.

Amir is a boy in my year at Cambridge who's been my crush for as long as I can remember. Look at him, standing there in an immaculately ironed shirt and chinos that perfectly frame his slender figure. He's always so elegant and flawless, like he's been groomed by a whole team of people. I'm not surprised to see him here—I've stalked Amir's social media extensively enough to know that he's come to support Wilbur, his old school friend who rows for our reserve crew.

I wonder if Amir's noticed me. I'm too nervous to catch his eye. Maybe if I drink approximately forty-five cocktails, I'll have the courage to go over and—

"Lucas!"

I turn to see my mum waving at me. She's wearing the purple dress she reserves for special occasions. Next to her is my younger sister, Casey, who's also in a dress and heels, looking as if she's ready to follow through on her threat to audition for the next season of *Love Island*. I don't have a clue about women's fashion, but even I can tell they've both got it slightly wrong. The other women in the room are much more casually dressed, in crew neck sweaters and jeans. They look at home in a way my mum and Casey never could. My heart breaks for them, but I'm also embarrassed. I feel bad, but now I'm actively hoping Amir hasn't noticed me as I cross over and greet my family. There's no chance I'm going to mention their faux pas. We might be common, but we're still British.

"I'm sorry, Lukey," says my mum. "I know how hard you worked for this."

I nod and bite my tongue. Damn all these posh people and their stiff upper lips.

"Thanks," I say. "Bet you wish you hadn't bothered."

I'm secretly touched that my mum paid for a Travelodge for her and my sister that she really can't afford. After all that effort, the least I could have done was win.

"Of course we don't," says my mum. "It was very exciting."

"What happened?" asks Casey.

I cast around the room and see George talking to the *Telegraph* journalist. He's answering every single one of her questions without letting his smile slip once.

"He did," I say, pointing. "He screwed up big time."

"Ooh," says Casey. "Is that the underwear model?"

I'm about to launch into a rant for the ages when George glances across and catches us looking at him.

To my horror, he excuses himself and walks straight over.

"You must be Lucas's family," George says with a smile.

My mum thrusts out a hand for George to shake and ward off any chance of him being a hugger.

"Just had a chat with that reporter," George says to me with a wink. "Making sure she's got her story straight."

I raise an eyebrow at him.

"I'm sure you had her falling at your feet."

George turns to my mum and sister. "How proud are you of this guy?"

"They're giving me two out of ten," I say.

"Don't be silly," says my mum.

"Yeah," says George, "you did so well."

I look at him dryly.

"George, we lost."

"We almost won."

"No, we didn't. We came dead last."

"We actually came second, if you think about it."

"What, like Harold came second in 1066?"

George pauses to process that one.

"You should still be proud of yourself," he insists.

"Of course he should," says my mum. "We all are."

"Cool, how about you all be proud of me and I'll blow my head off?"

My mum rolls her eyes at me.

"Don't worry," she says to George, "we're used to this. Do you have family here?"

George betrays a flicker of sadness.

"No. We're a long way from Wisconsin."

"Oh well," says my mum. "Maybe they can come see you win next year."

"For those of us who are selected," I say pointedly.

George looks uncomfortable and glances across the room. "I should keep doing the rounds. Excuse me, ladies. It was so great to meet you."

As George walks away, my mum looks like she's had an audience with the pope. "What a lovely young man."

"Join the queue, Mum. His reputation is legendary."

My mum tuts. "It must be hard, not having your family here to support you."

"Seriously, Mum, don't get sucked in by George. He's the worst."

"Why? What did he do?"

"He's acting like he's doing me a massive favor by getting the press not to focus on the start of the race. When actually, he's doing that because he knows that if they do, they'll realize he fucked up. He's getting away with it, like he always does. He's not even a proper Cambridge student."

Casey frowns. "What do you mean?"

"He'd never have got his place if he couldn't row. They bring in these athletes who literally can't pass their exams."

My mum looks shocked. "That can't be allowed."

"It's not. Not officially. But both sides do it."

"Then . . . what's the problem? Surely you want the best rowers."

"Yeah, you'd think, but it's not that simple. You need to do more than sit in a boat and pull your oar. You need to be smart, and George isn't smart. He's not smart enough to know we weren't straight at the start. He's not smart enough to know when to do the push. He's not smart enough not to have sex the night before the race. And the worst part is, he's convinced he's right every time. Like idiots always are. Until we get people like him off the team, we're never winning."

My mum nods and pats my arm. She knows that all I want is to be heard. Casey glances behind me and her eyes widen. I turn to see what she's looking at. It's Helen Wheeler from *The Daily Telegraph*, standing right there, recording on her Dictaphone.

SUMMER TERM

APRIL–JUNE

2

GEORGE

BRITISH PEOPLE LOVE TO THINK Americans are dumb. Sure, we've had a few presidents that haven't exactly enhanced our international reputation, but that doesn't mean we're all like that. I felt it as soon as I arrived in Cambridge—these people think they're better than me. I see their eyes glaze over as soon as they hear my accent. But hey, what's that if not an opportunity to prove them wrong?

Cambridge University is divided into thirty colleges, where students sleep, eat, and get personalized teaching. Lectures and seminars take place in a central building with the rest of the people enrolled in your major, but college is where you have an hour a week of teaching in pairs, known as a supervision. I'm a member of Trinity College, the largest and richest of all the colleges. Which I didn't know before I applied here, but turns out Trinity attracts the type of student who won't settle for anything less than the biggest and best. No one exemplifies this attitude more than Eleanor, my supervision partner, who also happens to be Tristan's girlfriend.

I've tried to like Eleanor, I really have. And I get it—the economics course is full of dudes, and I'm sure she's met her fair share of condescending assholes. But boy does she love to take it out on me.

Each week, we're given an essay title, which we have to write up and then discuss for an hour with our supervisor. Professor Mishri is a warmhearted woman in her forties with a large collection of knitted cardigans and a light Midlands accent (I thought it was Welsh, but Eleanor corrected me). When I googled Professor Mishri before our first supervision, I found this awesome article she'd written about amusement arcades and told her it was the best economics paper I'd ever read.

Was it also the only economics paper I'd ever read at that point? Sure. But she didn't know that.

After the supervision, Eleanor told me I'd mortally offended Professor Mishri by overlooking her vitally important work on econometrics. And honestly, Eleanor's been patronizing me weekly ever since.

"Hey, George," says Eleanor. "Bad luck in the Boat Race."

"Thanks," I say. "How's Tristan taking it?"

Eleanor grimaces. "He destroyed a patch of daffodils."

"Oh well, it's good to get out that negative energy. We'll come back stronger next year. So will the daffodils!"

It's the morning after the Boat Race and I'm back in Cambridge, ready to start the week with a clean slate. Eleanor and I are walking across Great Court, a large, cobbled courtyard famous as the site of an annual race featured in this awesome movie from the olden days called *Chariots of Fire*, where students try to run all the way around the courtyard before the clock finishes chiming twelve. Great Court is flanked on one side by Trinity's ancient chapel and centered around an ornate stone fountain. As I recently said on Instagram, it's giving Cambridge.

"How did you find this week's essay?" asks Eleanor.

"Oh, I just looked up Professor Mishri's email and copied out the title."

Eleanor smirks. "Clever. What did you make of the question?"

"I didn't really understand it, so I did what they taught me to do in high school—leave it blank and move on to the next one."

Eleanor stares at me. "But there was only one question."

Professor Mishri has a large study at the top of a staircase that looks out toward the spectacular college library, designed by . . . Sir Jonathan Blackbird? Sir Nicholas Thrush? Sir Christopher Wren! That's it. Eleanor and I have barely taken our seats before Eleanor launches into a monologue about everything she's learned this week. Professor Mishri is kind of like a therapist who sits and listens, then makes one very incisive point. That works for Eleanor, because she doesn't have an off switch. She could probably talk uninterrupted for this whole hour about asset pricing, whereas I'm just proud of myself for knowing what that is. True, I'm supposed to have read five separate books on the subject from cover to cover, then summarized my findings in a two-thousand-word essay with a carefully structured argument that I can vigorously defend, but I generally don't manage to get the books out of the library, let alone write the essay.

When I was approached by a Cambridge rowing scout, he promised me I didn't need to worry about the academic side of things. Since then, I haven't had any reason to doubt him. Not when I turned up to my first lecture and didn't understand a word, not when I failed to turn up to my second lecture, or my third. As my first-year exams approached, my rowing coaches urged me not to lose any sleep over them. I opened my paper on British economic history and wrote down some of the things I'd read on Wikipedia the night before. When asked to cite a source, I quoted my friend's dad who works for the Bank of England. Two weeks later, I was told that I'd passed, securing my place for the following year. I don't need to know what went on behind closed doors.

Now you're probably thinking I deserve everything I get from Eleanor. But I do at least turn up to supervisions, and I try my best once I get there. Even when I haven't done the reading, or been to the lectures, or understood the assignment—which is to say, every week—there's something satisfying about being in the presence of someone who knows what they're talking about. I am of course referring to Professor Mishri. Usually, I try to pay attention to what she says even if I tune out of Eleanor's monologues. Today, I'm not even managing that.

The past twenty-four hours haven't been the easiest. I've kept my phone switched off. My grandma always says, if you don't have anything nice to say, don't say anything, but I can't be sure everyone got the memo. People in this country can be so negative. I'm sure Tristan is going around telling anyone who'll listen that it's my fault we lost, and the only way to avoid it happening again is for him to take my place in the stroke seat. He's obviously entitled to his opinion, I'd just rather not hear it. Johannes reckons he's jealous because I've been signed by a sports agency who want to turn me into the Tom Brady of rowing—their words, not mine. There's a master plan that culminates in me winning gold for the United States at the next Olympics and signing multiple seven-figure branding deals. But I'm sure they'll understand that losing the Boat Race is a minor blip.

The only person whose opinion really matters is Deb. She will have watched the race footage dozens of times by now, listened back to the audio recordings from Lucas's cox box, and had multiple conversations with her staff about whose fault it was. I'm confident she'll have concluded that I wasn't to blame.

Either way, I think I'll leave my phone off for a few more hours. It's not like Deb is the type to provide feedback. Plus we all know the benefits of less screen time.

"Does that make sense?" asks Professor Mishri.

I jolt back to attention.

"Yes," I say. I've always been a yes-man.

Eleanor narrows her eyes at me.

"In an empirical sense, or hypothetically?"

"Both," I say confidently.

Eleanor scoffs, but Professor Mishri isn't going to call me out on it.

"Great," she says, "let's leave it there for today. I need to go home and get Tilly her dinner."

Professor Mishri talks about Tilly a lot, but I've never been able to figure out if she's referring to her wife or her dog. Eleanor says she refuses to answer such a stupid question, which I think means she's not sure either. As we get up to leave, I prepare to be told by Eleanor why the empirical sense is incompatible with the hypothetical, or whatever the hell she was going on about.

"George, could I have a quick word?" says Professor Mishri.

Eleanor pricks her ears, hoping I'm going to be yelled at and disappointed not to witness it. Professor Mishri waits for Eleanor to leave, then closes the door.

"I just wanted to say, I'm sorry about the Boat Race."

"Oh. Did you watch?"

"No, but I caught the result."

"Yeah. Disappointing. But there's always next year."

"Yes."

Hang on a minute. That wasn't a George yes. That was an English yes. The kind that doesn't mean yes at all. Professor Mishri squints out the window.

"Did you, er, did you see the *Daily Telegraph* article?"

"No?"

"I suspected you might not have," says Professor Mishri, scratching her neck. "Well, I don't want to keep you any longer, but I thought you should know."

I clatter out of Professor Mishri's study and sprint across Great Court. It's giving *Chariots of Fire*.

Over the past week, I've been featured in several newspapers' previews of the Boat Race. Did they use a photo of me training on the river? No, they used that same goddamn shot of me in my underwear. If I could go back in time, I'd never do that stupid modeling campaign. I was nineteen years old, and a scout slid into my Instagram DMs (people need to stop scouting me! I'm not that special). I didn't even know they wanted me in my underwear until I got to the shoot. I thought it was going to be all preppy, New England in the fall vibes, something my mom could show her friends. But when they asked me to strip down, I was too polite to say no, and now I'm the underwear model who rows for Cambridge.

Don't get me wrong, I look great in a pair of briefs. But do you know how embarrassing it is to have your bulge reprinted all over the press? It's not even *my* bulge—they made me wear this stupid cup that makes me look like a porn star. Now try imagining what my mom says about it to her friends.

I dash down Trinity Street to the nearest newsstand and buy a copy of the *Telegraph*. Tourists stream past me as I stand in the middle of the street and turn to the back page. They've used that photo again, because of course they have, but there's also a picture of me and Lucas at the start of the race that captures him shouting at me and me looking bemused.

Above it is a headline: CAMBRIDGE COX SAYS "IDIOT" FOREIGN ROWERS ARE RUINING THE SPORT.

Tag yourself—I'm Idiot. Don't love that. I know they say all publicity is good publicity, but even I'm struggling to see the positives here. This is hardly the first time the topic has come up, but usually it's the opposite argument, that foreign imports give their teams an unfair advantage. You can't please anyone. The article quotes Lucas extensively. The photo does the rest. Why wouldn't an American underwear model be an idiot?

With each new sentence I read, I get a nasty feeling brewing in my stomach toward Lucas. I've really tried to give that guy the benefit of the doubt. But come on.

I switch on my phone and am hit with a stream of messages too overwhelming to take in at once. Then I see an email from Deb consisting of nothing but a subject header: Emergency meeting, boat house, 4pm.

• • •

Cambridge's boat house is a plain redbrick building on the banks of the River Cam. We do our river training in the mornings on the much wider River Great Ouse near Ely, a thirty-minute train ride away, then meet here every afternoon for a gym session. I arrive to find most of the team already present. Tristan is chugging a protein shake while looking incredibly smug. Johannes is watching an episode of *Is It Cake?* on his phone, because that's how he stays calm. Rotter and Sprout are in the gym doing weights. Yes, you heard me. Rotter and Sprout are best friends who went to the same boarding school and have been known as Rotter and Sprout for as long as anyone can remember (their real names are Arthur and Jonathan). Lucas calls them meatheads with an endorphin addiction, but maybe they just really enjoy biceps curls. Ed and Ted, the bow pair, are mumbling in the corner. Deb claims their rhyming names have nothing to do with her decision to pair Ed and Ted at the back of our lineup, while I always tell them that last does not mean least. But they've always been slightly on the fringes of the team, finding reasons to grumble about the rest of us. I think I'll avoid them for now. Seconds before the meeting is due to start, in walks Dakani. He somehow combines being a rower with an exhaustive list of other activities, from playing the title role in a steampunk adaptation of *Hamlet*, to sitting on various impressive-sounding committees. Either he never sleeps or he has a body double.

"Sorry I'm late, guys," says Dakani, even though he's timed his arrival perfectly. "Been volunteering at a spin class for pensioners. Highly recommend."

A few moments later, the door swings open again, and this time it's Lucas. I feel a surge of anger as I see him. Why does he have to be so bitchy? I'm sure there's a nice person in there somewhere, but I've spent so much time in Lucas's company, and I still don't really understand him. He looks so funny sitting there in his cox seat, shouting at men twice his size. He doesn't smile much, except when he's about to crack a joke and gets this spark that reminds me of Tom Holland in *Spider-Man*. Lucas hates it when I say that. He hates most things I say. I do my best to stay positive, but that only annoys him more. I've tried to ignore the fact that he obviously doesn't like me, but it's hard to get past it when we spend so long looking into each other's eyes.

Behind Lucas is Deb, wearing her sponsored tracksuit and that blank look that keeps me craving her approval. But wait—Deb is not alone. Just behind her is a man in a suit. That's weird. I love a good suit, but I can't remember the last time I saw someone wearing one in the boat house. I'm expecting Deb to introduce him, but he hangs on the sidelines. Deb gathers us around and we all fall quiet.

"Lucas?" says Deb.

Lucas steps forward grudgingly.

"So about that *Telegraph* article," he says. "I didn't mean it."

Deb signals for him to elaborate.

"I was mad, I wasn't thinking, and I definitely wasn't expecting to be recorded."

"And?" says Deb.

Lucas grits his teeth. "I'd like to apologize."

"To?"

"George." He can't even look at me.

But Deb gives the team a thumbs-up. "Sorted."

She turns and starts muttering under her breath to the man she walked in with. At first, we all assume she's going to turn back and resume the meeting, but as it becomes clear that it's over, there's a hubbub of discontent.

"She made us come here for *that*?" Ed says to Ted.

I have to admit, that was short even by Deb's standards. But maybe that's the point. She wants to let us know there's not going to be any debate, any sharing of feelings, certainly not one of those showdowns we had in the locker room after the race. Lucas has apologized. What else is there to say? I think I'll go back to my room and watch *Mamma Mia! Here We Go Again*. I'm in the mood for some great cinema.

"Hold up," says Tristan. "Can we at least discuss—"

"No," says Deb.

"But—"

"Tristan."

The rest of the crew start chattering furiously. Then I see Deb beckoning me toward her. I cross over to her in confusion, and she leads me in silence up to her office. I turn and see that we're being followed by Lucas and the man in the suit. To my surprise, the man takes a seat at Deb's desk, while Deb turns and exits, leaving me and Lucas alone with him.

What the hell is going on?

"I'm here on behalf of the university," the man says. "I want to make sure we put a lid on this situation."

I breathe a sigh of relief. That sounds constructive.

"Do you understand the seriousness of your allegations?" the man asks Lucas.

Lucas looks at him coolly. "Yes."

"I gather you refused to give a retraction."

"I said what I said."

The man doesn't flinch. "The university has refuted the allegations in the strongest possible terms. We're confident that going forward, all rowers' exams will be marked according to the same criteria as their peers."

"So... is that how they've done it in the past?" I ask tentatively.

The man stiffens. "I don't have that information."

"It's just... sometimes I think I've not done that well in an exam. Like maybe not even written that much. Or really anything. But then I still pass."

The man shifts uncomfortably. "If you passed, you passed."

"So should I just... keep doing what I've been doing?"

"That depends what you've been doing."

"Jesus, George, read between the lines," snaps Lucas. "Up until now, they've given you a free ride, but that's going to end. Because I forced their hand."

The man looks at me. "I never said any of that."

"You're not denying it," quips Lucas.

I can't say I'm loving the turn this has taken. I'm in the third and final year of my degree. Deb has made it clear she wants me to stick around next year, and I'm being lined up for a master's in management studies. Professor Mishri says it's a great option for someone with my skill set. Lucas says management studies is for basic bitches.

"This is a bit sudden," I say, trying to stay calm. "My exams are in six weeks. My dissertation's due in two weeks. And that's without training. Six days a week, twice a day."

"I'm not denying it's a challenge," says the man. "That's one of the reasons people are so fascinated by the Boat Race."

Commentators are always gushing over the fact that those selected for the Boat Race combine the training schedule of an Olympic rower with the academic achievements of the country's brightest and best. I love it when they say that. At least, I thought I did.

"Look, I wish you the best," says the man, "but this is beyond my purview. Do you have any friends who can help you?"

"Not outside rowing."

"Then ask one of the rowers."

"But the only other guy who studies economics is—"

I look at Lucas.

The man realizes and gulps.

"I'll leave you two to figure that out. I trust you've taken my message on board." He leans in and drops his voice to a low volume. "Cambridge University has a reputation to uphold. I'm counting on you two not to embarrass us any more than you already have."

. . .

I really try hard not to visualize negative scenarios. But let's run through this one real quick. There's no way Deb can be planning to let me and Lucas both keep our places in the boat opposite each other after all this drama. And if not, it will be a huge decision which of us to demote. It would make Deb's life a hell of a lot easier if the decision was taken out of her hands because one of us wasn't around next year. And there's no doubt that Lucas will pass his exams. He's come top of our year twice in a row.

Remind me again why I came to Cambridge? After my junior crew won a national competition in a record time, I was inundated with offers from US colleges. I was deliberating between Stanford and Princeton when the Cambridge scout came calling.

That guy was so nice. He'd lost out on so many rowers to America that I felt kind of sorry for him. Plus I'd just watched *Bridgerton* and liked the idea of hanging out in a place where everyone had British accents.

Now it's not looking like the best decision. I've never failed at anything until this weekend. But I can't take all the blame for losing the Boat Race. Passing my degree? That's on me.

Lucas and I exit the boat house and walk down the tow path in silence. It's the first warm afternoon of the year, and the path is full of dog walkers and couples hand in hand. On any other day like this, I'd be scrolling through my phone, thinking about who I could take on a romantic walk to the Grantchester Meadows. I turn to Lucas.

"No," he says instantly.

"You don't even know what I'm going to ask!"

"You want me to help you pass your exams."

I raise a hopeful eyebrow. Lucas laughs.

"Why is that so ridiculous?" I ask. "We're on the same schedule. We're on the same team."

"And yet," says Lucas.

"And yet what?"

Lucas laughs again.

"Is that a no?"

This time Lucas gives a great big belly laugh, which makes me want to pick him up and throw him in the river. Not in a mean way. Just to make him see sense.

"What if I paid you?"

Lucas's smile vanishes. I instantly regret the offer. What was I thinking? British people are weird about money. I'm not sure I totally understand the phrase "a chip on his shoulder," but it definitely seems to apply to the little guy standing in front of me—or should I say, beneath me.

"No," says Lucas. "I don't care how many millions daddy's going to release from the trust fund."

Why do people think I'm rich? I was actually thinking I'd have to take some of my modeling money out of my savings account, but now doesn't seem like the moment to clarify that particular point with Lucas.

"Look, George, even if I wanted you on the team—and that's a big 'if'—you don't have a hope in hell of passing your exams."

"You don't know that."

Lucas folds his arms at me. "What are the pros and cons of low interest rates?"

The what and what of what what-y what? People at Cambridge think it's totally normal to throw questions like this into casual conversation.

"I haven't reviewed that topic."

"It was on the Cambridge entrance exam."

"Er . . . I think I took a different one."

"Yeah, I bet you did. So you're not even caught up on the things you were supposed to have learned before you got here."

"I'm a fast learner."

"Name one thing you've learned fast."

"How to gut a salmon."

Lucas does a double take. "How to *gut a salmon*?"

"Yeah! My parents run a restaurant at a country club in Wisconsin. I worked in the kitchen one summer. It's not easy to gut a salmon. Those guys are slippery!"

Lucas looks mildly amused but turns to walk away.

"I'm going to make one last pitch to you, Lucas. Please?"

Lucas turns back. "You make a compelling case. And I'm impressed with the way you presented the evidence and structured your argument. But it's still a no."

. . .

I spend the rest of the day glued to my phone. Usually when I have a problem, I google how to fix it, but I'm not sure I want to know what the results are for "How to pass your exams when everyone thinks you're an idiot." Instead, I catch up on the messages that have been streaming in since the race. There's an ominous email from my sports agent, proposing we touch base and debrief. There's a Google alert informing me that someone has posted screenshots of me in my Lycra in a gay forum and is using the available evidence to try and decide if I'm circumcised. Perhaps I ought to release a statement. There's nothing from my parents. Not even a "well done" or a "bad luck" or confirmation of whether they managed to watch. Maybe they tried calling while my phone was off? It's possible. Either way, there's no use in getting upset about it. If I don't come up with a solution fast, I'm going to be booking a one-way ticket home to Wisconsin.

3
LUCAS

IT'S MIDNIGHT IN CAMBRIDGE. I'm walking up a spiral staircase. I arrive at the top to find a locked wooden door. I step through it and emerge onto a stone balcony. I'm high up in one of the colleges, looking out across the skyline. It's a balmy summer night, but up this high, there's a cooling breeze. Then I realize I'm not alone. Someone's leaning over the edge of the balcony, gazing at the view. I approach him quietly, then stop as Amir turns and sees me. We hold each other's gaze.

"I can't believe I found you here," I say.

Amir looks at me, his hair blowing gently in the breeze. "I've been waiting for you."

My heart leaps. "I wasn't sure you even knew who I was."

"Are you kidding?" says Amir. "I've had my eye on you all year."

Amir steps forward and kisses me. His lips are warm and soft. I reach up to unbutton his shirt and it magically slips off his shoulders and onto the floor. His body is exactly how I imagined it, toned and smooth, his olive skin marked only by a wispy black treasure trail leading down toward an unmistakable bulge in his trousers. I drop to my knees and place my hands on his waistband. The cut of his hip muscles is right in my sight line. I pull down his trousers, feeling what's inside them strain against the material. Then I hear a sound in the distance, sharp and clear, ringing repeatedly.

"What's that noise?" I ask in annoyance.

Amir shrugs. "Probably a church bell."

"No," I say. "Sounds more like . . . an alarm clock."

. . .

I open my eyes. Damn. Should have known that was too good to be true. Deb has given us the week off training, but I forgot to turn off my alarm. It's 5:30 a.m. On any other day, I'd be blundering out of bed and striding through the darkness to catch a train to Ely and out onto the river for ninety punishing minutes. But today I have the morning to myself and I'm already wide awake. My thoughts return to Amir. You know when you have a crush so debilitating you feel physically weak? That's Amir. It's bad enough seeing him in person, but lately he's started haunting my dreams. Today was as far as we've ever got. Not even my subconscious will let me seal the deal.

In the absence of Amir, I pull up his Instagram profile. I get that it's curated, but no one could deny that Amir is living the quintessential Cambridge experience. Evensong at King's Chapel. Punting down the River Cam on a gorgeous summer day. Champagne picnics in the Grantchester Meadows. Black-tie summer balls. Parties at his palatial home in Tunisia or at his friends' who live in actual castles. Total *Brideshead Revisited* vibes, except that I once said that at a party and someone snootily reminded me that it was set in Oxford. All Amir's photos are carefully cropped or shot in sharp focus so that you can't quite tell who he was there with and can imagine yourself there instead. There's only one photo where he's in the frame himself: the one responsible for tonight's dream. I'm not sure where it was taken—possibly the St John's College clock tower. Who took the photo? How did they get up there? Amir's back is turned, so all you can see is his smooth tanned neck and immaculately cut hair. I always thought there was something incredibly alluring about this being the only photo he's posted of himself. Imagine being that hot and not feeling the need to announce it to the world. But after my dream, the freeze frame is almost an insult. Much better to close my eyes and picture myself back on the balcony with him.

Now where did we leave off? Ah yes. Just like that, I feel a stirring between my legs and slide a hand down my pants. Might as well make the most of being up this early.

. . .

A few hours later, I've showered and dressed and I'm scurrying over the Bridge of Sighs. It's a covered stone bridge with grated windows and ornate carvings—the jewel in the crown of my college, St John's, and never not being photographed by tourists. St John's College is a picturesque collection of grand sandstone buildings covered in ivy and courtyards with clocks that chime on the hour, situated in the center of Cambridge, right next to our biggest rival, Trinity. Trust George and me to end up at rival colleges. As I leave the grounds of St John's, I look over the river toward Trinity and wonder what George is doing right now. Maybe he's already found someone else to tutor him. I hope they're charging a lot. It's occurred to me that I could have just swallowed my pride and taken him up on his offer. It's not like I couldn't use the money.

The next college I pass is Trinity Hall, where my mum works as a cleaner. Or a "bedder," as they're called here, since Cambridge students are so pampered that we literally get our beds made for us. It's kind of awkward having my mum work at the same university I attend, even if I don't visit her nearly as much as I should. My dad used to work there too, in the kitchens, but he followed a woman to Newcastle soon after my sister was born, so we don't talk about him. I didn't think much about my mum's job until I got older. Then I listened as she came home with the most awful stories. Students who talked down to her, or expected her to clean up the full range of bodily excretions without a word of thanks. I couldn't bear the idea that these people thought they were better than her. So around the age of fifteen, I came up with a plan: I was going to get into Cambridge and prove I was as good as any of them.

I already did well at school, so it wasn't a pipe dream. Cambridge has always been heavily weighted in favor of private school students, but these days they admit plenty of people like me. Once I got my place, I could have happily found myself a nice group of down-to-earth friends with similarly modest backgrounds. But no, that would have been far too sensible. Instead, I was determined to get the stamp of approval from the privileged set. From my first day here, I tried to befriend anyone who looked like they might have grown up on the Saltburn estate, but surprise surprise, none of them had any interest in being friends with a weird little guy whose mum was a cleaner. Not that I ever mentioned that up front, but toffs are so good at sniffing each other out and excluding everyone else that I was doomed before I started. I failed so categorically to become part of that world that I convinced myself I was over it. That was until I met Amir.

I reach the other side of town and arrive at the coffee shop where I work a shift twice a week. There's a rule banning Cambridge students from having jobs during term time, but I'm not sure how strictly it's enforced, and I've got away with it so far. The coffee shop is a cute little place with a mint-green façade and hanging plant pots, owned by a retired gay man who spends most of his time in Yorkshire. A few weeks into the job, I was on the verge of quitting when Amir walked in. I recognized him instantly—he's also at St John's College, but at that point we'd never spoken, mainly because I'd never dare approach someone that beautiful. In the coffee shop, however, I had no choice but to look him in the eye and talk to him as I served him.

From that moment on, I was besotted.

I feared it was a one-off, but he came in the following week, and I realized it was a regular habit. He always comes in on a Wednesday afternoon, but there's no logic to whether he comes toward the start or the end of my shift, which keeps me on edge throughout. There's no such mystery about his order: a cappuccino with oat milk, not too hot. And no matter the time, whatever the weather, the script is always the same.

Just after 3:00 p.m., I hear the bell tinkle and there he is. Oh god. How does he get hotter every time? He's wearing an oversized knitted jumper and clutching a book like he so often is. One time he brought in a copy of *Maurice* by E. M. Forster and I immediately went to the library and read it in a day. It's the story of a young man who discovers his sexuality at Cambridge, before ultimately falling for Alec, a working-class groundsman. Obviously, I convinced myself that Amir is Maurice and I'm his Alec.

Today Amir is holding a poetry collection whose title I can't make out. I look up and attempt a casual smile.

"What can I get you?"

Why do I always say that? Does he think I'm rude or dumb because I haven't memorized his order by now? Somehow, I feel like admitting that would reveal something I'm trying to keep hidden.

"Cappuccino with oat milk, please. Not too hot."

I nod as if it rings a bell, but only vaguely. "No problem."

Over the weeks, I've tried out all sorts of responses, from "Sure" (too noncommittal) to "You got it!" (completely demented). But what if he's noticed I've settled on "No problem"? Should I have thrown in an "On its way" to mix it up? No, don't be silly—that would require weeks of rehearsal. I need to concentrate on getting the milk temperature right. I would die if I ever overheated it even slightly, but it also mustn't be too cold. And yes, I've conducted experiments on my days off.

While I flirt with the boundaries of clinical insanity, Amir stands there patiently. What's he thinking? I'd pay good money to know, although I am only being paid £10 an hour. Now would be the perfect time to ask if he enjoyed the Boat Race. Surely he knows I'm on the team? Surely he recognizes me? Tell me he recognizes me. It's the perfect icebreaker, but it's also a minefield. What if he watched the race and thinks it's all my fault? What if he saw me with my family at the boat house and decided I'm not the right sort? What if he read the *Telegraph* piece and thinks that was very undignified of me? How will I know if I don't ask?

I don't even have to mention the Boat Race. I could talk about the weather, exams, anything. But I can't. The words don't come out. Or they do, but not the ones I'm looking for.

"Cash or card?"

Amir looks me in the eye. "Card."

Shock twist—just kidding. Amir taps his card and I hand over his coffee. It's occurred to me that I could purposefully spill it, like some rom-com meet-cute. As if I'd risk scalding my precious Amir. Instead, we exchange that weird puckering of the dimples that passes for politeness in these situations, then he's gone for another week.

· · ·

I wouldn't say Amir is why I took up rowing. But the two things are not unconnected. Being part of the university rowing team grants me some kudos in certain circles, which, short of having gone to certain boarding schools or having a parent with a Wikipedia page, is the best someone like me can hope for. When I got approached by a rower at the freshers' fair, I thought they were joking until I realized they were thinking of me as a cox. Until that moment, I'd never imagined that the world of varsity matches and sports kit with matching crests might be somewhere I was welcome. It took one trial session on the river to realize I'd found my true calling: screaming at jocks.

It's weird to think of those guys as my friends. What other group of friends are so explicitly in competition with each other?

What other group of friends can you get kicked out of at any moment? On the other hand, it does give me a ready-made social calendar. Tonight, the men's crew are throwing a party in honor of the women's team's victory in the Boat Race. None of us are in the mood for a party, but it wouldn't be a good look for any of us to skip it, not when we get 99 percent of the world's attention.

As evening falls, I drag myself over to the Granta pub. It's a favorite of the rowers on account of its location, perched on the edge of a pond halfway down the River Cam with an open-sided pavilion that juts out over the water. Tonight, we're confined to a private upstairs room. I arrive to find it already heaving. There isn't a dress code, but plenty of people have chosen to wear their rowing blazers, the weirdos. There's a keg of beer, a vast plastic bucket filled with a cloudy white cocktail that has been optimistically labeled Tropical Punch, and several jugs of jelly whose purpose I'm not sure I want to know. The stereo system is pumping out a tropical house cover of "Wonderwall." Keep it classy, guys.

The atmosphere is as odd as it always is on these occasions. Male rowers are the type of men who will happily lick each other's balls for a laugh—I'm scarred for life by that memory—then get weirdly reserved around women. Sasha, the women's stroke, is valiantly trying to make conversation with Ed and Ted. She's paired a men's rowing tie with a bikini top and is jutting her hips from side to side as she talks to them. But no matter how hard she tries, Ed and Ted are desperate to retreat to their natural position on the sidelines, like two lazy dads at a family barbecue. Rotter and Sprout appear to be having a little more success, but only because they've found a pair of girls who share their obsession with weight training. They're set to spend the night getting paralytically drunk together while never once deviating from their preferred topics of protein supplements and resistance training. Dakani and Johannes are talking to each other, or rather Dakani is listing his day's achievements while Johannes nods along politely. I've always felt there's some kind of sexual tension between those two. Something about Dakani's dynamism and Johannes's compliance makes it all too easy for me to imagine what they got up to when they shared a room on the last training camp. But in truth, it's not like Dakani has the time for it.

"Punch?" asks Tristan.

I look behind me just in time to see Tristan hand me a paper cup and slap my back hard. Nobody warned me when I joined the boat club how regularly I could expect to be treated to the traditional greeting of the two-hundred-pound neanderthal. I take a swig of punch. Wow, that's disgusting—get me another one immediately.

"You been here long, old chap?" Tristan asks.

Old chap? I hate it here.

"Just got here."

Tristan surveys the room. "I thought no one would be up for a party, but people are going for it."

"Yeah, well, the girls deserve it."

"Totally," Tristan says stiffly. "Massive respect to these girls."

Massive respect is a stretch when it comes to Tristan and female rowers. From the way he talks about them when he's had a few more drinks, you get the impression he thinks they should limit themselves to artistic gymnastics and a light spot of badminton.

"You know we really shouldn't be seen together like this," I say to Tristan.

"Why?"

"Because everyone thinks me and you are plotting."

Tristan looks at me sharply. There was an email from Johannes earlier in the day imploring that no one discuss recent events at tonight's party. Several people replied concurring, but Tristan and I weren't among them.

"People can think what they want," says Tristan, finishing his drink with a scowl. "We both know I should have been in that stroke seat. We both know we would have won the race if I had been. It's a new season. It's damn near a whole year till the next Boat Race. And if George wants to keep his place, he can fight me for it."

I think I'm getting the "old chap" treatment because Tristan senses a potential alliance. There are plenty of reasons why it would make sense. It would mean I didn't have to sit in the boat opposite George, plus Tristan's parents have properties everywhere from the Cotswolds to Biarritz. Unfortunately, he's just too much of an arsehole. Nice to know I do have some standards.

I ditch Tristan and get chatting to Fran Macdonald, the women's cox and team captain. She's a sparky, red-haired Scottish girl who I clicked with the day I met her. It was Fran who made me fall in love with coxing, showing me how demanding and strategic it could be, like you're single-handedly in charge of a steam engine. Much as Fran takes her rowing seriously, she's always up for a laugh. As we start funneling down cups of punch, I tell her my theory about Johannes and Dakani.

"I don't see it," says Fran. "I get straight vibes."

"Yeah, no, they're definitely both straight. But that doesn't rule out a little fun in the bunks on rowing camp."

"Speaking from experience?" Fran asks with a grin.

"I wish."

"Careful what you wish for. The girls squad is a nightmare—we've always got at least two current couples and one set of exes."

"Maybe that's the secret to your success."

Fran laughs. "Sounds like you guys need to get fucking."

"Please, Fran, look at the material. It's not happening."

I notice people peering toward the door and chattering excitedly. There's only one person who could cause that reaction. I do my best to ignore it, but eventually I glance over and see George stride into the room. He's gone for a wet look with his side part, making him look like a member of the Rat Pack who causes teenage girls to be hospitalized for hysteria. He's wearing his blazer, but without a shirt. His shaved pecs glint out from underneath, displaying as much cleavage as any woman at the party.

I turn to Fran with a smirk. "Lock up your women."

Fran laughs. "Too late."

Unlike most of the crew, George doesn't struggle to fraternize with the women's team. He's slept with at least two of them that I'm aware of, which is impressive given how many of them are gay.

"Whose turn do you think it is tonight?" I ask Fran.

She smiles mischievously. "Mine."

Fran is as queer as they come, so I'm not sure what she's implying until she stands on a chair and calls the room to a halt.

"Thanks for coming tonight. Especially the men. You guys have had two hundred years of systemic bias, but we get a beer keg and a room above a pub, so I guess it all balances out."

Everyone laughs. Tristan grits his teeth. Fran smiles at George.

"I want to thank George in particular for making tonight possible."

George gives her a thumbs-up.

"I'm not talking about organizing the party," says Fran. "If you hadn't fucked two of our crew, they never would have known how to finish that fast."

The whole room gasps.

"Seriously, it's a good job half of us are lesbians," says Fran. "Really stopped that chlamydia outbreak in its tracks."

Oh my god, she's roasting him. This is delicious. Except that George is laughing along good-naturedly and doesn't seem remotely offended. What's wrong with him?

"But listen," says Fran, "I do understand that you boys' reputation is in the gutter right now. So we wanted to give you a chance to recover your pride."

She beckons off to the side. Two of her teammates step into the middle of the room with an outstretched rope. Everyone whoops in excitement as they realize what Fran is proposing—a limbo contest.

"You gonna win this for us?" asks Tristan, slapping me on the back even harder than the first time. "You could walk straight under there."

Hilarious.

The tournament gets underway with Fran as MC. Despite Tristan's claims, I'm probably the least flexible person in the room, and I'm sitting this one out. As men and women take turns, I see the ingenuity of the ladies' challenge. Most of the men who enter, with their larger frames and bulky legs, promptly fall like flies. The women generally find it much easier to slip under. But Fran hasn't reckoned on the physical dexterity and sheer determination of one man in particular. George sails under the rope with ease every time. To say he hasn't let his roasting get to him is an understatement. Pretty soon, he's made the top five with four other women, then the top three. It's remarkable how easily George can bend back on his legs and shuffle under. As another girl stumbles and falls in the bronze medal position, it's down to the final two.

Up against George is Katya, a Ukrainian girl who lives in the courtyard next door to me and is one of the rowing club's newest recruits. She's enjoying the attention as much as George, hyping up the crowd like a WWF wrestler each time she succeeds. The rope is lowered another inch, and George assesses it, then unbuttons his blazer and takes it off. The crowd whoops. George leans backward. Now that he's shirtless, it's impossible not to stare at his muscles. His body is so perfectly sculpted that it almost looks fake. He makes it under the rope and walks straight up to Katya until their faces are only inches apart. Katya doesn't flinch. They start to circle each other slowly. Their eyes are locked, the chemistry between them is electric, and the rest of us are rapt. I feel as if we're watching a mating ritual on a David Attenborough documentary.

Katya takes a sip of punch and stretches her arms, preparing to match George's marker. The crowd crescendos into a cheer as Katya lowers herself down. But the drink must have unsteadied her, as she has barely begun to shift beneath the rope before she stumbles and falls on her back. Everyone oohs, then applauds her. George reaches out a hand and pulls Katya to her feet. Someone rushes forward and places an inflatable crown on George's head. George grins gamely, but that's not the prize he cares about. He casts his eyes toward Katya.

. . .

I struggle to walk home in a straight line. I must have drunk about ten cups of punch in the end. At least the streets are quiet. The road back to St John's, which is usually filled with tourists, has the uncanny air of a film set, but I'm in no mood to appreciate it. I can't stop thinking about George's performance in the limbo. Not winning the contest, but seducing Katya like that, in front of everyone. They left the party together about an hour ago. How did he do it? Right after getting roasted in front of that whole room. If that had happened to me, it would have taken me months to recover. But George shrugged it off and got laid twenty minutes later. If he had a weekly coffee appointment with Amir, they'd be married by now.

It's only as I arrive back at college that I realize how devastated I am for letting that opportunity slip past me this afternoon at the coffee shop. Why couldn't I bring myself to start up a conversation? This week would have been the perfect time to do it. Next week it will be weird to say I saw him at the Boat Race. Creepy, even. But what if it's not too late? Dutch courage and all that. It's not *that* late. Amir seems like the kind of guy who'll be up at 1:00 a.m.

Colleges are patrolled day and night by porters—a cross between a butler and a security guard—who monitor who's coming in and out, deliver post to the professors, and shout at any students who walk on the lawn. The porters all know my face by now, but I feel like I'm committing a crime as I enter college through the Porters' Lodge and head straight past the turning to my room. I arrive at the courtyard where Amir lives and pad around the perimeter. Each staircase has a plaque with a list of names of the resident students, so it's really not that weird that I know Amir lives on the staircase in the far corner. As I stride toward it, I trip on a cobblestone and almost land flat on my face.

"Jesus, are you all right, dude?"

That voice is unpleasantly familiar. I glance up to see George looking at me in concern and offering his hand. Reluctantly, I let him pull me to my feet.

"What are you doing here?" I ask hotly.

George shrugs. "Katya's great, but the beds are tiny. For me at least."

George smiles, but I ignore him and turn away from him toward Amir's staircase. I can feel George watching me. My feet stay rooted to the spot.

"Are you lost or something?" asks George.

I don't know why I'm not more defensive. Maybe it's the alcohol, the tiredness, or the overwhelming sense of defeat.

"There's this guy I like, Amir. I was gonna go and, I dunno, knock on his door."

George stares at me. "Does he know you're coming?"

"No."

"Are you insane?"

I'm not answering that one.

George shakes his head in disbelief. "This is a guy you want to get with?"

"Yes."

"You can't just knock on his door in the middle of the night. That's not hot."

"What should I do, then? Since you're clearly the expert."

George bristles at my attitude. "That depends on a lot of things. And honestly, it's late."

He turns to leave. I feel cheated. It's as if he has the answers but is refusing to share them. You can hardly blame him, given the way I reacted to his request the other day. Then I have a brainwave.

"Wait—"

George glances back at me.

"What if we made a deal?" I ask tentatively.

George frowns in confusion.

"I'll do what you asked. I'll help you pass your exams."

George's eyes light up. "Are you serious?"

"Yes. But only if . . ." I glance around, embarrassed. "If you teach me how to get laid."

George looks amazed. "That's all I have to do?"

"No one said it's gonna be easy. But yeah. That's all."

Wait. Do I really want to do this? With George, of all people? Then I think of Amir. If there's even a chance that George can help me seduce him, I can suffer through anything. I hold out my hand decisively.

"Deal?"

George doesn't hesitate.

"Deal."

4
GEORGE

JEMIMA SAYS IT DOESN'T MEAN anything that she came to Cambridge. She works for the London office of the global sports agency that signed me after my modeling campaign. She's one of those posh British girls who never brushes her hair and is always having a good time. She didn't make it to the Boat Race—too busy doing promo with Emma Raducanu. But when the *Telegraph* article landed, she immediately arranged to come and see me. She's taken me out to lunch at Browns, a fancy chain restaurant on King's Parade, Cambridge's main tourist drag. She might be about to drop me, but this place does an awesome steak. So it's a win-win, if you think about it.

"Stonking Chardonnay for the price," says Jemima. "Do you want to try?"

"I have a lecture after this."

"Never stopped me! Did I ever tell you I was the inventor of a cocktail called the Nipple Tipple? Don't ask."

Jemima snorts and tops up her own glass almost to the rim.

"Look, George, I don't need to tell you how unusual it is for a company like us to represent a rower. A *student* rower. Opportunities like this don't come along very often."

I was approached by Jemima shortly after my modeling campaign went viral. At the time, I was feeling burned by having the whole world staring at my crotch, and Jemima made clear that one of the benefits of signing with her was that she'd be on hand for any future jobs to make sure I wasn't exploited. All I was hoping for was another campaign that my mom could be proud of, maybe modeling watches, something like that. But Jemima had bigger ideas. Apparently they're always looking for growth areas in niche sports. That's when she started calling me the Tom Brady of rowing. We plotted out a path that involved winning the Boat Race, then getting selected for the US Olympic team. I know when Jemima's excited about my career because she lets us pose for a selfie to post on the official agency account. No selfie so far today. Maybe after dessert.

"Do you remember Anna Kournikova?" asks Jemima.

I look blank.

"Too young. She was a tennis player. Massive hottie. Never won a tournament, but she was the most searched woman on Google back in the day. FHM Sexiest Woman. Huge star. Or look at Adam Rippon. Came tenth at the Olympics, but my god, the way he maximized his media profile."

Her admiring tone suggests that she sees this as the ultimate victory.

"Do you see what I'm saying? The sports side of things isn't necessarily that important."

She chugs her glass of wine and tops it back up immediately.

"But . . . I thought it was all part of the vision," I protest.

"It was. But then you lost. If you want to be a winner, you need to win things. That's why I'm worried about these exams."

"What's the alternative?"

Jemima doesn't miss a beat. "Drop out now. Transfer to a US college. I can find one who'll give you a degree for writing your name on the exam paper. Take every modeling job you can get and forget about the other stuff. Voilà."

I put down my fork.

"I'm two months away from finishing a degree I've been working on for three years!"

Jemima raises an eyebrow.

"OK fine," I admit, "maybe not *working*—"

"Exactly," says Jemima, "which is an issue at Cambridge. So glad they rejected me. I did fuck all for three years at Exeter!"

She snort laughs so loudly that the family on the next table look over.

"Jemima," I say firmly, "I want everything you want. The brand sponsorships. Olympic gold. But I also want a Cambridge degree."

"That's great, George. We all want those things. So did Kournikova, I'm sure. But you can't have everything. You need to decide what matters most. The woman is married to Enrique Iglesias."

She snaps her fingers at a passing man who definitely isn't a waiter.

"Mate, can we get another bottle?"

. . .

I'm choosing to see that meeting as a success. First and foremost, Jemima didn't drop me as a client. She even agreed to pose for a selfie, although she hasn't yet posted it on the agency account. But she must be so busy. True, the general tone of the meeting wasn't ideal, but Jemima's only asking me to choose between two things that are equally awesome. This is like the time my family went to Michigan's Adventure and there was so much traffic on the way that we only had time to stand in line for one big ride. I took so long to decide between Thunderhawk and Shivering Timbers that, in the end, I didn't get to go on either. But I did get a really cool baseball cap from the gift shop.

I'm not sure what the baseball cap is in this scenario, but I suppose the lesson is I need to make my mind up before it's made for me. Most people probably assume that my Cambridge degree is a means to a rowing career, but it's not that simple. I only got into rowing because a guy playing golf at the country club saw me carrying a crate of lobsters and said I had the physique for it. He was a dude in his thirties who turned out to be a rowing coach. I'm pretty sure he was hoping I had the physique for other things, but I showed up at the rowing club, avoided his advances, and never looked back. I guess you could say it fell into my lap, a bit like modeling and Cambridge. That happens a lot with me. But it's not like I haven't embraced all three. I'm planning to row at the Olympics. And I've loved being at Cambridge. I'd hate to quit now.

More than anything, I'd hate to have to tell my parents. Maybe they'll have some advice. We haven't spoken since before the Boat Race, which is weird, now that I think about it. I message them to arrange a Zoom.

Until then, it's all systems go on my deal with Lucas. He's promised to meet me after his lecture to get started, but I figure why not attend the lecture to show I'm committed. It'll be the first lecture I've made it to all year, but hey—better late than never.

The economics faculty is on the Sidgewick Site, a cluster of 1950s arts and humanities buildings that someone once described to me as a brutalist masterpiece. I guess there's something cool about the way the various faculties are housed in a rectangular quad raised on stilts around a grass courtyard. But it's basically just a load of concrete.

Today's lecture is on global capitalism. Nice! I forgot I'd even chosen that paper. The lecture is being held in a cavernous hall with enough scratched old benches to seat the entire year group of two hundred. I walk in and take a seat next to two students I don't recognize.

"I'm George," I say, offering my hand.

The first boy looks at my hand, then glances at his friend and turns back to me.

"David."

"Hi, David. So great to meet you!"

I smile at the guy next to him. "I'm George."

"Rav."

"Hi, Rav. Likewise!"

They share a look.

"So what's your favorite currency, you guys?"

David and Rav stare at me.

"Our what?" asks David.

"Your favorite currency."

Why are they looking at me so weirdly? Hello, we're studying global capitalism?

"Mine's probably the yen," I say. "Because damn, Japan is one impressive economy."

"The yen is doing terribly," says Rav.

"Is it? That sucks. How do we feel about the euro?"

I glance up and see Lucas enter the lecture hall. He spots me and crosses over, looking mortified.

"What are you doing here?"

I do a double take at his annoyance.

"We said we'd meet here."

"We said we'd meet after the lecture."

"Yeah, but I thought it was dumb not to attend. I saved you a seat."

As Lucas looks around to see if there are any other seats available, I'm seriously confused. Surely it's a good thing I'm taking the initiative? The room settles down as the lecturer arrives. Dr. Bastian Keller is a junior academic whose online bio I read on the way here. Now I feel equipped to talk to him about his primary research interests of industrial organization and regulatory governance. Well, maybe not equipped. But I can at least mention them. Show him how eager I am. I walk up to him proudly.

"Hello," I say, offering my hand. "I'm George."

Dr. Keller looks at me in confusion. "Right. Can I help you?"

"Sure can! Tell me everything you know about global capitalism."

Dr. Keller stares at me. "Is it OK if I start the lecture?"

"Yes," says Lucas, dashing up and yanking me toward my seat. "Ignore him."

I'm determined to absorb every word of this lecture. But from the start, Dr. Keller is making it hard for me. He keeps waving a book in the air and telling the class he's giving us a précis of marks. A what? Marks is what British people call grades, but what's a précis? The number of marks you need in order to pass?

The more Dr. Keller talks, the more unclear he becomes. Everyone else is nodding along as if he makes perfect sense. I bet they're faking it. Time for me to come to our rescue.

"But the point about the theory of alienation—" says Dr. Keller.

I shoot up my hand. "I'm gonna have to stop you there."

The entire auditorium turns and stares at me. Dr. Keller narrows his eyes at me.

"Could you break that down for me?" I ask.

I click my pen to show I'm ready. Next to me, Lucas puts his head in his hands.

"This is a lecture," says Dr. Keller. "I'm not taking questions."

"Just quickly," I say. "Tell me about this theory of alienation."

"That's what I just explained."

"I missed that part."

"Which part?"

"The theory. And the alienation."

There are snickers all around me. What's wrong with these people? I'm here to learn. I try again.

"I need to know how to get these marks you keep talking about."

The rest of the students chatter in amusement. Dr. Keller looks incredulous.

"I see what he's saying," Rav pipes up. "He wants to get marks."

I turn to Rav in gratitude. "*Thank* you."

Lucas lets out a faint groan.

"You don't get marks?" asks Dr. Keller in confusion.

"I mean, I'm hoping to. I haven't taken the exam yet."

"But hang on. Do you just mean . . . marks in general?"

"As many marks as possible."

"Might I suggest focusing on *Das Kapital*?"

I look blank.

"Das what?"

"It's the text I've just been discussing," says Dr. Keller. "By Karl Marx."

"Oh, *Karl* Marx. I thought you were talking about marks as in marks in an exam. That makes so much more sense."

I write the words "Carl Marks (person!!!!)" in my notebook.

Next to me, Lucas makes his hand into a pistol and silently blasts his brains out.

. . .

The rest of the lecture is a blur. I can't shake the feeling that Rav deliberately tried to embarrass me. Maybe it was no less than I deserved, but I've never understood why so many people at this university are allergic to being nice. I hate feeling stupid. It's the reason I stopped going to classes in the first place.

At the end of the lecture, as everyone files out, I wait until Rav is out of earshot, then turn to Lucas. "Was Rav making fun of me?"

Lucas gives me a droll look. "No, George. He sees you as a scholar and a peer."

I frown at Lucas with suspicion. "Why do I feel like you don't really mean that?"

Lucas chuckles and shakes his head. "You are honestly unbelievable."

"Why?! What did I do?"

As Lucas starts speeding away, I race to catch up with him.

"Where are we going?"

"You really don't get it, do you?"

"No! That's the problem."

"You will. Once we get there." Lucas points directly ahead. Rising above us in the distance is the tallest building in Cambridge: the University Library.

"Wait, we're going to the library?"

Lucas nods tersely. Is he still mad about the Boat Race or something? I try to think of a subtle way to find out.

"Are you still mad about the Boat Race?"

Lucas stares straight ahead.

"Is that a yes or a—"

"No."

We walk on in silence. There have been many days out on the river when Lucas goes all quiet and grumpy like this. I've learned from experience that the best thing to do is leave him alone. Maybe he'll cheer up once he gets some action. I can't wait to get started on my plan. I've never thought of myself as an expert on dating, but seeing Lucas outside Amir's room like that, drunk and desperate, I knew instinctively what he was doing wrong. I am so going to Drew Barrymore in *Never Been Kissed* that boy. Except that Amir will be the one to kiss him. Obviously.

A few minutes later, we arrive at the University Library. I've always wanted a reason to go inside. As we get close, I realize just how massive it is. Along the front, floor-to-ceiling windows stretch the entire span of five or six floors. In the center is a thrusting brick tower at least twice as high. It looks more like a factory than a library.

"Wow," I say. "How many books do you think it holds?"

"Nine million."

"You're kidding."

"Every single book that's ever been published in this country."

"No way. So they'd have like, the whole Diary of a Wimpy Kid series? And Tom Brady's memoir?"

Lucas turns to me, deadpan. "It's your lucky day."

Lucas leads me into a cavernous lobby with two librarians behind a desk. I'm all set to greet them, but Lucas goes through a side door and down some stairs to a basement locker room. He gestures at my bag.

"You're not allowed to take that in."

"You're not allowed bags? This is so cool. It's like the Pentagon or something!"

Lucas rolls his eyes and throws my bag into a locker. We go back upstairs and swipe through the turnstile to find ourselves in a drafty corridor.

"Right, meet me in the economics section," says Lucas.

"Where are you going?"

"I need to get out a book."

"What book?"

"It doesn't matter."

"But if it's on our syllabus—"

"It's not," says Lucas. "I'm reading around the subject."

"What does that mean?"

"Seriously, George—"

"I'm trying to get into the right mindset! Help me out here."

Lucas sighs. "I've already read everything on the reading list. But Dr. Keller mentioned how Marx was influenced by Hegel, who was influenced by Descartes. So I thought I'd get out some Descartes to see how it all fits together."

I keep my mouth shut, because I don't want to sound any more stupid than I feel.

"I won't be long," Lucas says. "See you upstairs."

He walks off down the corridor, and I look up at the wall in front of me, which has a big map showing the library's complex layout. Economics is on the fifth floor. This place is huge. I can't think why I haven't been in here before now. You can literally smell the knowledge that's contained in these walls, all these books full of facts and theories that will soon be second nature.

I follow the directions to the economics section, walking down to the end of the corridor and heading up to the fourth floor in a creaky metal lift. Around every corner, there's a desk and a student nestled quietly, turning pages and making notes. I've always thought there's nothing more calming than sitting in a rowing boat and pulling an oar, but now I'm not so sure. Then again, it's not like I have to choose between the two—if Lucas can do both, so can I. Not that Lucas can row.

I arrive at the economics section and stop in my tracks. What now? There are stacks of books that stretch as far as I can see, but no one to guide me. I feel as lost as I did in the lecture. I need a starting point, but I don't think I'll ever live it down if Lucas arrives to find me reading *Economics for Dummies*. Better order that one on Amazon.

I look around to see if I can find a librarian. But there's no one in sight, and I'd rather not go all the way back down to the lobby. Maybe I can ask one of these students. They can't all be hell-bent on humiliating me. I walk along the row of desks, but the first student glares at me and the second is so engrossed by her book and a giant set of headphones that I don't want to scare her. Then, in the far corner, I hear a noise. Someone is sniffling. I step behind a stack of books and peer through a crack.

Seated at the desk is a brown-haired girl in a strawberry-colored sweater. She has a book open in front of her, but she's not reading it—she's trying desperately to stop herself from bursting into tears. Let it all out, I want to tell her. I can picture her, weeping gently as I hold her in my arms.

No, George, stop it.

After all the drama last week, I promised myself I wouldn't sleep with anyone until my exams were over. But what was I meant to do about Katya, slinking under the limbo rope like that? I was powerless to resist. But right now I'm sober. I'm in a goddamn library. I'm going to ask strawberry sweater girl for help finding books and that's it.

I step into the aisle and smile at her in sympathy.

"Are you OK?"

"Yeah," says the girl. She wipes her eyes. "Sorry, this is so embarrassing."

"What are you sorry for? We're in Cambridge. It's exam term."

"Yeah," she says gratefully.

"You don't have to explain yourself to me. I'll leave you alone. But if you want to take your mind off everything . . . I could actually use some help."

The girl—Danae is her name—accepts my request to help me look for books. I'm so excited to have found someone who's willing to help, it takes me a while to realize I have a bigger problem.

It's hard to put a finger on where it starts. Maybe the moment our arms graze against each other for just a little too long. Or the time I make some random comment and Danae laughs loudly.

I like to back myself, but I know for a fact that what I just said wasn't funny. There's only one explanation: this girl likes me.

To be honest, I knew it from the moment she looked at me. Let's just say it's not an uncommon occurrence. It's not that I don't think she's cute, I just really need to focus on my studies. But she *is* being so helpful. I don't want to seem ungrateful.

Danae has taken us down this narrow gap between two shelves of books. It's too close for comfort, so I crouch down, pretending to examine a book on the bottom shelf. How do I get out of this? Just act like it's not happening. But when I stand back up, Danae has taken a step toward me, so she's closer than I was expecting. She gives me a look to let me know she's not bothered by our proximity. Oh wow, she's so pretty up close. One kiss can't hurt.

There's nothing quite like that first touch of the lips. Which is good, because I need to keep this quick. Except . . . the second and the third touches, those are quite good too. And the fourth. And the fifth. Now that I've committed, I need to put in a good performance. What if Danae knows who I am? I've got a reputation to uphold. I'll give her the kiss of her life, then leave her wanting more. But Danae's hands slide down to my pants and start to unzip me.

Damn. I've never done it in a library. At least if we go all the way, we'll have a satisfying end point.

Then I hear a cough. I look up to see Lucas staring at me. Danae turns and sees him too.

"Lucas," says Danae, mortified.

"Wait," I say, hastily zipping up my pants. "You two know each other?"

"Yeah," says Danae. "We—"

She hurries off without finishing her sentence. I want to follow her, but I know it's best that I don't. Lucas and I are left facing each other.

"How do you know her?" I ask.

"She's in our year, George. She just got really badly dumped. Were you taking advantage?"

"No! I would never!"

Lucas shakes his head in disbelief.

"Danae was helping me find some books," I insist. "No, she was, really!"

I don't want to tell Lucas I was only going along with what Danae wanted, because that makes both of us look bad. Plus, it's not like I wasn't enjoying it. Luckily, Lucas has already forgotten about it. He tells me to follow him and leads me to the very back of the economics section, deep in the stacks. He kneels and starts poking around the back of one of the bookshelves. I hear a click, and he removes part of the wall.

"Is that—"

"A secret compartment."

"No way! Told you this was like the Pentagon."

"I hope you never get to visit the Pentagon," says Lucas. "I feel like you're going to be very disappointed."

He removes the panel and pulls a book from inside the compartment. It's a bit dusty, but at this point, I'm expecting him to produce an ancient papyrus scroll. Instead, it's just a dog-eared edition of the economics course handbook.

"What's that?" I ask, trying not to sound disappointed.

Lucas dusts it off.

"This is the only book we need to get you through your exams."

"Isn't that just the course handbook?"

"No. This is a . . . special edition."

I squint at it. Doesn't look special to me. "Why's it kept in there?"

"So it can be found by the people who need it, and not by the people who don't know it exists."

Lucas hands it to me and I turn the pages. I quickly realize this isn't just any edition. It's been tampered with extensively, with dozens of notes scribbled in the margins and various maps glued in the back. It tracks not only which topics are likely to come up in any given year, but where the exam scripts are stored at each stage of the process and the codes to the buildings. It tells you which professors might be open to a bribe or two, and which would rather lose their jobs than break a rule. There's even a section that tells you where to hide your phone in the exam hall toilets so you can check it on a break.

"Who wrote this?" I ask in amazement.

"Different students over the years. There's all sorts of reasons people might not be able to pass their exams the traditional way."

Lucas glances around and drops his voice to a whisper.

"I'm not going to help you study for your exams, George. I'm going to teach you how to cheat."

5
LUCAS

I'M NOT THE KIND OF person you'd think of as a cheater. My mum was pretty strict with us growing up, and there was never any need to cheat at school. The thing that radicalized me was World Book Day, when everyone had to dress up as their favorite character. The first year, I must have been nine or ten, and I didn't overthink it. My favorite book at the time was *Charlie and the Chocolate Factory*, so I just wore what he wore—jeans and a jumper. When I got into school that day, I couldn't believe what I saw. This was a regular state primary school, but the kids from nice homes had never stood out more. There was a girl in elaborate face paint done by a professional, plenty who had purchased expensive-looking costumes for the occasion, and this one girl, Rachel Holden, who was dressed as the Gruffalo, complete with a giant papier-mâché head. That afternoon, the teacher announced that Rachel Holden had won the prize for best costume—a £10 book voucher that she obviously didn't need. I was furious. I never stood a chance.

The next year, I was determined to be competitive. From the moment they announced the date, I pestered my mum about my costume. I was convinced that papier-mâché was the key to victory and begged her to help me dress as the peach from *James and the Giant Peach*. She said I was being overambitious. The stand-off continued until the morning of World Book Day, when a doomed clump of soggy cardboard led to my mum borrowing my grandpa's glasses, scribbling a zigzag on my forehead with eyeliner, and calling me Harry Potter. Which was so unfair, because I've never liked those books. When I got to school, there were at least three other Potters, one of whom had purchased the official wand from the Harry Potter studio tour. I wasn't even best in category. Then Rachel Holden came in dressed as Charlotte from *Charlotte's Web*, with a web made from coat hangers that fanned out behind her like a peacock. She won by unanimous consent for the second year in a row.

If I disliked her before, I now openly despised her. It just didn't seem fair that we were in competition when it was never going to be an even playing field. Then that summer, we were both invited to a mutual friend's birthday party. There was a game where you had to put a pin on a map to find the buried treasure. I wasn't interested until, toward the end of the game, I happened to spot two adults pointing out where the treasure was buried. I rushed up and asked to take my turn. I went deliberately off target, but only slightly. When they announced the winner, I acted shocked. Rachel Holden didn't look as mad as I hoped, but then she hadn't spent the past two years secretly resenting me. Scared as I was of being caught, I didn't feel remotely guilty. Just like Rachel on World Book Day, I'd used all the tools available to me.

Once I got to Cambridge, I realized that Rachel Holden was nothing. Of course, I'd always known that things weren't easy growing up, but I hadn't fully appreciated how much easier some people had it. I hadn't understood that going to private school meant tutors and after-school clubs, foreign exchange trips and teachers who gave you one-on-one attention. As we've approached graduation, I've found new things to be annoyed by. I hear people announcing that a family friend has lined them up with a job interview, or their parents have bought them a flat in London so they can avoid the horror of renting. It's not an even playing field and it never has been. Which is why I don't feel bad about suggesting that George cheats.

OK, maybe that's not totally true. When I think about what we're actually going to have to do, it does make my pulse race. That's why I was in such a weird mood on the way to the University Library. In fact, when I went to get that Descartes book, I didn't really need to get a book. I needed to go and hyperventilate because I was so nervous about picking up the cheat book. I didn't believe it was real until I saw it. I heard about it from a grad student at St John's, who claims it originated from a professor who had to cut a lot of corners with his teaching because he was too busy presenting a TV show. It would be funny if this all started not because students didn't want to learn, but because a teacher didn't want to teach.

George doesn't know any of this. In fact, I think he sees me as a lot more hard-edged than I am on the inside. I can easily convince him that cheating is all in a day's work for me. I don't have a choice. I meant what I said to George—there's no way he can learn three years' worth of economics in one term.

That lecture with George was excruciating, but I was impressed by how honest he was about what he doesn't know. George didn't seem thrilled about the prospect of cheating, but he's clearly aware that the way he's been passing his exams up until now hasn't exactly been above board. He can't really argue with my strategy. And I'm determined to deliver on my end of our deal. As for me, I'm under no illusions that I can cheat my way to a boyfriend, but George has promised he'll do whatever it takes to get me there. In fact, we're starting tonight.

What the hell have I agreed to?

George has instructed me to meet him at his room dressed as a superhero. Is this some kind of confidence-building exercise? I hate dressing up. I spent over an hour at the costume shop in the Grafton Centre, trying on every superhero outfit imaginable. In the end, I went with one of the classics: Batman. This version sits in copyright purgatory halfway between Adam West's comical black underpants and Christian Bale's bulked-up bat suit. The main thing is that it's black. And that it has a mask that will stop anyone from recognizing me. Still, I can't believe I'm willingly submitting myself to this humiliation. Thank god George's college is next door to mine. I jog over to Trinity, looking less like Batman on a mission than a man dressed as a rat on a charity fun run. I find George's staircase and knock on his door. As the door swings open and George sees my outfit, his face lights up, and he bursts into song.

"Da-na-na-na-na-na-na-na-na-na-na-na-na-na-na—"

He holds a fake microphone up to my mouth.

"Batman," I say weakly.

"Nice!" says George. "I thought you might go for Spider-Man. Because you look so much like—"

"No, I don't."

"Tom Holland is cute!"

"Exactly."

George laughs and shrugs it off. "Can you guess who I am?"

I look George up and down. He's paired a Viking helmet and hammer with the skimpiest pair of shorts I've ever seen, plus a harness that seems expressly designed to showcase his nipples. I would love to say he looks ridiculous. But George is the one man on earth who can pull this off.

"No idea," I say.

"I'll give you a clue—it rhymes with score."

"Does it also rhyme with man whore?"

"Hey! No sarcasm tonight."

I look at him indignantly. "Sarcasm is my superpower."

George invites me in and offers to fix me a vodka and Coke. Like many final-year Cambridge students, George has what's known as a set—a living room and a separate bedroom. The living room has a low ceiling with exposed wooden beams that are probably several hundred years old. I'm surprised to see that George has made the most of the space. The rest of the rowing team can barely bring themselves to put their dirty clothes in the laundry basket. But George has put plants on the windowsill, candles on the coffee table, and a framed photo by his bed of some people who I presume are his family. That must be the country club in Wisconsin. And that looks like an older brother. The parents each have an arm around the brother, and George is squeezing in at the side like they made him press the camera timer. That isn't how I would have pictured George with his family, but then I realize I don't really know anything about him. Unnerving to think that there's a human being behind Sexy Thor.

"We should make this quick," I say. "I'd love to be in bed by midnight."

"Are you kidding?" says George. "The night won't even start to get good until midnight."

I look at him in disgust. "The night?"

"Yeah, the club night. What did you think we were doing?"

"Honestly, I hadn't ruled anything out."

"That's the spirit!"

I feel a tiredness that is almost existential. George drapes himself over his sofa, spreading his legs wide in that way that straight men love to do. Luckily, I've had plenty of practice out on the river at avoiding any unfortunate glances in the direction of his crotch. I perch tentatively in an armchair, my knees pressed together like a Victorian widow.

"Why do we have to go to a club night?" I ask.

George grins. "We'll get to that part. First, I have a bunch of questions."

I audibly groan.

"I need to know what I'm working with," says George. "Can you give me a brief summary of your dating history?"

"Sure."

George looks expectant.

"I just did," I say.

"Huh?"

"There's your summary. Nada. Niente."

"Your ex was called Nada Niente? Was he Spanish?"

"George, I don't have an ex!"

"So who's Nada Niente?"

"Allow me to translate. I've never had a boyfriend. I've slept with three different guys. Hand jobs and blow jobs only. The first guy asked me to stop. I was giving him a blow job and he *asked me to stop*. I'm a flop, George. A flop like his dick flopped the minute he got into bed with me. This is what you're working with."

George considers this for a moment. "Maybe he was tired."

"Who?"

"Nada Niente. Maybe he wanted to go to bed."

"Yes. Maybe."

You have to pick your battles. It's not like I remember the guy's actual name.

"So is it a choice not to sleep with more guys?" asks George.

"Oh absolutely. After Nada I thought, I've peaked. It doesn't get better than this."

George narrows his eyes at me. "Why do I feel like you're being sarcastic?"

"Because you're a genius. Only explanation."

"Lucas, stop! I'm trying to help!"

"Sorry. No, obviously I'd love to bang more guys. That's why I'm here."

"And why haven't you?"

"Banged more guys? I don't know, George. There isn't a feedback form."

"So it's mostly men rejecting you?"

"No! There's plenty of guys I could have got with. Just . . . not the ones I want."

"Yes!" says George, his face lighting up. "The unattainable! So hot!"

"Is it? 'Cause I find it incredibly frustrating."

"You just have to persevere. This one time in high school, I had a crush on a girl who had a boyfriend. But then me and her were paired on a science project, and her boyfriend was like, 'You know what, I can see how this is going to end, I'm just going to cut my losses.' And we had sex the same night he broke up with her."

I shake my head at him. "You and I are not the same."

George looks guilty. "Tell me what you like about Amir."

At the mere mention of his name, I feel a rush. "Obviously, he's hot. Like seriously hot. But I think the thing that really does it for me is his intelligence."

George looks surprised. "So is that what you look for in a guy?"

"I mean, it's not the only thing, but if they're not seriously clever, it's never going to work."

"Interesting. Anything else about Amir that does it for you?"

I stop to think. "He's so . . . understated. Like he's clearly very handsome, but he doesn't show it off. He's never even posted a selfie."

George tightens up. "What's wrong with selfies?"

"Oh come on, every selfie is a cry for help."

George frowns and glances at his phone.

"And he's rich, but he doesn't show it off. He's never posted a photo of his house or his pool."

"Wait, so how do you know he has a pool?"

"Google Earth."

"Hold up, back up a minute. How do you know this guy?"

I blush and tell George about my weekly rendezvous with Amir and the fervent obsession it has inspired. I don't go quite so far as explaining how a single Instagram post allowed me to track down the precise coordinates of Amir's family home in Tunisia, because I'd rather not be reported to the police, but I give George the general idea.

"This is incredible, Lucas! We can totally plan the perfect meet-cute."

"Since when are you a rom-com guy?"

"I watched all the classics with my mom growing up."

"Right, well you know how rom-com heroines have a misanthropic best friend who never gets a romantic arc of their own?"

"Yeah! Love that character!"

"OK, well that's who you're working with."

George nods solemnly.

"George, you're not meant to agree with me!"

"Oh. Right. I just can't believe you see this guy every week and you thought it was a good idea to crash his dorm at night."

"Don't remind me."

"Let's let it be a teachable moment."

"I'm too English for phrases like that."

"Then tell me why it was a bad idea."

"Because Amir thinks I'm an idiot loser?"

"Wrong," says George, leaping up from the sofa in enthusiasm. "Because the circumstances weren't right."

I feel like I'm at some sort of self-help seminar. But George is on a roll.

"Here's my first piece of advice," he declares. "You can't just make something happen because you want it to happen. You have to react to the situation. That's what makes it all so exciting. Anything could happen tonight."

. . .

That's what I'm worried about. Cambridge doesn't have its own gay club, but there have been various attempts to establish a weekly queer night, some more successful than others. This one claims to be bringing back cheesy music, which I wasn't aware had ever gone away. I've never attended, but I've sneaked several peeks at their Instagram page. I always click on it with the aim of convincing myself I'm not missing anything, but it just reminds me there's a world out there full of people having fun without me. Which is very rude of them. I haven't told George this, but there's a part of me that's excited to finally cross the threshold. And when I say excited, I mean I'm totally shitting myself.

As George and I make the short walk to the club and join the end of the queue, I check out my fellow clubbers. There are a couple of Spider-Mans, several Iron Mans, and another Batman who has opted for the Christian Bale fake six-pack and looks reassuringly stupid. I catch someone smiling at me, then realize they're looking at George. Of course. When you're an underwear model dressed as Sexy Thor, you're not going to go unnoticed. There can be few men able to stand next to George and not feel like an inferior physical specimen. I'm starting to doubt the wisdom of going clubbing together when George clocks my expression.

"Hey," he says.
"What?"
"What are we here for?"
"Ritual humiliation."
George laughs.
"George!"
"What?"
"I thought you banned sarcasm!"

George looks astonished that I'm holding him to account. "But that was funny. I didn't want to *not* laugh."

"OK, but you know the only thing I want to do right now is turn around and walk home. Do not let me. Even if I beg you."

George looks at me in admiration. "I'm so impressed by your commitment."

"No, no, no. I'm a failure. A total failure. And you are *not* going to let me get away with it."

As we descend into the basement, I feel a rush of excitement. It evaporates the moment we enter. One random glance from a guy at the bar is enough to convince me the whole room is staring at me and wishing I'd fuck off.

The club has an industrial look, all exposed air vents and stainless steel, which feels as if it might have been stylish twenty years ago. It's only half full, but there's already a crowd of people on the dance floor, flawlessly reciting the lyrics to a song that may or may not be by Ariana Grande. As George goes to the bar to buy cocktails, I spot some space on a bench next to an Aquaman who has gone a bit overboard with his wig. Aquaman gives me a spaced-out nod, seemingly high and unaware of his resemblance to Dolly Parton.

"Cheers!" says George as he crosses over with our drinks.

I take mine and try to angle my straw through the gap in my mask.

"OK, that's the first rule," says George. "Mask off."

"I thought the first rule was no sarcasm."

"Then the second rule is mask off."

"The mask's the best bit!"

"But then we can't see your handsome face."

"That's the point of a mask."

George pauses, as if he's really struggling to triangulate.

"You wanted me to be strict with you. So I'm only doing what you asked. Take off the mask, Lucas."

"Very good."

I remove the mask and tuck it into my pocket sulkily.

"How many more rules are there?"

"Don't think of it like that."

"I don't even know what we're doing here."

George smiles. "Nor do I."

"What?"

"You're not ready to hit on Amir. I know that much. But the rest... you can't teach it. Switch off your brain. Tell me what you feel. What you hear. What you smell."

I sniff the air pretentiously. "Top notes of aftershave and sweat. Undertones of beer and tequila. The delicate hint of a fart that a boy did on the dance floor and is now trying to dissipate with some overenthusiastic breakdancing."

"Very observant!" says George.

I look at him dryly. "I was taking the piss."

"Well, joke's on you, because there are no wrong answers."

"Oh, then please explain how smelling a fart is going to help me seduce the man of my dreams."

"Because it gets you out of your head. It puts you into your body. And honestly, whoever successfully hit on someone in a room that smelled like that? Your body would send you signals. This one time, I was at a barn dance and—"

"Do I want to know where this story is heading?"

"Totally. I was at Big Bertha's Barn Dance."

"Of course you were."

"And for once I wasn't really in the mood to meet girls."

"Shocking."

"I know, right? My parents were there, and we'd had a busy weekend at the country club."

"Gutting lots of salmon?"

"Exactly. So I'm planning to just have some corn dogs and do some line dancing, when I smell this scent."

"Don't tell me—Big Bertha let rip."

"Lucas! Ew! No, the scent was this incredible perfume. And I was transfixed. I followed the smell, and eventually I realized that it's this divorced woman who runs the candy store in town. Never given her a second glance. But that night, she just smelled so amazing, I asked her for a dance. And well, we ended up making out in the hay bales."

I give George a droll look.

"Do you have any stories that don't end with you successfully seducing a woman?"

George looks surprised. "I thought they might inspire you."

"Yes, I can't wait to get sniffing."

"Lucas! It's not about that. I just want you to go into the crowd and . . . be open to anything. Forget about smells. Just let it wash over you. And if you catch someone's eye, talk to them."

My mouth drops open. "You want me to hit on a stranger?"

"No. Yes. It doesn't matter. It literally doesn't matter what you talk about."

"What if they reject me?"

"It doesn't matter. Watch."

George leaps up to speak to a woman who's standing on the edge of the dance floor dressed as Black Widow. I can't hear what he's saying, but I can see that he's turning on the charm. I watch her face turn from surprise to fear to a desperate attempt at politeness. George shrugs and crosses back over to me.

"What was that about?" I ask.

"I hit on her. She wasn't interested."

"She's probably gay."

"Maybe. The point is, I put myself out there, she said no, and it was fine."

I look back at Black Widow. She's pointing out George to her friend and laughing. He definitely said something outrageously cheesy. I'm sure it's easy to handle rejection when you know that half the club would pay to sleep with you. But point taken.

"I really don't want to do this, George."

George pauses to think. "But you'll be mad at me if I don't help you push past your desire not to do it, because deep down, you actually do want to do it?"

"That's the one."

George gives me a friendly shove and I stumble to my feet. Every part of me is longing to argue and sit back down, so I try to remember what George told me. Be in my body. Respond to my senses. But regardless of what they smell like, how can I get past the fact that these are real people? Am I really going to just walk up to one of them and start talking? What if the conversation goes well? Then I'll have to go home with whoever I choose. It's the law.

I eye people up one by one. For every committed Thor or Captain America, there's an apologetic Wonder Woman or a half-hearted Hulk. I feel bad for all the Spider-Men, because that costume is unforgiving, and there's one guy who is blatantly hotter than the others. He's got those triangular shoulders that really pop in Lycra, plus the kind of face card that would be wasted behind a mask. I can't possibly approach him. I glance around and try to find someone more on my level, but I'm terrified of catching the wrong person's eye and being co-opted into some sort of prenuptial agreement.

Then I freeze. Someone's looking at me. Worse than that, he's smiling. And he's only meters away. I wouldn't say he's hot, but he's all right looking. For want of a better response, I smile back. At least, I intend it as a smile—god knows if my facial muscles are capable of cooperating. But it works—the guy is walking toward me. Shit. Shit. What do I say? It's only as he reaches me that I realize who he's dressed as.

"Ant-Man?"

Ant-Man beams proudly. I glance back and see George watching intently from the bench, willing me on. This feels like the gay Olympics. I try to recall the three rules.

"That's cool," I say.

"What?"

"I said, THAT'S COOL."

The music is so loud that I have to shout to be heard. I wonder how George would proceed. Probably by saying something extremely basic without a hint of embarrassment.

"Are you having a good night?"

"What?"

"ARE YOU HAVING A GOOD NIGHT?"

"Oh. Yeah! Très bon!"

Très bon. I'm going to let that one slide.

"What are you drinking?" I ask.

"Rum and Coke. You?"

"G&T."

Ant-Man frowns. "Green tea?"

"Yes, I'm drinking green tea on ice with a straw in the club. Trend alert!"

Ant-Man stares at me.

"It's GIN and TONIC."

"Oh, right. I love gin."

"It's great, isn't it."

"So good."

There's an awkward pause.

"And tonic," says Ant-Man.

"What?"

"Love a bit of tonic."

"Oh yeah, tonic's the best. And when you put them together? Wow."

Listen, it's not a Socratic dialogue. But I've passed George's test. More to the point, I'm realizing it doesn't matter that much what we talk about. We've connected. And now I can feel the music vibrating through me. I can taste the G&T on my lips. I picture myself kissing this guy, and I can't say I hate the idea.

"Hey, do you want to dance?" I ask with what I hope is a suggestive smile. Ant-Man returns it with a pitying look.

"Aww, I'm actually just waiting for my boyfriend to get back from the loo. But we can all go together when he gets here if you want?"

"That's OK, I'm going to go and poke my eyes out."

But Ant-Man is no longer listening.

"Cool," he says. "Enjoy!"

Back over at the bench, George raises his hand to high-five me. I leave him hanging.

"What's the matter?" asks George. "That was incredible."

"He has a boyfriend."

"Who cares?" says George with a shrug.

"I do! He must think I'm a loser."

"It doesn't matter what he thinks."

"I should have walked away sooner."

George reaches behind him and hands me a napkin.

"Great," I say, "I knew I looked sweaty."

George laughs. "That napkin is for you to crumble up your negative feelings and toss them over your shoulder. So you can forget all about them."

"You're joking, right?"

"No! My mom taught me this trick when I was working as a waiter in the restaurant and my brother got his friends to come in and prank me."

"OK . . . a lot to unpack there."

"Not really. The napkin trick helped me forget all about it."

George offers the napkin again. Purely to get him off my back, I screw it up and throw it over my shoulder.

"There!" says George. "Let's go celebrate."

Obviously the napkin thing was lame. But I will admit it was nice to have someone force me to get over it. I could have wallowed for hours.

George takes me up to the bar and racks up no less than six tequila shots. I was hoping my reward might be permission to leave, but as each shot goes down, Ant-Man fades into the distance and the club starts to feel a little more inviting.

A Dua Lipa song comes on the sound system. It gets a whoop from the crowd, and even I have to admit that I know it.

"Let's dance!" says George.

"Let's not go wild."

"Pretend I'm Amir. It will be fun."

I'm not a great dancer at the best of times, but I can't deny the lubricating effects of tequila. George drags me onto the dance floor. It's totally packed, but it's fun to be part of the throng. George finds a little pocket of space, where we have no choice but to dance right up against each other. I close my eyes—because it's awkward, not because I'm planning to do what George told me. Then I feel George's hips grind against me.

I instinctively tighten.

"Come on, Lucas, I'm the man of your dreams. Enjoy it."

Easier said than done, but what the hell.

I close my eyes, put my hands around George and imagine that I'm dancing with Amir. I almost can't bear it. If these hips were his. If we were this close to kissing. If we'd somehow succeeded in trading those clipped exchanges in the coffee shop for something this intimate and sensual. I open my eyes and George smiles at me. Now I'm unnerved. Because he's not Amir, is he? He's George. None of what I just imagined is real. And somehow, this is making it feel further from my grasp, not closer.

I'm relieved when the song ends and George goes to the bathroom. I wait for him at the bar and get another round of shots. I'm damp with sweat and my head is starting to spin. For some reason, these are pleasurable sensations. I spot a cute-looking Mr. Incredible. I catch his eye, and he smiles back, then looks away. We repeat the cycle. My heart is beating fast. This is actually quite exciting. Before we can get any further, George gets back.

"Feeling good?" asks George.

"I'm not hating it as much as I thought I would."

"Great, you should check out the bathroom. Everyone's so friendly! I turned down a blow job, but then I felt bad, so I said you might be up for it."

"George!"

"What?! He was hot."

I laugh at him in incredulity.

"I thought we were taking baby steps tonight."

"But you said you wanted me to push you."

"I didn't mean lining up blow jobs in the toilet."

"That's fine. I was just, you know, reacting to the situation."

"Cool," I say, "me too. I just caught someone's eye."

"That's amazing, Lucas. Where?"

I look around for Mr. Incredible, but I can't see him anywhere. Instead, my gaze falls on a boy who has just walked in dressed as Rorschach from Watchmen. That's a pretty cool choice of costume. I do a double take and my heart almost stops.

"Fuck," I say, yanking George behind a pillar.

"What?"

"It's him."

I peer back round and take in Amir. He's with his friend Yasmin, a fact I know only through my extensive internet stalking. Amir is wearing Rorschach's iconic Panama hat and trench coat. He hasn't bothered with the mask, but that only makes his look cooler. It's so simple and stylish, committed to the part yet effortless. Yasmin is dressed as Silk Spectre in a '60s-style yellow mini dress, her hair in an elegant bob. I'm surprised to see Amir at a theme night, but of course he's found a way to transcend it by dressing as one of the Watchmen, the anti-superheroes. If only I'd had that idea.

"Don't panic," says George.

Great advice. What else am I meant to do in this situation? Now Amir and his friend have spotted us.

"Why don't you go over?" says George.

I stare at him in disbelief. "I can't speak to him!"

"Why not?"

"You said I wasn't ready."

"You're not ready to hit on him. That doesn't mean you can't say hi."

I can't believe what I'm hearing. "I'm dressed as fucking Batman."

"You look good."

But good isn't good enough. Not when Amir is over there looking like a film star.

"No. No way. I'm not doing it."

George sighs. "Fine."

"George! You can't let me give up that easily."

"But . . . I can't force you if you really don't feel ready. What would you make you do if you were me?"

I pause to think. "I'd get me past this place of defeatism."

George processes this. Which takes him a moment, but let's not be mean.

"OK. I'm not going to make you approach Amir if that doesn't feel right in the moment. I think you can show him you're not scared another way. By hitting on someone else. Where's that guy whose eye you caught?"

"I can't go after him now."

"Yes, you can. Now is the perfect time. Nothing will make you more attractive to Amir than seeing you show interest in other men."

I look out and sure enough, there's Mr. Incredible. There's no denying that he's looking in my direction. But the whole thing now feels impossible.

"He's too hot for me."

"You didn't think that a minute ago."

"What if he rejects me in front of Amir?"

"He won't. He's blatantly into you!"

"I've never even made out with someone in public before. I can't do this."

I glance over at Amir and Yasmin. This is all too much.

"I'm leaving." I stand up.

"No, Lucas. I don't want us to end on this note."

"Tough."

"Lucas! Please! You'll thank me!"

George yanks my arm so hard I fall into his lap. I look into his eyes in shock. What happens next defies all logic.

We start kissing. I'm so taken aback that I don't stop to think. Is he doing this out of sympathy? Tactics? A teachable moment? I couldn't say.

All I can tell you right now is how it feels.

George's tongue is darting in and out of my mouth. I can taste the tequila on his lips. Smell his aftershave. Feel the stubble on his chin. We're *kissing*.

I run my hand through George's hair and down over his rock-hard abs. I've always wondered what those felt like.

Then, just for a split second, I open my eyes. George opens his eyes at the exact same time.

I catch his expression, and suddenly I'm not so sure he knows what he's doing. He reacted in the moment, sure, but who's to say he reacted correctly? I'm making out with George. *George*. In front of Amir. Am I insane? I leap to my feet, and this time George doesn't try to stop me. I stumble toward the exit. Before I leave, something compels me to turn and look at Amir. He and his friend are staring at me in fascination.

6

GEORGE

I HAVEN'T KISSED A MAN in a very long time. Not since high school. His name was Travis Clark, and we were on the football team together. We were best friends from day one. We went together like potato chips and mayonnaise—seriously, you have to try it! I was quarterback and Travis was tight end. The fact that we were always whipping each other with our towels in the locker room was just what boys did. Then one night, we won a big match and Travis and I went to a party. We spent the whole night talking about girls but didn't leave each other's side.

By 2:00 a.m., we were nestled together on a sofa, too drunk to move. By 3:00 a.m., we were the last people there. For most of that time, our legs were touching. I can't remember which of us first admitted that we had a boner. It was all a big joke at first. Travis claimed he wouldn't be able to fall asleep if he didn't jack off. Then he pulled down his pants and there it was. Hottest moment of my life up to that point. We were only planning to do it side by side, but we ended up making out, then giving each other a helping hand. I couldn't think about anything else for days afterward. Travis and I never spoke about it. I wasn't ashamed, but it felt easier to leave it in the past and keep doing what I'd been doing with girls. Which brings me to last night.

I'm not talking about Lucas. Listen, this whole reacting to the situation thing isn't foolproof. Kissing Lucas felt like the right thing to do in the moment, and it's possible that it wasn't, but I'm not going to sweat it. Lucas and I haven't been in contact since, but he's the kind of guy who needs time to cool down. I'm sure it will be fine once I see him.

After Lucas fled, I returned to the dance floor. Pretty soon, I was approached by Spider-Man. The hot one. He knew who I was, but he didn't go on about it. Everything else that needed to be said we said with our eyes. Maybe it was being in a gay club. Maybe I was looking for a loophole after promising myself no more girls until after exams. Or maybe I was just horny. Either way, Hot Spider-Man came home with me. In fact, he's still here now.

He's fast asleep, on his side facing the wall, his rib cage rising and falling. I'm curled up behind him, fighting for my life. These single beds are small enough when it's just me. Fair to say I haven't had the best night's sleep. I'm on the verge of dozing off when Hot Spider-Man stirs and turns to look at me through hazy eyes. He mumbles as if he's dreaming, then reaches down and grabs my dick. He's a big fan of it. He wouldn't stop complimenting it last night. It's not *that* big, but it's perfect, according to him. Yesterday he said he was tired and wanted to focus on me, which I wasn't going to complain about. But this morning, I want to return the favor. Something I never got to do with Travis. Something I've always wanted to try.

Actually, I did once try sucking my own dick when I was a teenager, but I was too busy to really appreciate it, if you know what I mean. As I shimmy down and Hot Spider-Man realizes what I'm doing, he grins in delight and lies back.

Why did I wait so long to try this?

No one told me how hot it is when you feel them getting harder in your mouth. When they mutter and moan in a voice they've never used before. After a while, Hot Spider-Man flips around and returns the favor. I close my eyes, and suddenly I'm not in a dorm room in Cambridge. I'm in the club last night with Lucas.

I didn't really process what was happening at the time—I was too drunk, then it all fell apart so quickly. But looking back, that was kind of hot. We really went for it. Sure, it wasn't a typical kiss, but it was still a kiss. It still felt good. And now I'm thinking there was only one reason I came home with Hot Spider-Man last night, and it's because I wanted to finish what I started with Lucas. Lucas got me horny, believe it or not. I recall him drifting his hand over my abs, and now I'm picturing him going further, sliding a hand up my shorts and closing his lips around what he finds.

I tense, then let out a gasp and jet all over my chest. I open my eyes and see Hot Spider-Man smiling at me. I'd almost forgotten about him.

• • •

Crazy the places your mind will go when you're turned on. Did I really just imagine me and Lucas doing that? I must still be drunk. Feeling guilty, I help Hot Spider-Man finish, then get out of bed and pull on some clothes. As he gets the message, his face falls.

"It's Sunday," he says. "Come back to bed."

"I need to do my laundry."

"What about next week? We can go for a drink, see the new Marvel?"

He's trying to sound casual, but failing. I hate to disappoint him, but I don't usually double dip. People are never as impressed by me the second time.

"I've seen it," I claim.

"What?" says Hot Spider-Man. "But it's not out yet."

Damn. Think fast, George, think fast.

"I went to a special screening."

"Whoa, how come?"

"Er . . . I'm not allowed to say."

"Oh my god, do you have connections at Disney?"

How have I made myself *more* attractive to him? This is what happens when you can't bear to say no. I've never been very good at lying. All I can think to do is mime zipping up my lips.

"Wow," says Hot Spider-Man. "We *need* to go for that drink."

"I'll have to check my schedule. Give me your number and I'll let you know."

I stay in bed for the rest of the day, wondering how I'm going to explain my way out of that one. What's wrong with me? Why couldn't I tell him I wasn't interested in seeing him again? How have I gotten into this habit of seeing people only once?

Last night was fun. There's no reason to think Hot Spider-Man wouldn't be into it a second time around. In fact, he already texted me saying he's looking forward to it, but if I reply, I'll feel obliged to keep the conversation going. How long do I have until it's ghosting?

I'm embarrassed to admit I've done that to a couple of girls in the past, but only because I couldn't figure out how to let them down without upsetting them. It once took me three months to draft a text to a girl explaining why I found it stressful when she trauma dumped on our first date. By the time I finally sent it, she'd blocked me.

. . .

The next morning I'm up bright and early, ready to resume training. After the past week, I'm relieved at the thought of getting back into a familiar routine. When I arrive at the train station, the first person I see is Lucas.

"Hey!" I say. "How fun was Saturday?"

Lucas looks aghast and drops his voice to a mumble. "Don't talk about that when we're with the team."

I look around. Most of the guys aren't here yet, and Dakani is busy on his phone, so I guess that means I'm OK to proceed.

"You made some really good progress. Plus you're a great kisser."

Lucas looks even more mortified. "Shut up, George!"

"I'm just saying. But hey, if you need any more practice."

"You think I need practice?!"

"No! I just—"

"George, can we drop it, please?"

"In a minute. Lucas, I watched Amir as you left. He wasn't laughing. He wasn't upset. He was curious. I think the guy likes you."

Lucas shakes his head. "I blew my chance. I should have just gone and said hi."

"You'll see him at the coffee shop! You'll have tons of chances."

"I'll never be brave enough to approach him when I'm sober."

"You will, Lucas. I'll make sure."

"OK, great, now shhhhhh."

I turn as I hear someone approaching. It's Fran Macdonald. What's she doing here? Everyone keeps going on about her roast as if she ran me over with a car, but she was only having a laugh.

"Have the girls switched to morning training?" I ask.

Fran smiles. "The other girls haven't."

"Huh. So you're training on your own?"

"Nope."

It's too early for guessing games. Then it hits me. "You're joining the men's squad?!"

Fran shrugs. "I need a new challenge. I'm gonna give it a shot."

"Did you know about this, Lucas?"

"Of course I did," he says quickly. "I'm all for it. Bring on the competition."

If I know Lucas—which I'm starting to think I do, a little bit—he's freaking out internally but determined not to show it.

Still, those two are friends, and I'm sure Fran got his blessing. Lucas links arms with Fran and chats happily with her for the whole train ride to Ely. I sit with Johannes and we try to figure out what this means for the lineup. Is Fran going to be paired with me in the first boat, meaning Lucas has been dropped? Or will she be started in the second boat, and I've been demoted to join her?

When we arrive in Ely, Deb briskly announces that Fran will be coxing the second boat, with Tristan as stroke. Tristan looks happy—he's always wanted to be tried out in the top seat—but a trial is all it is. Lucas and I are safe, for now at least.

As we carry the boats down to the water, I'm dying to ask Lucas how he really feels about the threat of Fran, but he's avoiding my gaze and it's clear he doesn't want to talk. It feels like we've slipped back into our old dynamic. Hard to believe that two nights ago, we were making out dressed as superheroes.

We get into our seats and push out onto the water. The Great Ouse is a wide stretch of river in the middle of the Cambridgeshire Fens, a flat expanse of former marshland on England's east coast. In winter, arctic winds blow all the way from Siberia. On days like today, when the sun is shining, the scene is majestic. It feels good to be back doing what I do best. The other boat is behind us on the river, so I have no idea how they're faring. Lucas is the one who has a clear view. He looks pretty stressed, but if I try to reassure him, he'll snap at me.

So much tension in such a little guy. I wonder what he'd say if I offered him a massage.

"Right," Deb shouts on her megaphone as she cycles along the tow path. "Sprints."

I can hear Ed and Ted muttering in disgust from here.

Making us race on the first day back in training is an ice-cold move, but I love it when Deb keeps us on our toes. The other crew pulls up alongside us. Tristan is in my periphery, but I'm determined not to glance over and give him the satisfaction of thinking that I care. Which I don't. Deb blows her whistle. As Lucas cranks up the stroke rate and I pull on my oar, I have a serious case of déjà vu. Only we aren't out there on the Thames, being watched by millions of people. And we're not racing Oxford. It's Tristan and Fran, who've been paired together for all of ten minutes. Compared to them, Lucas and I know each other's game perfectly. He's guiding me like magic. And with a week's rest in my legs, my rowing is flawless.

This is why I was made stroke. This is what Deb wants to see from me. I glance over at the other boat. Tristan is trying desperately to keep pace, but he's not quite managing. As we cross the finish line narrowly in the lead, I look at Lucas and grin. For the first time that I can remember, Lucas smiles back.

. . .

"Anyone sitting here, old chap?" asks Tristan.

"No," I say, before I know what's happening. Tristan slides in beside me. I was determined to sit with Lucas on the train home, but he already made a beeline for Fran.

"That was close," Tristan says.

"Yeah, you did great!"

"We almost won. First time rowing with Fran. You've had months of practice with Lucas."

These facts are indisputable.

"I guess it's official," says Tristan. "I'm your competition."

"Bring it on. It will push me to be my best."

"Well, you'd better get on with it, cos it looks like you've lost Deb."

I frown at him. What's he talking about?

"Don't you think it says a lot, the crews she chose today?" asks Tristan.

"No," I say, suddenly uncertain. "I mean, if she'd dropped me or Lucas from the first boat, that would have said something."

Tristan looks at me slyly.

"You know that's not the only option. Look who else was in your boat today. Half of them aren't even around next year."

"What are you saying?" I ask, trying to sound casual.

"Maybe you shouldn't be so sure which was the first boat out there," says Tristan. "Maybe Deb dropped you both."

. . .

I'm not going to panic. Tristan is trying to fuck with me, because that's what he does. No one knows what Deb is thinking. Until she tells us otherwise, I'm going to assume that I haven't been dropped.

I definitely won't say anything to my parents, who I've finally managed to pin down to a Zoom call this afternoon. The country club is closed on Mondays, and it's the only time I have any chance of getting their attention. Once I get back to my room after lunch, I pull on a shirt my parents gave me for my birthday and dial in. But as the call connects, it's not my parents on the other end.

"Oh," I say. "Hey, Chuck!"

"Surprise," my older brother Chuck says blankly.

There's green all around him and it looks like he's floating. Then I realize he's sitting on a lawn mower. Chuck also works at the country club as a groundskeeper.

"Mom and Dad sent me the link, but I've only got five minutes. There's a golf tournament tomorrow, and Pete is not happy with the fairways."

I'm secretly pleased to hear that Chuck won't be taking up too much of my precious time with Mom and Dad. He always claimed he'd never end up working at the country club like them, until one summer his holiday job became permanent. No one's ever said a word about the change of plan.

"Hey," says Chuck, "saw you in the Boat Race."

I feel my whole body tense. "Thanks for watching!"

"What happened?" asks Chuck.

"It's complicated."

"You think I won't get it?"

"No, it's just—"

"Relax, George. I saw the headlines."

My heart sinks. "You did? You mean—"

"That article? Yeah. Jeana Hampton sent it to mom."

Damn. I'd hoped it hadn't crossed the Atlantic, but it's OK. It's not a big deal.

"How's it going with you?" I ask Chuck.

"Awesome." He frowns at his screen and brushes at his bald patch. "I just got a raise."

"Very nice. How's Natalie?"

Chuck tenses. If Mom's to be believed, Chuck and Natalie are never more than a few days from their latest argument.

"She's great," says Chuck. "Everything's great."

Just then, another rectangle is added to the call.

"Mom? Dad?"

"Just a minute, boys," says my mom. "We're at a very risky stage."

"Of what?"

"The pavlova."

It takes several more seconds of my mom dashing in and out of frame before she's seated in front of the camera. My mom was a stunner when she was my age and I still think she's beautiful, but she's always claiming she's lost her looks. She's got the same curly brown hair, round face, and plump cheeks as Chuck, and they both look so jolly when they smile. Which isn't very often.

"There, Ron, I think that's stable."

My mom catches her breath. She's stressed out of her mind.

"I thought today was your day off," I say sympathetically.

"It is." My mom wipes her brow. "There's a wedding tomorrow."

"Who gets married on a Tuesday?"

"Lots of people these days. Better rates."

"Which means they're worse for us!" says my dad, entering the frame. "Brenda, you might want to watch that coulis."

My mom dips out and my dad takes over. He's the one I take after, just like he takes after his ancestors who originally came over from Norway. We're the exact same height, and though his stomach has filled out, he's still got a full head of hair.

"Hey, Dad," I say. "Did you watch the race?"

"Now that was a whole operation," says my dad. "What channel was it on, BBC World? We don't get that on our TV. We had to get Maureen Carlsberg's boy to come and set it up. It took him forever. I think he was stoned."

"Well, I hope it was worth it."

"Ron," says my mom. "It's looking unsteady."

My dad leaps out of his seat. My mom tags back in.

"Six tiers," she says. "It's like the Leaning Tower of Pisa."

"Can we see?" I ask.

"I'll send you a photo when it's done."

She'll never remember.

"Mom, Chuck said you read that article about me."

"What? Oh, that. Yes, Jeana Hampton sent it to me, but I didn't really get what it was saying."

Plenty of times I've wished my parents would show more of an interest in my life in Cambridge. Right now, it's a relief.

"Don't worry about it. But I do have to decide—"

"What's the weather like there?"

"It's a bit gray today."

"Ron," says my mom, "try removing those strawberries."

I don't know why, but I'm having the strangest reaction. I'm having to try really hard not to cry. It's not because I'm sad. I'm always happy to see my family. I guess it's that they're so far away and don't really have time for me.

"Mom, I have to decide about next year."

"Plenty of jobs going here."

"He's too good for us now," says Chuck. "He's at Cambridge."

I clear my throat. "I want to stay on and do a master's."

Chuck scowls. "Why?"

Surely Chuck's five minutes are up by now?

"Because I like it here. And I want to row in next year's Boat Race. If I do, will you guys come this time?"

My dad has rejoined the call. My mom gives him a look.

"We can't just leave the restaurant. We'd have to take at least four days off."

"At least," says my dad.

"You guys need a vacation."

"Then we'd be losing money and spending it."

"Flights aren't that bad if you book in advance."

My mom gives me a smile. "We'll definitely look into it."

I'm getting that feeling again. Which is ridiculous, because my mom just said she'd look into it. I'm sure she means it. I'm sure she's not just saying it to get me off the phone.

"Thanks, Mom. That would be amazing."

"Ron!" says my mom, looking off-screen in horror. "It's gonna fall!"

. . .

I always feel weird after speaking to my parents. I think I just miss them so much. It's a long way from Cambridge to Wisconsin, and I get that it's another world to them. That's why I wish they'd visit. The last time I went home, they were so busy and distracted that I couldn't really deal with it, and I haven't been back in a while. But now we have a plan. They're going to be at next year's Boat Race. Almost certainly. Maybe. Hopefully. It's not like I'm in a position to make firm plans yet. First, I need to pass these exams.

I message Jemima to let her know I'm sticking to my original plan. She replies with a thumbs-up emoji. Love that emoji! Next, I text Lucas and tell him it's about time we got started on my dissertation. He texts back telling me not to worry about it. I'm trying to think of a polite way to tell him that we probably do need to start worrying about it, when he sends another message telling me to come to his room at 6:00 p.m.

That can only mean one thing—an all-nighter!

I've never been able to motivate myself to stay up all night working, but I've always liked the idea of starring in my own studying montage like Reese Witherspoon in *Legally Blonde*. I go to Sainsbury's and load up on Red Bull and Haribo—that should keep us going until dawn. At the appointed hour, I head over to St John's. As Lucas opens his door, I hold up the Red Bulls in one hand and the Haribo in the other, pulling the kind of winsome expression I imagine Reese Witherspoon doing.

Lucas chuckles. "Tell me you've never pulled an all-nighter without telling me you've never pulled an all-nighter."

The smile is wiped from my face. Lucas softens.

"Seriously, George, people have died from drinking that much Red Bull."

Lucas allows me to follow him inside. Wow, his room is huge. After your first year, rooms are assigned by ballot, with those who get the best exam results being awarded first choice. Which means that Lucas got the best room in college. It's not a typical set of rooms, but one vast one that looks out onto a cluster of weeping willows bordering the River Cam. There's a sturdy wooden desk in the window, a sofa, an armchair, and—

"A double bed?!"

Lucas glances over at it bashfully.

"I believe it's king-size."

"Lucas, you are living the dream."

"Yes, George. Alone in my king-size bed every night."

He sits down on the sofa and opens his laptop. On the screen is a photo gallery that shows some young people at a party in London. I recognize one of them.

"Is that Amir?"

Lucas sighs dreamily. "He was at the opening of the Royal Academy Summer Exhibition. Joe Alwyn was there. FKA Twigs. Imagine if I got to be his date."

"Yes, Lucas! Let's visualize it!"

Lucas laughs. "It's a bit late for that. But we have both been invited to this garden party at St John's. The whole college has. It's meant to be like, the last hurrah before exams."

"That's perfect!"

Lucas looks at me in disbelief. "I'm not approaching Amir at a public event."

"Then do it in the coffee shop."

"What do you mean?"

"Mention the garden party. Find out if he's going or not. Break the ice."

"And then what?"

I smile at Lucas. "Part of your problem is you're always thinking two steps ahead. Let's cross that bridge when we come to it."

"Are you sure we shouldn't conduct a full structural assessment of the bridge to prepare for the eventuality that we come to it?"

"Yes, Lucas, I'm sure. Apart from anything else, tonight is about me."

Lucas looks relieved to change the subject. He pulls up a document on his laptop.

"What's that?" I ask.

"Your dissertation."

"What do you mean?"

"I wrote it this afternoon."

I laugh, before realizing he's serious. "What?! How? That's ten thousand words."

"This was the easy part."

"What's the hard part?"

"We can't hand it in like this. It has to sound like you."

"You mean, make it sound American?"

"Well, not just that. Have a seat."

I sit down next to Lucas on the sofa. Judging by the way he shuffles over, I'm guessing he was expecting me to sit on the chair opposite, but if we're going to be working on my dissertation together, isn't this better? It's only as I sit down that I'm reminded of how big I am. And how I kind of need a whole one of these sofas to myself. This is cozy.

"OK," says Lucas, scanning the document, "what words would you use to explain that comparative advantage depends on an assumption of constant returns?"

"Er . . . what?"

"Like how Ireland has comparative advantage over most countries in dairy production. But you can't just assume that will go on forever."

"Of course you can't. You don't get unlimited refills from a cow."

"Perfect!"

I assume he's being sarcastic, but Lucas types what I just said into the dissertation. He explains his rationale: a low-grade essay that sounds like my voice is far preferable to a perfect essay that risks being caught for plagiarism. As we work through the dissertation, concepts that have never meant anything to me suddenly become crystal clear. Opportunity cost? That's the price of FOMO. Conjoint analysis? That's Twitter polls for geeks. This is cheating as an art form. A seamless production line between Lucas's mode of understanding and mine. It's more than any of my professors have managed over the last three years. No wonder Lucas is first in our class. There's nothing this boy doesn't know, but he's not showy about it. When I confuse the scarcity principle with the exception that proves the rule, Lucas doesn't laugh or make me feel bad. He gently walks me through the difference until he's sure I understand.

Who *is* this Lucas?

"You're so good at explaining!" I exclaim after his latest demonstration.

Lucas shrugs it off.

"I always used to help my sister with her homework."

"That's so nice of you."

"That's just what a big brother does."

Images from my childhood flash through my mind. Chuck pummeling me for borrowing his dinosaur egg. Convincing me that milkshake tastes nicer if you drink it through your nose with a straw. "Accidentally" slipping my SAT results into the menu of someone I was serving at the restaurant.

"Was that your brother in the photo?"

Apparently Lucas is psychic.

"What photo?"

"In your room."

"Oh. Yeah. Charles. We call him Chuck."

"You guys get on?"

"Sure. I don't see my family that often."

Lucas looks curious, but I'm not in the mood for this conversation.

"What's next on the dissertation?" I ask.

Lucas smiles at me. "We're done."

I look at him in surprise.

"What about the math part?"

"I can do that myself. You can go."

Suddenly we're not engaged in a secret assignment. We're just two guys sitting way too close to each other on a sofa. Two guys who kissed the other night. And let's not forget the part where I thought about him during sex. I really don't know what's gotten into me lately. I'm going to leave before I start overthinking it.

As I stand up, I spot Lucas's rowing kit. "Hey, Tristan said the funniest thing to me today. He thinks Deb dropped us."

Lucas shrugs. "I doubt she's made any decisions."

"That's what I thought."

"Then what are you worried about?"

"I'm not worried. Tristan deserves to have his shot."

Lucas looks at me in disgust. "Are you insane? Fuck Tristan."

"But—"

"I'm serious, George. You are not in a good position right now. Focus on what *you* want."

. . .

I used to not be able to cope with Lucas's bluntness. But when he's on my side, it's refreshing. That guy is surprising me more and more. It's so nice of him to finish my dissertation on his own. Plus, he's right—it's quicker if he does it. As I leave St John's, I look at my phone to figure out what to do with the rest of my evening. At the top of my chats is an unanswered message from Hot Spider-Man. I don't have any particular desire to see him, but I feel bad about leaving him on read, plus what else would I do tonight? Wash my hair?

I reply to his message, and he texts back within seconds. A bit too fast, if I'm honest, but who am I to complain? We make a plan to meet at a bar on Trinity Street, and I go back to my room to make sure I'm looking good and smelling better. I'd have been happy for Hot Spider-Man to come straight here, but I guess a drink first is classier. It's only as I walk toward the bar that I feel a sense of regret at my abandoned night with Lucas. Yes, it's great that I'm going to have a finished dissertation by morning, but it felt so good to bask in Lucas's brilliance and let it rub off on me. Is that what it feels like to be top of the class? Is this what I've been missing out on all these years?

I arrive at the bar and see Hot Spider-Man already seated inside. His hair is still wet from the shower, and he's wearing a shirt with so many buttons undone it would be rude not to keep going. Instead I find myself dashing past the window before I'm spotted.

What am I doing? He's gorgeous.

But I'm just not feeling it. What was it that Lucas said? Focus on what you want. And now that Hot Spider-Man is being offered to me on a plate, it's clear he isn't it. I'm sure I'll come up with a good way to let him down gently.

I turn around and head back to college. Back in my room, I sit at my desk. Earlier today, I had a delivery from Amazon. It's nothing if not a good place to start. I turn to the first page and begin to read *Economics for Dummies*.

7
LUCAS

OUT ON THE RIVER, when you can feel the wind rush against your cheeks and the boat move through the water, rowing makes sense as a sport. But every weekday after lunch, the rowers have to come back from their lectures and complete a timed session on a rowing machine, known as an ergometer, or erg for short. There's something oppressive about the sight of the whole team on ergs, putting in just as much effort as they do on the river but going nowhere. I know I have it easy, but if anything, it's even more mind-numbing to stand and watch. There are times when rowers can't motivate themselves and need me to shout at them like I do in the boat. But on days like today, when they aren't exhausted from weeks of training, pushing out 2k on an erg is second nature.

"Tempted to join them?" asks Fran, walking up behind me.

"I don't want to make them look bad."

"Yeah, no, same."

We share a grin.

"Why don't you shout at Tristan a bit?" I ask. "He loves it when women do that."

Fran laughs, then her expression turns serious. "What about you?"

I frown, not catching her drift.

"Are you OK with me being here?"

"No, Fran, I think women should stay in the kitchen where they belong."

"Lucas—"

"We talked about this."

"I know," says Fran. "But now that I'm actually here . . . is it weird?"

Of course I'm not thrilled that I'm suddenly facing competition for my place. But I'm glad it's Fran. Genuinely. I'd much rather she bump me from the boat than someone I hate. I understand why she's doing this. Her victory in the women's Boat Race was virtually ignored by the media. She's the only member of the women's crew who has the opportunity to join the men and share the limelight. I can cope with a bit of awkwardness. It's not like we're being asked to jelly wrestle.

"It's fine," I say to Fran with the widest smile I can muster. "Honestly, I have bigger things to worry about."

. . .

I'm not just saying that. Today's the day of the garden party, and my first shift in the coffee shop since I saw Amir at the club. I've been dreading this moment, but as it's got closer, something weird has happened—I've dreaded it less. Don't get me wrong, I'm still dreading it. But I'm trying to take more of a George approach to what happened in the club. It was embarrassing, but mainly because of the way I reacted. I don't think George was wrong that it was good for Amir to see me being interested in another boy. Especially someone as hot as George. When I look back on that night, I can't quite believe it. I hit on one guy and kissed another. Sure, one of them was George and he was only doing it to make me feel better, but still, it happened. I put myself out there and shit happened. There's a lesson there somewhere.

As I arrive at the coffee shop, I remember George's advice. Mention the garden party. That's it. Then the ice will have been broken, and Amir and I can pick it back up with a glass of wine among the rose beds. Or, if he reacts badly, I'll know not to show up. And, you know, retire to my chamber to impale myself on a ceremonial sword. But all I have to do for now is this one simple task.

Except that as the clock ticks past 4:00 p.m. and then 4:30, Amir still hasn't shown. It's getting close to 5:00, the end of my shift and the start of the garden party, and I'm starting to give up hope. Amir's not coming. He's never coming in again.

Then, as I'm about to hang up my apron and lock up, the bell tinkles and there he is.

Shit. Shit shit shit. Don't think about what happened in the club. Don't think about how hot he looks. Just do it. Amir walks up to the counter.

"What can I get you?" I ask.

"Cappuccino with oat milk, please. Not too hot."

"Coming right up!"

Not "coming right up." That was not in the script. I need to ask him now, before I say something genuinely insane.

"Are you going to the garden party?" I manage to splutter.

Amir looks astonished. It's a mad thing for me to have asked. We've never even acknowledged that we go to the same college. But maybe it's better to cut to the chase.

"Actually, yeah," says Amir, "I was thinking of going."

Fuck. He was thinking of going. Say something normal.

"Me too."

Amir smiles. "Nice. Wanna go together?"

What? WHAT?

"Uh, yeah," I say. "That would be awesome. I'm almost done here."

As I turn to make his coffee, it's hard not to whoop and punch the air. What just happened? I'm going to the garden party with Amir! I stick the milk frother in the coffee by accident and it spurts everywhere. For god's sake. I should have asked him after I made his drink. Now we have to make small talk. What would George advise? Instinct, react, look around you, book! He's holding a book!

"What are you reading?" I ask Amir.

He holds up a copy of *Giovanni's Room*.

I roll my eyes. "Not still in that bloody room, is he? Loser!"

Amir looks slightly startled. "Er, no. He just got arrested for murder."

What's wrong with me? I'm serious, I need a diagnosis. As I focus on making Amir something vaguely wet and caffeinated, I attempt to think of a less crazy response.

"I'm so bad at reading novels during term time."

"Really?" says Amir. "I find it easier to read in Cambridge than at home."

Interesting. Is he referring to the flat his parents own in Mayfair, estimated value £2.2 million, or the family home in Sidi Bou Said, a charming coastal town in Tunisia?

"Why's that?" I ask.

"I'm from Tunisia. It's too hot out there to think, let alone read."

I hand Amir his coffee, and it's a miracle I don't ask him why he doesn't try cooling down in that lovely swimming pool of his with the green tiles.

"It sounds gorgeous."

No, it doesn't! He doesn't know you've seen it. Concentrate.

"Yeah," says Amir, "it's all right."

He taps his card and smiles at me.

"We should go."

I'm unsteady on my feet. Five minutes ago, we'd never even had a proper conversation. Now he's proposing a trip together? I smile at him in amazement.

"Yeah! I'd love to go to Tunisia."

I watch as Amir's expression crumples into one of sympathy.

"Oh. I meant go to the garden party."

I turn bright red.

"I know. Obviously. I didn't think—kidding!"

I start frantically mopping with a cloth. I can feel Amir staring at me. That's good—he'll be a crucial police witness when I spontaneously combust.

"Are you coming, then?" Amir asks.

"Me? No."

Amir looks surprised. "Oh right. I thought—"

"Yeah, no, I forgot I have a doctor's appointment, so I can't—in fact I have to close up here. You should probably—"

I step out from behind the counter and bundle Amir toward the door.

"So great to talk finally. Enjoy the rest of the book. Fingers crossed for Giovanni! Everyone makes mistakes!"

. . .

I run to the nearest cliff and jump off it. If only. That would be infinitely preferable to replaying the conversation with Amir in my mind for the rest of the day. Each time, it only gets more mortifying. How could I have been so stupid? Why would Amir have been proposing a trip to Tunisia with someone he'd just met? And once I realized my mistake, why didn't I style it out? I can't possibly speak to Amir ever again. If he comes back to the coffee shop, I'll quit on the spot, get a taxi to the airport, and start a new life in Bulgaria.

I'd quite happily spend the rest of the week lying in bed and planning my own funeral. Sadly, every year, the winning Boat Race crew invites the losers to a formal dinner. This is supposedly done in a spirit of gentlemanly bonhomie, but really it's an opportunity for the winners to gloat. That part is bad enough, but the fact that it's a black-tie dinner makes me actively dread it. There's nothing like these formal Oxbridge occasions to dredge up my insecurities. I might be able to dress the part, but I swear people can tell I don't belong. Even before I open my mouth, I just don't feel at ease in these spaces in the way they so clearly do. It's something about the way they hold themselves with such confidence—not that I can put my finger on it, let alone mimic it. Following the catastrophe with Amir, I decide I'm in no mood to put myself through any more humiliation, and message the crew to say I can't come to the dinner because I don't own a tux. George isn't having it. He tells me to meet him at the local suit rental shop.

"You really don't have to do this," I say to George.

"I do," George says cheerily. "I don't want you to miss out."

He turns to the sales assistant, a girl around our age.

"Do you have this a size smaller?"

"Let me check."

As the sales assistant walks off, I grimace.

"She has to check. Can you imagine being so small that the shop assistants don't even know if you belong in the adult section?"

"Lucas, you're the only one who cares about your height. You need to own it."

"Why? What's the point? I've fucked it with Amir."

I told George what happened as soon as I got here. Unsurprisingly, he's refusing to see it as the disaster it so clearly was.

"You didn't fuck it."

"I don't want to talk about it."

George nods and turns back to the suits.

"George! Obviously I want to talk about it!"

"Oh. Yeah. Right. Look, you made a mistake, but the main thing is, Amir asked if you wanted to go to the garden party together. That's huge."

"It's not huge. The garden party was yesterday."

"That doesn't matter. It's a really good sign. I honestly think you can salvage this."

The sales assistant returns with my suit. George thanks her and gets me to put it on. I'm expecting him to leave me to change alone, but he just stands there in the door of the dressing room.

We've seen each other naked before, but for some reason, taking off my trousers in front of him feels way more exposing.

Once I've got the suit on, George examines me carefully. He feels along both of my arms with his hands to check the fit, then crouches down and slides his hand up the inseam, right up to the danger area. I flush red and feel the hairs stand up on the back of my neck. I'm not sure how helpful it is to have a dating coach who's quite so beautiful as George.

"Yes," says George. "Much better."

I peer at my reflection doubtfully.

"Seriously," says George, "you look so handsome."

"You sound like my mum."

"You look hot. Is that better?"

I blush and reappraise myself in the mirror. "I don't see it."

George nods. "I think I see the problem."

"I'm a short arse."

"I don't mean physically!"

He looks at me earnestly. "You've learned how to break the ice, and that's great. But you don't see yourself as attractive. That's probably why you panicked with Amir."

That is way more insightful than I would have expected from George. But maybe I'm being judgmental. He is an expert at this.

"OK, so we're agreed," I say. "This is never going to work."

"No," laughs George, "we can totally fix this. Pick something you like about yourself."

I look back at my reflection.

"I have two working knees."

"Lucas, I need you to take this seriously."

I smile at George. "Well done. You're being very strict."

"Because I actually want this for you."

I've never been able to handle sincerity. "What do I have to do again?"

"Pick something you like about how you look."

I stare at the mirror. I know I'm not ugly. I could even take handsome on a good day. But I just can't see myself as hot.

"Well?" says George.

"I got nothing. No tengo nada."

"Forget about your ex. I'll say a few things about you that I think are attractive, and you tell me if you find any of them convincing."

George stands back and examines me like I'm a painting.

"Your hair is a great color. It reminds me of maple trees back home."

I feel self-conscious, and my hand shoots up to tidy my hair. George reaches out his hand to stop me. The moment he touches me, I tingle all over.

"And it suits being messy," George declares, holding my gaze.

"Your eyes are very striking," he continues. "That green against your skin, it really works. Your freckles are adorable."

I can't take this many compliments in a row, especially not with George so up close. Perhaps detecting my unease, he takes a step back and surveys me.

"You have a great body. You can tell even when you're in a suit. Especially when you're in a suit. Your shoulders are naturally broad, but it's all in proportion. Oh, and best of all, you have a seriously cute butt. I've always thought that."

George looks at me innocently.

"How was that?"

. . .

I'm not sure what I succeed in mumbling in response to George. That whole moment caught me off guard. Pretty sure he was just being nice. Thankfully, we've run out of time and need to go and meet our teammates. In spite of the storied rivalry between Oxford and Cambridge, the journey between the two towns is far from convenient. It requires taking a bus along several country roads, which tend to be clogged with traffic. George and I arrive at the boat house to find the bus already waiting and half the team boarded. I get on and look around for a seat.

"George!" calls Johannes, waving his iPad at him. "I've downloaded the new season of *Is It Cake?!*"

"Cool," says George. "I'm going to sit with Lucas."

I follow George to the back of the bus. Johannes is not the only one staring. I realize this is probably the first time any of the crew have seen me and George spend time together voluntarily.

"Jesus," says George as we take our seats. "You'd think they'd caught us fucking."

I laugh a little too loudly and glance around to check that no one is in earshot.

"You haven't told anyone about this, have you?"

"About what?" asks George.

"Our deal?"

"Who would I tell?"

"We've gotta be careful," I say furtively. "They're already suspicious."

"Who cares? This will all be over soon."

My demeanor darkens.

George looks surprised. "Because we'll both have everything we want."

I let out a laugh. "I don't get how you're always so positive. What makes you think this is going to work out?"

"I've visualized it."

"It's not that simple."

"Sometimes it is. Come on—what's your ultimate fantasy of you and Amir?"

I roll my eyes, but George isn't letting me off the hook.

"I dunno. Hanging out in his flat in Mayfair, reading books and having sex."

"Great. Hold that image in your head."

I try. I really do. But I can't see myself in the flat in Mayfair. It's like these black-tie university events. I just don't belong there.

"Hey," says George.

"What?"

"You're not holding that image in your head."

"You don't know what's in my head."

"True, but based on your facial expression, I'm guessing it's not your ultimate fantasy."

I frown and try again. I suppose I can see myself in the flat in Mayfair if I really try, ruining its perfectly folded towels the moment I touch them. It's the part where I'm lovingly entangled in Amir's arms that I'm struggling with.

"What's the problem?" asks George.

"I don't want to talk about it."

"Why do you think I trapped you on a two-hour bus ride?"

I narrow my eyes at George. "You've changed."

"I learned from the best," George grins.

"I could lock myself in the loo," I say dryly.

"Yes, Lucas, you could do that."

I let out a long sigh.

"Fine. It's like you said earlier. I just don't feel attractive."

George looks encouraged by the confession. "And why do you think that is?"

"Because why would someone like Amir be into someone like me?"

"I told you, a lot of guys are into short men."

"That's not what I mean."

I tell George about my upbringing. How my mum's experiences at work made me aware from a young age that people will always look down on me because of my background. How it made me desperate for their approval and simultaneously convinced that I'll never be good enough for them. How it's nothing to do with how much I have in my bank account, but a far more deep-rooted sense of inadequacy.

"I get it," says George.

"No you don't."

"How do you know?"

"Because you actually like yourself. You're not trying to be something you're not."

"Maybe not right now, but I know what it feels like." George pauses and goes somewhere else in his mind. "When I was at high school, I had the pick of the girls."

"There's a common theme to these stories."

George ignores me. "When I say I had the pick, I mean the pick. It was ridiculous."

"Feeling soooo good about myself right now."

"Please just listen," says George.

Something about his tone snaps me out of it. This is clearly not one of George's typical high school anecdotes.

"There were all these girls who were into me," says George. "But I had a crush on Carly Rosen. She was cute, but not in an obvious way. We took English class together."

George smiles wistfully as he recalls her.

"She was so smart. I wanted to impress her. So I'd ask her what she was reading, and she'd tell me. *Little Women. Wuthering Heights*. 'But you wouldn't get it,' she'd say. 'It's not your thing.'"

Even as he says it, I can see how much the memory pains him. I spent so much of my childhood cursing being a geek that it never occurred to me that anyone would actively long to join the club, let alone a jock like George.

"I wanted so badly for it to be my thing," says George. "I wanted to be the guy who understood. So I begged Carly for a recommendation, and she told me to read *Murder on the Orient Express*. It took me more than a week, but I did it. I told Carly all my thoughts. And she was really encouraging. I felt so good about myself. Carly said I should pick that book for my class presentation, so I did. She helped me after school. And I felt like we were really bonding. I did my presentation, and I was so proud of myself. But as I started the presentation, everyone started laughing at me. I had no idea why. So I just kept going. And afterward, the teacher told me that I was pronouncing Hercule Poirot's name wrong. I was saying it like 'Poy Rot.' Dozens of times. Hercule Poy Rot."

I'm this close to laughing. That's objectively funny. But one look at George's wounded expression and my face floods with sympathy. I hope he knows I'm not on the side of his classmates. It hurts me to think how much that must have devastated him.

"She knew all along," says George. "She knew and she never corrected me. She wanted the whole class to hear it. So yeah,

I know what it's like to try and be something you're not. It can be really humiliating. And the worst part is, you don't stop wanting it."

. . .

The feast is being held at Christ Church College, one of the richest in Oxford. If I hadn't known, it becomes obvious as the bus pulls up outside the college's ludicrously grand entrance gate. It has several domed turrets, an octagonal clock tower, and a stone statue of Henry VIII, the college's founder. I only need to take one look at it all to convince myself I'm going to be turned away at the door. At least I'm not the only one who's nervous. As the team gets off the bus, we straighten each other's bow ties and clear our throats. Whatever animosities have raged between us in recent days, nothing unites us more than our hatred of the old enemy.

"Why do we put ourselves through this?" groans Ed.

"We're actually in a better position than they are," claims Dakani.

Everyone frowns apart from Johannes, who is naturally inclined to feel that all is equal on balance.

"What did they even win?" Dakani continues. "The chance to lose next year."

"That's exactly the kind of thing a loser would say," scoffs Tristan.

We enter the Porters' Lodge and are directed toward Maynard's Chamber, which sounds like something from a Victorian anatomy class, but turns out to be the reception room that's hosting welcome drinks. It's the typical room lined with gold-framed paintings of bearded old men that you find all over Oxford and Cambridge. But it's empty.

We walk into the center of the room, confused about where our hosts are. The moment we're all inside, the room is plunged into darkness. What the fuck? It feels like we're about to be attacked. Instead, there's a low humming sound that I gradually realize is chanting.

"What are they saying?" George whispers.

I listen until I can make it out.

"Fuck the Tabs."

"The who?"

"Tabs. Cantab. Cantabrigia."

Even though I can't see him, I can feel George's look of confusion.

"They're telling us to go fuck ourselves in Latin."

It's at times like this that I think I should have got over myself and gone to a more normal university. Who the hell invites people to a black-tie dinner, then welcomes them with this pathetic excuse for intimidation? Posh twats, that's who.

As the chant reaches its climax, the lights come on and there they are, the victorious Oxford team, dressed in their tuxedos and looking like pricks. They burst into a round of self-congratulatory laughter. By the look of things, their drinking started a while ago.

I'm already counting down the hours until we can get the bus home, but George spots a waiter with a drinks tray and hands me a flute of champagne.

"Down this," he says. "It's time to get flirting."

I take a doubtful look at our hosts. "Do you really think this is a good place to pull? We're in enemy territory."

George flashes me a smile. "Enemies always secretly want to fuck."

He scans the room. "Based on my intelligence, three of the Oxford crew are gay."

"Are you sure we want to base anything on your intelligence?" I quip.

George shoots me a look.

"That was mean," I say. "Sorry."

"It's OK," says George. "I just didn't want to freak you out by not having a plan. So I texted one of the Oxford women's crew I slept with last year, and she got me the intel."

"Wow, George. Not just a pretty face."

George chuckles and pulls out his phone. "Option one is Daley. Canadian guy."

"I remember him. There he is." I gesture at a huge muscular guy who's laughing with Tristan.

"Apparently he has a massive dick and he's very proud of it," says George.

"But he laughs at Tristan's jokes. Automatic no."

"Fine. Option two is Magnus." George points out an extremely tall Norwegian.

"Magnus is gay?"

"Apparently."

"Way too tall."

"Not your thing?"

"He won't be into me."

"You need to get over this! He'll think you're small and cute." I'm surprised that George seems so sure.

"But we do have a third option," says George. "Felix."

Felix is the Oxford cox. I haven't thought about him in weeks, but in the lead-up to the Boat Race, I developed a minor obsession with him. Despite all my moaning, I'm not actually that short as far as men go. But Felix is tiny. He's so small in comparison to the rest of the crew that the media developed an obsession with photographing him, catching him at the angles that most capture the difference. When his team threw him into the Thames at the end of the race, as is tradition, they flung him so far, they had to pull him back to shore with a life ring.

"There he is," says George.

Felix is talking to Rotter and Sprout and looks bored out of his mind. He has this wicked glint in his eye, kind of like a yassified Chucky, but that's more attractive than it sounds. I've heard he's a bitch, but I'm sure he's heard worse about me.

"Yeah, fine, I can have a crack at Felix."

"Great," says George. "Make sure you sit next to him at dinner. And remember what we talked about earlier.

"Correct pronunciation of Poirot?"

George laughs and gives me a playful wink. "Cute butt."

Dinner is being held in Christ Church's Great Hall. It's a cavernous room with stained-glass windows and vaulted ceilings thirty feet high. As we take our places at a long wooden table, I stand next to Felix. The tables are so wide that you can barely hear the person across from you, or even see them amid the gloom. But here, side by side, Felix and I have our own private candlelit dinner for the next hour or so. I'm about to take a seat on the bench when Felix taps me on the shoulder.

"Not yet. Gotta stay standing." He gestures to the end of the room, where a man in a gown starts to sing in Latin.

How could I be so uncouth as to forget about grace?

"I can tell you haven't been to one of these dinners before," Felix whispers.

Great. I've been found out already.

But Felix smiles. "Don't worry about it—I've got you."

Oh my god. This is far worse than him being a bitch. He's actually nice. Suddenly I'm feeling the pressure. As soon as grace concludes, I excuse myself and go to the bathroom. I look at my reflection and try to remember what George said earlier. The stuff about my eyes and hair was all a bit obvious. And you're never convincing me that freckles are anything other than overproductive melanin cells. But that comment about my butt . . . that was convincing.

Do I really have a cute butt?

I stand on my tiptoes and examine it in the mirror. That is a cute butt. Why have I never noticed? I hear a wolf whistle and turn to see that Daley from the Oxford team has caught me in the act.

I turn bright red. "I was just—"

"Hey, don't let me stop you."

Daley smiles, then stands about a foot from the urinal and whips out—Jesus Christ! You could feed a family of four with that thing.

"What do you make of Oxford?" Daley asks, glancing downward.

I hold his gaze.

"Nothing special."

I turn and walk out. Call me old-fashioned, but I'd rather be wined and dined than flashed at the urinal. Still, there's no denying what just happened. A man hit on me. Because I have a cute butt. Even though I wasn't up for it, that was hot.

As I get back to the dining hall, my mood has transformed. I grab another glass of champagne and take a seat next to Felix. He looks kind of cute in the candlelight. That suit's a great fit. I remember being in the rental shop with George and have an idea for how to play this.

"That suit looks great on you," I say coyly.

"Thanks," says Felix.

"Where's it from?"

"Can't remember."

"Let me check."

I signal for Felix to swivel so I can read the label on his collar. As I lean in close, I see the hairs go up on the back of his neck. Oh my god. It worked.

"Well?" says Felix, turning to face me. There's a spark in his eyes that wasn't there a moment ago.

"John Lewis. Wool and polyester blend."

"Fascinating."

We both laugh. I sip my champagne.

"So are you guys as boring as we are in your free time?" I ask.

Felix looks confused.

"My friend Fran was telling me that half of the girls' team have slept with each other. But nothing that exciting has ever happened with the men."

Felix raises an eyebrow. "The night is young."

I feel our feet touch beneath the table. Holy shit.

"But to answer your question," says Felix. "Daley is kind of the village bicycle round here. So yeah—me and Magnus have both had a ride."

"Wow."

"That's not the word I'd use. Daley will hit on anyone."

I'm not going to take that personally. It was all down to my cute butt. Felix glances down the table and sees Daley talking to George, who is making an effort to be friendly but not too friendly.

"Case in point," says Felix.

"Ha," I say. "I don't think that's George's thing."

"Oh well," says Felix. "They can bond over being thick as shit."

I visibly bristle.

"Oh come on," says Felix. "I saw your quotes in the *Telegraph*."

"I was in a pretty bad mood that day."

"But did you lie? I mean look at him. You can feel the stupidity from here."

I'm getting annoyed now. Who does this twerp think he is?

"George is actually smart. In his own way."

"Sure."

I'm starting to understand why Felix's teammates threw him into the river with such gusto.

"You can be honest with me," says Felix.

My irritation has completely passed him by. It would be so easy for me to just agree with him and head off back to his room together. But that's no longer what I want. Not even slightly.

"You want me to be honest? Fine. You're being a douche."

• • •

After dinner, the Oxford boat club president formally invites the Cambridge team for drinks in the Junior Common Room, yet another wood-paneled reception room, this one boasting an enormous portrait of a peacock, for some reason. Our hosts have laid out a selection of cheese and port from the college cellars, as if we're a load of middle-aged bankers. George comes rushing up to me.

"How did it go with Felix?"

"Do you want the good news or the bad news?"

"Good news, good news!"

Why did I even ask?

"I saw myself as attractive," I say. "Genuinely. My butt has been causing havoc."

"That's amazing!" says George. "What's the bad news?"

"Felix is a cunt."

George laughs, then glances behind me.

I spin around and standing there is Landon Hughes, the Oxford rowing coach. Landon Hughes is an Australian Olympic silver medalist and a gold-star media whore. He once somehow schemed his way onto a diving reality TV show where he always seemed disappointed at having to execute a dive, much preferring the part where he got to strut up and down the diving board in his Speedo. From the look of things, he spent too much time on Bondi Beach in his twenties and has been making up for it ever since with Botox and fillers.

"Felix means well," says Landon diplomatically. "Did you guys have a good dinner?"

"It was entertaining," I say. "You?"

"I was getting to know one of your teammates. Tristram, is it?"

"Tristan. Don't get it wrong to his face, he might slap you."

Landon chuckles and looks around. "Sad not to see Deb here this evening."

"She's busy. Her words, not mine."

"Her loss, more like," says Landon. "It's such a shame you guys come all the way here and barely get to see our beautiful town. Can I offer you a tour?"

I don't trust this guy. Not for a second. "We're good."

"We'd love to do it another time," says George.

"There won't be another time," says Landon. "Come on, it won't take long."

. . .

This man is definitely up to something. But I'm intrigued to find out what. Landon leads us away from the drinks, across a courtyard and down through a gate to a poorly lit meadow.

"Is this where you take your rivals to murder them?" I quip.

"Ha!" says Landon. "No. The opposite."

I look at George in alarm. Does Landon want a threesome? Has my cute butt claimed another victim?

"I don't get it," George says matter-of-factly.

"I don't see you guys as rivals," says Landon. "Far from it."

We cross the meadow and arrive at a brand-new sports center. It's closed, but Landon scans a key card and shows me and George in. As he turns on the lights in the gym, twelve state-of-the-art ergometers gleam back at us. George's eyes light up.

"Are those Hydrow Pros?"

"Custom made," Landon says proudly.

"No way!" says George. "Can I try one out?"

"Be my guest."

George strips off his jacket and jumps onto the erg. He puts it on the hardest setting and starts pulling away. Landon turns to me and smiles.

"Someone's happy."

"Like a pig in shit."

Landon laughs. "Organic manure."

I watch George in action. I've never seen someone this excited about an ergometer, exclaiming about how smoothly it runs and pulling like he's in the final straight of the Boat Race. It's actually quite sweet how happy this makes him, when here I am, distrusting everything Landon says. I do wish I could live in George's head sometimes.

"This is just the start of it," says Landon. "Downstairs, we have massage rooms, ice baths, cryotherapy booths. You guys use cryotherapy?"

"Isn't that what Walt Disney used to freeze his corpse?"

Landon laughs again.

"You're funny. Look, mock me all you want, but Deb is using training methods she learned in the '80s. We treat our rowers like Olympic athletes here."

George crosses back over, sweating and pumped with adrenaline. Landon places a hand on his arm.

"You like that, big guy?"

"It was incredible!"

I fold my arms at Landon.

"Why are you showing us this?"

Landon smiles coolly. "I think you should come and row for Oxford."

I burst out laughing.

"Why not?" asks Landon. "I've heard rumors you're both being dropped from the first boat."

George looks panicked, but I scoff.

"Did Tristan tell you that? He's dreaming."

"He mentioned something about having to pass your exams, George."

"I'm working on it," George says proudly. "I was reading all about fiscal deficit bias just this morning."

I look at George in surprise, but Landon isn't interested.

"But if you fail, you'll be out, and Lucas, you'll be stuck opposite Tristan. That's if you aren't bumped by Fran Macdonald."

I narrow my eyes at Landon. "And why would you want such a pair of proven losers?"

Landon gives us yet another flash of his Cheshire Cat smile. "Because I didn't fall for Tristan's bullshit. I can see you guys have talent. I'm just not sure it's being appreciated."

I share a look with George.

"Am I wrong?" asks Landon. "Or has Deb given you her vote of confidence?"

Neither George nor I answer.

"Listen," says Landon. "I'm about to take Oxford to the next level. I've been having some very exciting discussions with broadcasters. We're going to do for rowing what *Drive to Survive* did for Formula 1."

Landon hands us his business card.

"Just think about it, OK? Imagine what a moment it would be if you both defected."

"Has it happened before?" I can't help asking.

"Only three times in two hundred years. But the last guy to do it lost at Cambridge, then won at Oxford. You know what to do."

8

GEORGE

I TOOK LANDON'S CARD, but I was only being polite. Lucas told him to get stuffed. Don't you love British insults? Lucas said he'd take Deb's blink-and-you'll-miss-it responses over Landon's slimy pickup lines any day, and I agree. I'm not even sure Landon's offer was serious. Lucas says that man will do anything to get in our heads. I'm trying not to just go along with whatever Lucas thinks, but it's so nice to have a proper friend on the rowing team. Last night was the first time I truly appreciated it. I feel like Lucas and I have really bonded.

There were a couple of moments yesterday when it felt like more than that. All those compliments I gave Lucas . . . I wasn't lying. Maybe I should be subtler about the fact that I find him cute. But it's important for Lucas to know that's how people see him. He's finally ready to seal the deal with Amir, and I don't want to get in the way of that. Lucas is just my friend with a really cute butt.

"It's very impressive," says Professor Mishri.

I snap back to attention.

"Sorry, what is?"

"Your dissertation."

She hands it back to me. We've spent most of the past hour discussing it, and I don't think Eleanor can believe the praise that Professor Mishri has been lavishing.

"Let's end it there today," says Professor Mishri. "Actually, George, could I have a word?"

Not again. Eleanor looks smug as she leaves—she knew there had to be a catch. Professor Mishri closes her door and looks at me sternly.

"George, this dissertation is head and shoulders above anything you've written previously."

I give her a modest shrug.

"I guess all the reading I've been doing paid off."

Professor Mishri glances down.

"That's not to say there aren't some ... interesting metaphors in there."

"That's what helped me understand the concepts."

"Yes, it's not a criticism. And I think it will help convince the examiners that this is your own work." She gives me a long look. "It is your own work, isn't it, George?"

"Of course it is."

"Only I wouldn't want you to have had the wrong reaction to this whole drama around the Boat Race."

"It kicked my ass into gear. I thought you'd be pleased."

Professor Mishri lets out a little laugh.

"I'm delighted. But your coursework is not the same as your exams. You're going to be on your own there." She gives me another searching look. "Do you feel like that's going to be an issue?"

I smile at her. "I don't see why it would be."

"Great." She goes to open her door. "I'm dashing home to Tilly. She gets ever so grumpy when she's hungry."

My ears prick up. I'm this close to cracking the Tilly mystery.

"Does she? How does she, er, communicate that?"

"Oh, she's very passive-aggressive. She huffs off and has a nap."

Try as I might, the only thing I can picture is a lesbian in a dog basket. It's occurred to me that I could just ask a question that would answer the mystery once and for all. Does Tilly like dog biscuits? Who's her favorite composer? But it's not that I can't picture a woman eating dog biscuits or a dog who loves Mozart. As she opens her door for me, Professor Mishri hesitates.

"George, there's only one thing you can do at this point, and that's try your hardest. If you do that, you'll get the result you deserve. You can't just wave a magic wand."

. . .

The following morning, Lucas and I meet up on the train to Ely. I've been desperate to tell him about the mark I got in my dissertation, but I wanted to wait until I could do it face-to-face. As soon as we're seated, I recount my conversation with Professor Mishri.

"We did it!" I exclaim.

Lucas looks at me with concern. "You mean, we got away with it."

"Yeah!"

"George, do you not understand? She was warning you."

"She said don't use a magic wand. And we won't."

"What do you think cheating is? We need to be really careful going forward."

I observe Lucas as he looks out of the window and picks at his nails.

"I don't get it," I say. "You made it sound like cheating was going to be so easy."

"Yeah, George, I was bluffing."

Huh. That does make more sense.

"Look," I say, "if you're worried, maybe I don't have to cheat. I've been reading some textbooks, going to lectures. I'm starting to understand more."

It's not just that. Ever since I told that story to Lucas about Carly Rosen and Hercule Poy Rot, I've been reminded of something I'd managed not to think about for a long time.

I want to feel smart.

I try not to dwell on it, because it's obvious no one thinks I'm smart, and why waste time worrying about the one thing I'm not good at? But like I said to Lucas, the feeling hasn't gone away. Maybe I should explain that.

"George, no offense, but we do have to cheat. You feel like you're learning a lot because you're starting from nothing."

This hits me in the gut, but I swallow hard. "So what's the plan now?"

Lucas glances behind us. Ed and Ted are only a few seats away.

"I'll tell you after rowing."

"Why so mysterious?"

"Because the plan, George, is to not take any more risks than are necessary."

. . .

As the train pulls into Ely, there's only one thing anyone's talking about. Henley Royal Regatta, the jewel in the crown of rowing regattas, is only a few weeks away and Deb still hasn't announced the teams. Henley usually takes place in July, but it's been moved into the middle of exam term to accommodate the World Championships. Deb has ignored the calls of various university honchos to avoid such an unfortunate clash of timetables.

For most of the squad, the main opportunity presented by Henley is a rematch with Oxford, but Jemima emailed the other day to let me know that Rick Toledo, the US Olympic coach, is flying out to watch me row. If I can win in his presence at Henley, that will give a huge boost to my Olympic hopes.

"Two words," says Deb as she gathers us at the boat house.

"Wow, she's really spoiling us," quips Lucas.

"Seat racing," says Deb.

A scandalized murmur passes through the team. Seat racing is one of the most brutal and controversial training methods in rowing. It involves running repeated sprints while swapping out one rower for another to see if they make the boat go slower or faster. It's usually done in fours, rather than eights, since that way it's easier to measure the impact of each rower. Its effectiveness is disputed, as crews are notorious for trying to influence the results. If someone gets swapped into the boat in favor of your friend, you're incentivized to pull slower and make it look like your friend was the difference. That's why the first boat out is so important. Those four rowers don't know which of them will be swapped out and for whom. Even if you think you've figured out the coach's plan and want to mess with it, it's a huge risk not to pull your hardest and see your scheming backfire.

Deb announces the first boat out—Tristan, Johannes, Ed, and Ted, with Fran in the cox seat. The rest of us trade glances and gather on the bank to watch. If Tristan is right, and he's in contention for my place, the next boat out will be the same lineup, only with me instead of him. In theory, that should show Deb which of the two of us is faster. But if Ed, Ted, or Johannes would prefer me over Tristan as first team stroke, all they have to do is pull harder the second time, making it look like I'm stronger. Except it's not that simple, because what if Deb surprises us all by swapping out Johannes for Dakani? Then Johannes would regret not having pulled his hardest when it was actually him who was being tested.

Do you see what a mind fuck it can be?

But let's not overcomplicate things. Everyone knows it's me versus Tristan. And Johannes wouldn't dream of taking sides. Ed and Ted are more of a wildcard, since they're both at Peterhouse College with Tristan. That's a potential point of allegiance, but I've always gotten the impression they don't like him. I cross over to them casually.

"Hey, guys. You ready for this?"

"I guess," says Ed.

"We're gonna row fair and square, right?"

Ted gives Ed a look, then shrugs at me.

"Why wouldn't we?"

If I was more calculating, I'd cut them a deal to be sure of it. But they don't have any reason to lie to me. Plus, after my conversation with Lucas, I'm not taking any more risks than are necessary. As Deb sets the first boat off, they speed away from us and out of sight. When they row back a few minutes later, no one apart from Deb knows what time is on her stopwatch. She orders me and Tristan to swap places. I get into the boat opposite Fran. The boys on the bank are going wild at the sight of the two of us in the boat together. I give her a smile.

"You gonna crack a joke about how if you get any closer to me you'll get an STI?"

Fran raises an amused eyebrow.

"I think you just did. Not bad."

I feel absurdly proud of myself. "You're not gonna get that kind of banter with Tristan."

"Well then, you'd better show us if your rowing matches your comedy skills."

I take a deep breath and slide forward on my seat. Deb blows her whistle. For the first few dozen strokes, I get that rush of adrenaline that comes every time I race. But as I settle into a rhythm, something feels off. Is it Fran? Am I not used to her style? No, we're perfectly in sync. Then I realize—I'm doing more of the work than I should be. There's drag at the back of the boat. When you've rowed as many times as I have, you have a feel for these things. But it can't be that Ed and Ted aren't pulling their weight. They told me they would. It must be the river current. It was probably like this when Tristan went out. There's nothing I can do about it. All I can do is keep pulling on my oar, harder and harder and—

"GEORGE," Fran yells.

As I snap into focus, I feel my oar clatter into the oar behind me. I'm still rowing, but everyone else has stopped. What's going on? Oh, wait—we've crossed the finish line. That was quick. Surely I did enough?

I glance over at the bank just in time to see Tristan give Ed and Ted a wink.

. . .

"A wink doesn't mean anything," I say to Lucas. "That could just be Tristan trying to mess with me again."

"Yeah," says Lucas. "It could be."

We're walking from the train station to the economics department. It's crazy to think we went three years without once coordinating our schedules like this.

"This one time in high school, a girl kept winking at me in class, so I hit on her at lunch break. Turns out she was a Mormon with conjunctivitis."

"Wow, George. A high school story that doesn't end with you getting laid. What's going on?"

What's going on is something I'd rather not dwell on. I'm slightly concerned that the wink did mean something, and Tristan just screwed my chances of making the first boat for Henley. If I get dropped from the first boat, I can't see Jemima sticking with me as a client. But I'm not going to worry about that based on one wink.

"How was Fran?" asks Lucas.

"She was really nice. She didn't roast me once."

"I meant as a cox."

"Oh yeah, she was awesome. I mean, she's the only person in our whole squad who's actually won the Boat Race."

Lucas looks offended. "So she's better than me?"

"I didn't say that. You're both very talented."

"Which one of us would you save from a burning building?"

"Both of you," I say. "One under each arm. But I'd get you first."

I thought that would at least earn me a smile, but Lucas is deep in thought. As we arrive at the economics department, he stops and turns to me. "Do you ever think about what Landon said?"

"About moving to Oxford? I thought you told him to get stuffed."

"Obviously I told him that. But Deb hasn't given us one word of reassurance since the Boat Race. I feel like she's getting ready to drop us."

"If she wanted to drop us, she'd drop us."

Lucas shakes his head at me in wonder. "You're incredibly relaxed about the possibility that Tristan just cheated you out of a place in the first boat."

"It would be a bit much for me to get mad at someone for cheating. Now, are you going to tell me what we're doing here?"

. . .

Lucas leads us up to the economics department library. Like most of the Sidgwick Site, it has an ugly shell, but the interior is much more welcoming. It's set over two floors, with a central aisle that spans the height of both. All the desks are occupied with students hard at work. But rather than enter the library,

Lucas perches near the entrance, which looks out onto a corridor lined with the offices of various professors.

"There he is," says Lucas.

He gestures toward a door bearing a metal sign with the name Dr. Vasilis Civeris, and a paper one announcing that it's office hour, when students are invited to drop in to discuss any issue that might be troubling them. Just then, a man who I presume is Dr. Civeris gets up and lets a student into his office. He's in his thirties, with a sprinkle of silver hair and designer stubble. He welcomes his student warmly, bursting into animated conversation as he shuts his office door.

"Who's Dr. Civeris?" I ask Lucas, intrigued.

"Made his name during the Greek financial crisis. Now he's mad he doesn't get to appear on BBC News every five minutes. Has a finsta where he posts topless selfies from Mykonos. Once shouted at a canteen worker about the correct way to serve moussaka. Oh, and he has a foot fetish."

"And why do I need to know all this?"

"Because he's on the exam committee. Apparently, he keeps the exam papers locked in his study in Queens'."

I follow as Lucas heads along the corridor toward Dr. Civeris's office.

"Did that book tell you that?"

"It's no secret who's on the exam committee. But that book told me why it's so great that *he's* on the committee this year."

Lucas raises an eyebrow.

"He has . . . a reputation."

"For what?"

"Getting close to his students."

"How close?"

Lucas grins. "Only one way to find out."

I look at him in surprise. "You mean me?"

"Are you happy to flirt with a guy?"

Lucas and I have been getting to know each other pretty well. There's no reason not to tell him about Hot Spider-Man, or even Travis. But now is not the moment.

"Sure. If you think he'll be into that."

"Why wouldn't he? Apparently, he loves twinks."

I laugh out loud. "Then he's not going to like me."

Lucas looks surprised. "You're kind of a twink."

"Please—I'm a twunk at best."

Lucas looks blank. "What's a twunk?"

"A hunky twink."

Lucas frowns. "I'm not even totally sure I know what a twink is."

"You're a twink, Lucas! Young, skinny, cute. How do you not know this?"

"How *do* you know this?" Lucas asks in amazement.

"I have a lot of gay fans. You should read my Instagram comments."

Lucas chuckles.

"Seriously though," I say, "if twinks are what he's into, you're our man."

Lucas is incredulous. "He's not going to prefer me over you."

"Yes, he will, if that's his taste. What's our goal here?"

"Get an invite back to his study in Queens', but there's no way he's going to invite—"

Lucas is cut short as Dr. Civeris's door swings open and the previous student exits. The student is a total twink, and Dr. Civeris smiles at him fondly as he says goodbye. This is definitely Lucas's time to shine.

Dr. Civeris spots us. "Can I help you boys?"

"Yes," I say.

"Great. Who's first?"

I glance at Lucas. He's frozen in fear. I turn to Dr. Civeris.

"Er . . . can we come in together?"

Dr. Civeris looks surprised but nods and shepherds us into his office.

Lucas shoots me a confused look, and to be fair, I have no idea what I'm doing—I just knew there was no point in sending Lucas in there on his own when he's in this state.

Dr. Civeris's office is modern and fairly impersonal, but he has pinned up a couple of postcards on a bulletin board, a Matisse reprint, and a view of Mykonos at sunset.

"Mykonos," I say, gesturing at the postcard. "Nice."

"That's Poggibonsi," says Dr. Civeris.

"Oh."

He definitely isn't attracted to me. I can always tell when someone is. Dr. Civeris takes a seat and surveys me and Lucas.

"So how can I help?"

I glance at Lucas, but his eyes are fixed on the wall, and he appears to be dissociating. I try to remember some of the facts from my latest lecture.

"We just had some questions about the Brainard principle."

"Right," says Dr. Civeris. "That's not really my field, but go ahead."

"Er . . . it's really the way that it runs into a pitfall when you apply it to central banks."

Dr. Civeris does a humorless "voilà" with his hands.

"I think you just answered your own question."

Lucas shoots me an impressed look. I have to admit, I'm impressed with myself too. But this isn't about me. It couldn't be clearer that Dr. Civeris has no interest in a twunk like me, and is quite reasonably wondering what he's been dragged into. I give Lucas an urgent look. Finally, he snaps into action and sits forward on his seat.

"We know this isn't your usual area," says Lucas, "but we were discussing your paper on capital structure and felt there was some interesting cross-pollination."

Just like that, Dr. Civeris's eyes light up.

"That's a fascinating point. You're Lucas Bradshaw, right?"

Lucas blushes. "How did you know that?"

"People talk about you highly in the department."

This is amazing. Lucas's reputation precedes him. Dr. Civeris is now perched on the edge of his seat, hanging on Lucas's every word. I nod at Lucas to keep going.

"That's good to know," says Lucas with a smile.

"So what can I tell you about capital structure that you don't already know?" asks Dr. Civeris, trying not to drool.

Lucas gives him a coy smile.

"I find you can always go deeper when the desire is there."

Dr. Civeris shivers with delight.

"And is it?"

Lucas holds Dr. Civeris's gaze.

"Very much so."

I feel like I'm watching my student graduate. Lucas has Dr. Civeris in the palm of his hand. I'd be thinking about making a subtle exit if Dr. Civeris hadn't completely forgotten about my presence.

Lucas leans forward on Dr. Civeris's desk. "So do you think we can find a time to talk more?"

Dr. Civeris tries to look nonchalant.

"I'm a busy man. And I'm heading to a conference in Japan tomorrow."

Lucas pouts his lips in disappointment.

"Can you not squeeze me in later today?"

Dr. Civeris pulls up his calendar on his computer and frowns.

"I'd be happy to come to your study in Queens'," Lucas says. "So we can really ... put our feet up."

Lucas glances downward and slips one foot out of its shoe.

As Dr. Civeris clocks it, his expression turns grave. He sits up tightly. "I'm guessing you've heard certain rumors."

Lucas is stunned into silence.

"There's a fair amount of homophobia in this university," says Dr. Civeris, "not to mention cultural stereotypes. I've never been to Mykonos. I don't even like moussaka."

He gives Lucas an almost pitying look.

"That all came from one of my students who got, shall we say, a bit overinvested. I know how stressful exam term can be. But this isn't the answer."

Lucas looks mortified.

"I'm so sorry. I didn't mean to offend you."

Dr. Civeris smiles at him kindly. "It's OK. It happens."

He stands up to leave and starts chattering to Lucas about equity capital. Lucas looks like he's got whiplash.

As I follow them out, I notice a set of keys on Dr. Civeris's desk. There are no guarantees that one of them is the key to his study in Queens'. But what if it is? Before I know what I'm doing, I swipe the keys and put them in my pocket.

. . .

Once we get outside and I show Lucas the keys, he can't believe it. He's terrified that Dr. Civeris will know it's me who stole them, but I assure him that people always blame themselves for losing their keys. It's not like Dr. Civeris was paying me any attention.

I'm worried that Lucas is going to be convinced his seduction attempt failed, but even he can't deny that Dr. Civeris was into him. I tell Lucas he really ought to update the cheat book and explain that Dr. Civeris is a decent guy, but Lucas says we can worry about that later. We have to break into his study in Queens' tonight. We make a plan to meet outside Lucas's college at midnight.

I count down the hours and wait for Lucas at Trinity Gate. As he arrives, he gestures for me to go back the way I came.

"Through Trinity?"

"Yeah."

"But . . . Queens' is that way."

"If you're going on foot."

"How else are we going to get there?"

Lucas leads me through the shadowy courtyards of Trinity and down to the river. Tied there is Trinity's collection of punts, which are basically the British version of gondolas, and a popular tourist attraction on the river. I stare at Lucas.

"We don't have a choice," says Lucas. "If we go through the Porters' Lodge, they'll have our faces on camera."

"There must be a gate we can jump over."

"There isn't. Trust me, if there was an easier solution, we'd be doing it. The only way to get there undetected is by river."

As he says it, Lucas starts breathing rapidly.

"Are you OK?"

"Yeah, I'm just—it only just hit me what we're about to do."

I give him a reassuring arm rub.

"It'll be fun. It'll be like *Ocean's 11*!"

"Maybe for you. This is going to be hell for me."

"No, it's not. Do you know why?"

Lucas shakes his head. I hold his gaze earnestly.

"Because I'm here."

We pull the tarp off one of the punts and push it down a ramp to the edge of the water. I offer to punt, but Lucas says he'll feel less nervous if he has something to do. I get in the punt and Lucas pushes us off. It feels weird that he's the one steering when I'm twice the strength and size of him, but he knows what he's doing. He feeds the punt pole through his hands until it hits the river bed, then pushes off and drags the pole behind him in the water. He explains that he once had a summer job giving punt tours.

I can't help but be charmed by the image of a teenage Lucas, dropping one-liners for his customers and puncturing their romantic visions of Cambridge. They'd never have guessed what a sensitive soul lurked beneath. Lucas might not like it when I'm sincere, but I hope he knows I meant it when I said I'm here for him.

I'm starting to think I'd do anything for that boy.

On warm days in Cambridge, the river is chaos, but tonight, the water is eerily quiet. I tick off each college as we pass it—first Trinity Hall, then Clare, then King's. If you don't think too hard about what we're doing, the scene is magical. The colleges look spectacular from the river, lit by moonlight. Cambridge isn't a huge party town at the best of times, but this close to exams, it's silent. The only chance we have of being caught is by someone walking back from the library late at night. As we pass under the bridge at King's, I catch sight of a student, but they stare vaguely at our punt, then keep walking. For all I know, they're high on Ritalin and think they're hallucinating.

After a few minutes, we arrive at Queens' College. Lucas guides the punt into the bank, then sticks the pole in the ground to secure it. We disembark and vault over a low brick wall. I look around to get my bearings. We're in a deserted courtyard, though there are lights on in a couple of rooms, which makes my heart jump.

Lucas leads us across the courtyard and down a passageway until we arrive at a stairwell with Dr. Civeris's name on it. At his door, I pull out his keys and try the lock. Lucas is focusing on his breathing, but even my hands are trembling a bit. The first key doesn't work. But the second one opens the door with a satisfying click.

We step into Dr. Civeris's study. It's messier than his faculty office, but in a way that feels like a choice. Books are stacked high on all surfaces, and there are piles of paper strewn across his desk and half the floor. The exam papers could be anywhere. Lucas has already started looking. I click into gear and join him.

This is insane. But it's also amazing. We could be out of here any minute with the exam papers in our hands. I turn over a pile of papers. First-year dissertations. I check the next set. Some sort of book manuscript covered in scribbles.

"Oh my god," says Lucas, holding up a piece of paper in triumph.

"Is that them?"

"No, but it's a list of the exam topics!"

As he says it, I freeze. Someone is coming up the stairs.

"Lucas! Listen!"

"Shit!"

I run toward the door before realizing it's too late to escape. Lucas is frozen in fear. Then I spot a broom closet. I bundle Lucas inside and pull the door shut behind us. Lucas almost cries out in surprise, but I muffle his mouth on my chest to quiet him.

Inside the closet, it's pitch black. There's barely room to move. Our legs are intertwined, and I can smell the zesty scent of Lucas's shampoo. My heart rate is going crazy.

Through the door, I hear someone enter the room. It's Dr. Civeris. But he's not alone. There's someone else—a younger, male voice—they're laughing and chatting.

"Can you hear what they're saying?" whispers Lucas.

"Not really."

I notice a gap in the closet door and stretch to peer through it, even though it involves shifting even closer to Lucas. I can just about make out Dr. Civeris on his sofa, and next to him—

"Oh my god."

"What?"

"That's the guy who went in before us! The twink!"

I look at Lucas in indignation. "So the rumors *are* true."

"Oh my god," says Lucas, "do you think he's brought him here to—"

The chatter in the room outside has stopped. I'm not sure I want to know what's happening in its place. Now that it's quiet, I'm even more aware of just how tightly Lucas and I are packed together. I can feel his heart pounding beneath his ribcage and his breath on my cheek. Our crotches are almost touching. That's a recipe for disaster, but I'm just not going to think about it.

Except now it's all I can think about. And it's causing me to have an unfortunate reaction. Why is this happening? Nerves are meant to prompt the opposite response down there, although that's never been a problem for me. But the more I think about it, the more turned on I am.

I need to be careful. I don't want to make Lucas uncomfortable. Except... he must be able to feel me pressing into him, and he hasn't reacted.

Apart from his breathing.

I swear it's got faster.

And sure, that might be because of the situation on the other side of the door. But what if it's because of what's happening on this side?

It's then that I feel it.

Lucas is getting hard too. It's like a domino effect. Within seconds, we're both as hard as each other. There's a lot going on down there for a little guy.

This is at once the most embarrassing situation I've ever been in and the most exciting. Should I say something? No. That would only make it more embarrassing. And less hot. Now I know I've lost my mind, because I'm hiding in a professor's closet and all I can think about is how badly I want to jerk off.

Worse than that, I'm picturing Lucas unzipping me and doing the honors. Needless to say, it's not helping matters. I feel like I'm going to burst if I don't do something. At the very least, I need to adjust myself so I'm not straining against my pants quite so much.

I can't do that without touching Lucas, unless I shift my position slightly. As I try to adjust, my leg gives way. I fall forward and come clattering out of the closet.

"What the fuck?!" yells Dr. Civeris.

He leaps up from the sofa, frantically buttoning up his shirt. The twink is rooted to the sofa in shock. It takes him several seconds to come to his senses and pull up his pants from around his ankles.

"What are you doing in my office?" Dr. Civeris demands.

As I awkwardly adjust my crotch, Lucas steps out from behind me and stares down Dr. Civeris.

"What are you doing in your office, more like."

Dr. Civeris's expression hardens.

"That's none of your business."

"I see," says Lucas. "Would you like to keep it that way?"

Dr. Civeris is too astounded by Lucas's gall to answer.

"Thought so," says Lucas. "Then I suggest you don't worry about what we were doing here. We got lost. And now we're leaving."

I can't believe how cool Lucas is being. I would have folded immediately, apologized, confessed. But Lucas is killing this.

He turns to the twink. "Don't throw it all away for this loser."

Before anyone can say anything else, Lucas strides into the corridor and I follow him out. We don't say a word until we get back to the punt.

I let out a gasp of relief. "You were incredible, Lucas. How did you do that?"

Lucas shrugs. "I was trying to impress you."

We share a smile. I blush as I recall the moment in the closet.

"Shame about the exam topics," I say.

Lucas grins, then lifts up his shirt. The piece of paper is wedged right there.

9
LUCAS

WHEN I GET HOME THAT NIGHT, I jerk off immediately. That was unbelievably embarrassing, but I'm sure George understands. It was a heightened situation. Men aren't in total control of our equipment. You can get an erection from riding a bus, for god's sake. I mean, George was rock hard and he's not even into men. At least, I don't think he is. He did make that comment about my butt, and he was very cool about the idea of flirting with Dr. Civeris. But that's irrelevant. It's a sign of how close we've become that this is not going to be an issue between us. I felt way more awkward after the kiss in the club. Look, I'm not denying it was hot. George is hot. That's just a fact. But it's not going to affect anything. I'm not going to let it.

Still, when I walk into the economics department the next morning and see him standing there, I turn bright red.

"What are you doing here?" I ask in surprise.

"I told you," says George, "I've been coming to lectures. I've been learning so much."

"That's great, but you can stop now. We've got the exam topics."

George looks aggrieved. "It's not just about passing my exams. I'm enjoying it. The other day I had a whole conversation with Dr. Janacek about general equilibrium."

I smile at George, impressed. "I wish this wake-up call had happened a year ago. Then we might have got away without cheating."

George looks momentarily wistful, but snaps out of it. "Better late than never," he says with a shrug. "So, what's the plan?"

"I'm guessing they haven't written the questions yet," I say. "We might have to break into the department a bit closer to exams."

"*Ocean's 12!*"

"Sure. In the meantime, I'll try to guess the questions based on these topics and draw up some essays you can start memorizing."

"Cool. What about Friday night?"

"What about it?" I ask in confusion.

"I thought we could watch a movie."

"Why?"

"I have this tradition that when I make a new friend, I make them watch the greatest rom-com of all time: *Notting Hill*."

George looks at me solemnly and puts on the worst British accent I've ever heard.

"These carrots ... have been murdered."

There's something risky about the idea of me and George sitting on a sofa and watching a rom-com together. But there's also something comforting about the idea of cementing us as friends.

"Sure," I say.

"Awesome." George goes to leave.

"Hey, George."

He turns back.

"I've got my date with Amir this afternoon."

"You're going on a date?!"

"No, at the coffee shop. First time since . . . don't remind me. If he doesn't show, I'll know I've fucked it."

"I feel like he'll show."

"And then what?"

"Just go with the flow."

That's a recipe for disaster. I frown at the idea.

"Sorry," says George, "that's a bit vague. How about this—ignore the voices in your head and read the signs he gives you."

That's slightly more helpful, but I'm still not feeling ready, and George can tell.

"Lucas, I know you don't feel it deep down. But you've come so far. The way you flirted with Dr. Civeris was amazing."

"Only because you were there."

"I'll be there this afternoon."

"What, squatting underneath the counter, giving me a thumbs-up?"

George sticks his thumb in the air and beams at me. I laugh.

"In spirit," says George. "I'd be there in person, but that might be risky."

"I'm the risk," I say dolefully.

"Stop that," says George. "You've never been the risk. Ant-Man, Felix, Dr. Civeris . . . you risked every one of them. And you survived, just like you'll survive whatever happens with Amir. Now go get your man."

. . .

It feels so good having George in my corner. Maybe this stopped being a deal a long time ago. George wants me to succeed. He believes in me more than I do. I'm really not sure what I'd do without him. Except that I'm without him right now.

It's 4:15 p.m. and Amir has just walked into the coffee shop. As usual, I can't believe how good he looks. He's wearing a loose-fitting vintage shirt, his hair is tucked behind his ears, and his eyelashes look longer than ever.

"Hey," I say.

"Hey."

I think that's relief on his face.

"The usual?" I ask.

Amir smiles. I've finally admitted it.

"Yes please."

I start to make his coffee. This is going well. Don't drop the ball.

"How's the exam prep going?"

Amir sighs. "It's a lot."

"Tell me about it."

"Yeah, I could do with a break." Amir hesitates. "There's this concert on Friday. Trinity choir, singing on punts. It's meant to be beautiful."

"That sounds awesome."

There's an awkward pause. Why is he telling me about the concert? Is he just making conversation? Surely if he wanted to invite me, he would. Then I remember George's instructions: ignore the voices in my head and read the signs.

Amir's here. He came back. He came back to tell me about a concert. He's not just making conversation. He wants to go with me, but he's too shy to ask—probably because of how it went last time. The ball's in my court, but I'm still too scared to seal the deal.

I glance down and picture George squatting beneath the counter, giving me his goofy thumbs-up. I might not be able to envisage a positive outcome, but he can. Then it comes to me. The perfect response. The only possible response. I look up at Amir.

"We should go."

Amir double takes.

"To the concert," I clarify.

A grin spreads onto Amir's face. "I'd love that."

. . .

For an hour or so, I'm so in shock that I forget to text George. When I'm finally about to, I remember that the concert clashes with our movie night. For some reason, I can't bring myself to tell George I need to cancel. I'm 100 percent sure he'd be happy for me. OK, maybe 99 percent. The other 1 percent of me is convinced that I detect a slight note of envy whenever I talk about Amir. It's so subtle that I'm not sure George is even aware himself. But that's crazy. I must be imagining it.

Even so, I decide not to tell him about my date. Instead, I wait until the day itself, then tell him I'm feeling sick. It's a risky lie, given that the concert is taking place in George's college. But a classical music concert is the last place I'd find him. He tells me to get some rest and that he'll pass on my apologies to Julia Roberts.

It's still only 10:00 a.m. and there are hours until the date. I have nothing to do all day except panic. Since I've been trying to cut down on my panicking, I go to the shops and buy a new shirt I can't afford. When that only takes an hour, I decide on a whim to get a haircut. The barber has barely started to cut my hair before I regret it. Not only does he cut off way too much as usual, but it's going to be obvious I got my hair cut for the date. As I survey the wreckage, I look at the barber ruefully.

"Shave it all off, why don't you?"

"Really?" says the barber. "I don't think that would suit you."

The resulting look is so awful that it's essential I avoid all mirrors for the next few hours. It's like that episode of *Fleabag* where her sister gets a disastrous bob, except that I need to be giving main character energy, not supporting comic relief. On my way back to college, I accidentally see my reflection in the window of Dorothy Perkins. I'm so appalled I think of texting Amir to cancel. I'm in desperate need of a pep talk from George, but I've shot myself in the foot on that count. That leaves me with one option.

"You look lovely," says my mum.

"Be honest."

"I am being honest."

"You're my mum. It doesn't count."

"Then why did you come here?"

"I don't know, Mum! I can't be accountable for my actions following the trauma that was unleashed on me this afternoon."

"It's a haircut. Do you want a cuppa?"

I can't remember the last time I came to see my mum at work. She's delighted, I can tell, but she can see the state I'm in and is trying not to look too pleased. We're in a tiny little cubicle that is insultingly called her staff room. It's a joke when I think of the grand old rooms that are reserved for Cambridge's academic staff. But right now, it's perfect. I perch on the counter as my mum makes me a cup of tea.

"What if he's doing this as a prank, Mum? I know a girl who was invited to a drinking society by a guy and then she found out it was Pull a Pauper night."

My mum looks appalled.

"If he does that, you send him to me, and I'll give him a good slap."

I laugh but my mum doesn't join me. "So he's rich, then?"

I sip my tea. "He's not poor."

My mum raises an eyebrow and says nothing.

"How do you handle them?" I ask. "I mean, you're surrounded by these people."

My mum looks at me with a shrug.

"If they're nice to me, I'm nice back. Is this boy nice?"

"I think he is."

"Then you'll be fine."

"What if I'm not? What if I blow it? What if I'm so nervous I can't speak?"

My mum gives me the look of a woman who has heard approximately four thousand of these freak-outs from her son over the past twenty-one years.

"Then he can send you to me and I'll give you a good slap."

. . .

Before I know it, it's seven o'clock and I'm racing to meet Amir outside Trinity. He's waiting for me when I get there, carrying a wicker picnic hamper and dressed in wide-cut trousers and a brilliant white shirt. Perhaps he sees me looking him up and down, as he gives me a similar once-over.

"Nice shirt," he says.

I think of my mum and sister at the Boat Race and decide that the only possible reason Amir could be saying this is out of sympathy.

"My mum bought it for me."

"Cute," says Amir. "I hope you're hungry."

"Starving."

"Perfect."

We cross Great Court and follow a steady stream of students heading toward the river. As we arrive, the choir are taking their places in four punts that have been tied together and moored to the far bank. An audience has started to gather on the lawn on the bank opposite, passing around bottles of wine and packets of Kettle chips. Amir pulls out a tartan rug from the hamper and unfolds it with a flick of the wrists. He places it on the grass, making sure there are no creases.

"Have a seat," he says.

I sit on the rug, unsure if he's expecting me to take my shoes off. I feel like I've entered one of his Instagram shots, only unlike in my dreams, it's a maze of potential faux pas.

Amir gets out two glasses and a bottle of champagne. "Sorry it's not Pol Roger. I didn't have time to go to Waitrose."

I smile and say nothing. Is this what George feels like in lectures? Amir proceeds to get out various cheeses and crackers, unwrapping them from expensive-looking boxes and placing them side by side. He hands me a plate and fork. I reach for one of the cheeses. Amir makes a little noise. What did I do wrong?

"I'd start with the caciocavallo if I were you," Amir says. "Followed by the pule, then the Époisses de Bourgogne."

I give him a gormless look.

Amir smiles. "Mildest first. Left to right."

"Got it."

"And don't worry. I got them out of the fridge a while ago."

Can't say I was worrying about when he got them out of the fridge. It's not just cheese—there's Ibérico ham, smoked salmon blinis, and three different sorts of pâté. No word on when they came out of the fridge or what order you're meant to eat them. I'm dreading what Amir's going to pluck out of the hamper next, convinced that I'm going to panic and snort some caviar or find another way to expose myself as the uncivilized oik I am. Amir glances up and sees my look of dread.

"Is everything OK?"

"Sure," I say, leaping to my feet. "I just need the bathroom."

. . .

Before I even know what I'm doing, I'm pounding up George's staircase and knocking on his door. It swings open and there's George, wearing a dressing gown and a clay face mask. Behind him, I can hear Julia Roberts attempting to emotionally blackmail her way to a chocolate brownie. As I catch my breath, George looks at me in confusion.

"What are you doing here?" he asks. "I thought you were sick."

"OK, don't be mad but . . . I'm on a date with Amir."

George's jaw drops open.

"We're at the river concert," I say, blushing. "He thinks I've gone to the loo."

George tries to process what he's hearing.

"Jesus, Lucas, what the hell? When you didn't message me after your shift at the coffee shop, I figured he hadn't shown."

"Yeah, no, he did, and now we're on a date. I thought I could handle it without you, but I can't."

"You can!"

"I can't, George. He's making me eat three different kinds of cheese in a certain order and I feel like he's judging me."

George looks protective. "Did he say something?"

"No."

"Did he give you a funny look?"

"No! He's been nothing but sweet."

George's expression fills with sympathy. "Lucas, I know it feels like he's judging you. But that doesn't mean he is. How many people do you think Amir knows who eat cheese in a certain order?"

"Loads!"

"And who did he choose to be on a date with?"

I feel silly as I realize George's point.

"Me."

"Exactly."

I get a surge of gratitude toward George. This is why I came here.

"You see? I couldn't have done this without you."

"Yes, you could, Lucas. You've done the hard part. Just be yourself."

George looks at me sincerely.

"Now get back down there before he thinks you've got a serious bladder problem."

. . .

When I arrive back at the river, Amir has a look of relief that I can't help but find reassuring. To be fair, it's not inconceivable that I might have done a runner if I hadn't had George to calm me down. I tell Amir I got caught in a queue, then settle in next to him in time for the start of the concert. The choir makes a beautiful sound, but it's all the same to me. Amir listens intently, as if he's at a church service. He can tell I'm not familiar with the program, so he leans in occasionally to tell me little nuggets about this or that composer.

As darkness falls and I sink my third glass of champagne, the atmosphere becomes sultrier. The choir finally does a song I know, a jazzy version of "Moon River." I smile at Amir, and he slides his hand into mine.

How is this real? How am I holding hands on a date with Amir? I'm getting a cramp, but I don't want to let go. I don't want to wake up from this dream.

The choir does a Broadway medley for their finale, and everyone applauds. For the encore, four gondoliers step onto the punts and start punting the choir away down the river as they sing one last number. As the choral music fades into the darkness, the effect is haunting.

Following a final round of applause, everyone starts to pack up their picnics and leave. But Amir sits in silence, still enraptured. I don't want to interrupt the moment, but eventually, once we're more or less alone, Amir turns to me.

"How good was that? I love that they did the full version of 'Ne Irascaris.' And that tierce de Picardie at the end of the Willbye was outrageous."

I smile and nod.

"Which one was your favorite?" Amir asks.

I pause to think. I should probably reference one of the composers he mentioned, to show I was paying attention. Who was that one I liked, Pearson or Parsell or something? I've drunk too much and my mind is swimming.

Then I recall George telling me to be myself. If Amir wanted to go on a date with a musicologist, he would have.

"My favorite part was when we held hands."

Amir smiles at me with affection. "You're adorable."

He leans in and kisses me. Amir kisses me. Amir.

He's so tender. So delicate. I knew in my gut this was worth chasing after, but I didn't realize it would feel this good. After a while, I pull back and let out a little laugh.

"What?" asks Amir.

"I can't believe this is happening. I've liked you for a while."

"Same."

I look at him in amazement.

"I could never tell what you thought of me!" he says. "Then when I saw you in the club with George, I thought I'd missed my chance."

"Oh god, that? That was nothing."

"Yeah, I asked my friend Wilbur, he said George is straight."

The knowledge that Amir has also been airing his anxieties over our interactions is unimaginably reassuring.

"And the whole garden party thing didn't put you off?"

Amir laughs. "I mean, it kind of confirmed that you liked me."

I feel a rush of adrenaline as he says it. I look around and see that we're the last people left on the lawn.

"What do you want to do now?" I ask hopefully.

"I have a mock exam in the morning," says Amir. "I should get to bed."

I can't help feeling a pang of disappointment.

"I mean, I have training at 6:00 a.m., but sleep is overrated."

Amir smiles softly. "There's no rush."

. . .

As my alarm goes off the next morning and I blunder my way to the train station, I'm so tired I'm almost euphoric. Despite getting home at a sensible hour, I barely managed to sleep. I can't believe that date was real. It was perfect. I didn't even masturbate once I was in bed. Amir is right—there's plenty of time for us to have sex. Last night was about the romance.

I barely make it through the training session. I crash into the bank twice, and much as I regret skipping breakfast, I'm fairly sure if I'd eaten anything, it would have ended up in the river. I'm so focused on holding it together that I don't say a word to George about my date. I'm well aware that he's looking at me with curiosity and concern, but it's only when we make it back onto land after our session that he pulls me aside.

"Are you all right?"

"Yeah. Why?"

"You were a mess out there. How did the rest of the date go?"

I burst into a smile. "We kissed!"

"Lucas! Oh my god!" George whoops in delight and scoops me into a hug. Is it me, or does his reaction feel a little forced? I laugh stiffly, then hear someone behind me. I turn and see Fran.

"What are we celebrating?" she asks.

George puts me down and I give Fran a wry look.

"Local man not as hideous as previously believed."

I expect Fran to laugh, but she doesn't.

"Deb wants a word with you two."

"Just the one?" I say, still grinning.

Fran remains sober. "I'm around later if you want to talk."

That's ominous. George and I cross over to Deb. She takes a deep breath, which means only one thing: she's going to say a full sentence.

"Boys . . . I've been sensing you're both a bit distracted."

"It's exam term," I say. "Everyone's distracted."

"Not everyone. Some of the squad have been posting PBs. But George, you've been way below your usual standard recently."

"The seat racing wasn't my fault."

"I'm not talking about that. I'm looking at the whole picture. Same for you, Lucas. I'm not sure *what* you were doing today on the river."

I look at Deb in panic.

"It was a blip."

"Right. Well I'm afraid until you're over that blip, I'm giving you both a rest from the first boat. Fran and Tristan will be taking your places for Henley."

10
GEORGE

I'VE FOUND THE ONE PLACE outside Cambridge where I'm a celebrity. Ever since my modeling campaign, I've been recognized on and off, even if people can't quite place where they know me from. It happened a bit after the Boat Race, though not as much as I expected. But I've been at Henley for less than an hour and I've already been clocked four or five times. I'm in the steward's enclosure—an exclusive VIP area next to the river with marquees full of food and drink, and a bank of deck chairs to watch the races from. The dress code is strict: jacket and tie for men, skirt below the knee for women. And the drinks code is even stricter: Pimm's, Pimm's, and more Pimm's. I hadn't even heard of Pimm's before coming to England, but here you can't escape it. It's a liquor that's mixed with lemonade, pieces of fruit, and, bizarrely, cucumber. I'm not drinking any alcohol until after my race. Not everyone is being so restrained.

"I can chug this stuff like water," says Jemima. "Faster, if anything. Pimm's, Rick?"

"Not right now," says Rick. "Just checking the wind speed."

Rick Toledo, the US Olympic coach, is in his fifties, with slick gray hair and a leathery tan. Rick is known for being a master technician, but rather than focusing on his rowers, like most coaches, he's obsessed with external influences such as river current and wind direction. Jemima introduced me to him about ten minutes ago, but he's so engrossed in his portable anemometer that he's barely acknowledged me.

"Mild southwesterly breeze," says Rick. "Shoot."

"What does that mean?" asks Jemima.

"Slight advantage for Bucks."

Jemima frowns and sips her Pimm's.

"That's the left-hand side," I say.

"What side are you rowing on?"

"Right."

Rick casts me a look.

"No, Cambridge are on the left-hand side."

So here's the thing. I haven't actually told Jemima that I've been dropped from the first boat. She's been so excited about Henley that I couldn't bring myself to do it. And now I've left it too late. They're going to discover one way or another in the next few minutes. I can't bear to see the look on their faces.

"You'd better hope the wind drops," says Rick.

"George can cope with a bit of wind," says Jemima.

"Yes," says Rick. "I remember you winning Head of the Charles. Gale-force winds that year, if I remember correctly."

"Sounds right," I say. "Feels so long ago."

"You were the talk of the town. Every college wanted you."

"He went for the best," says Jemima, picking out a piece of strawberry from her glass with a cocktail stick and sucking on it.

"Oxford might have something to say about that," says Rick. "This year at least."

Damn. I was hoping we wouldn't have to discuss the Boat Race.

"That was unfortunate," I say. "We did our best."

"Not your fault," says Rick. "The flood tide favored Middlesex more than usual this year. Not many people talking about that."

He looks at his anemometer.

"Wind has dropped. Perfect. You'd better go get ready."

I freeze. "I, er, I've still got a bit of time."

"The race is at 2:30."

"There's a race then, yes."

"So shouldn't you be with your team?"

"Well, not really."

"Why not?"

"It's just that . . . I'm actually rowing with the Cambridge second team today."

Jemima almost spits out her drink. Rick's expression curdles.

"Wait, what?"

"Yeah, did I not mention?"

"No," says Rick, glaring at Jemima. "No one did."

Presumably he's wondering why he's flown out from America to watch a guy who just lost the Boat Race and has now been dumped from the Cambridge first boat. It's a good question. Jemima lunges for a jug of Pimm's and pours herself another glass.

"Rick, have I told you about George's social media metrics? He's really bringing rowing to a new audience. Aren't you, George?"

She gives me a crazed look halfway between panic and murderous rage.

"Yes, you already mentioned," says Rick. "Twice."

"Great," says Jemima, "just checking."

She chugs her glass of Pimm's, swallowing whole pieces of cucumber.

"George, can we get you to pose for some photos?"

Jemima shuffles me over in front of a branded backdrop and puts me into a designer blazer. Is this a punishment, or just a rapid strategic diversion? I want to apologize to her, but I don't know what to say.

I pose for a photo with a cast member from *Dancing on Ice*, followed by some male models who claim to be combatting homophobia in sport by promoting their naked calendar. Most of the people I'm photographed with are representatives of brands or random marketing consultants in need of LinkedIn content. Everyone is very excited to get a picture with me, but none of them are remotely interested in what I'm doing at the regatta. Call me the Anna Kournikova of rowing.

"Looking good, George."

I turn and see that I'm being addressed by Eleanor. Always strange seeing her outside our supervisions. She's standing next to Tristan and his mother and father, that politics dude who lost his job and still looks mad about it.

"Hope you're steering clear of the Pimm's," says Eleanor.

"Of course I am. So nice to see you here."

"I wasn't going to miss Tristan's big moment." She turns to Tristan and squeezes his hand.

"Why don't you treat yourself?" Tristan says to me, gesturing at the bar. "The pressure's off."

I've done my best to avoid Tristan since the announcement of the new lineups, but he's managing to look even more smug than I feared.

"Let's have a drink afterward," I say warmly. "Toast your success."

"That's such a great attitude," says Eleanor.

"Yes," adds Tristan's dad. "Jolly well done for keeping going."

His mother looks wistful. "One can be tempted to jump ship."

"Don't worry about me," I smile. "Tristan deserves this."

Tristan grimaces. He can't cope with how nice I'm being.

"Didn't I just see Rick Toledo?"

I try to look casual. "I heard he was in town."

"Bit of a wasted opportunity for you."

"I'm sure he knows what I'm capable of."

"Yes, I think we've established your limits. Now watch and learn."

. . .

I exit the steward's enclosure and wander through the regatta. It's been a week since Deb broke the news to me and Lucas about our demotion, but it didn't really hit me until today. It's not that I mind rowing in the second boat. It's an honor to be at Henley in any capacity. But obviously I'd prefer to be in the first boat. I've been telling everyone that Tristan deserves it, but I can't forget how he winked at Ed and Ted after seat racing. What if I'd done a deal with them instead? Would I be sitting in his place? Lucas has taken the news extremely well, but maybe that's no surprise. What does a rowing race matter when you've just pulled the man of your dreams?

I'm happy for him—at least, I am in theory. For some reason, I don't feel as happy for him as I should. Throughout this process, I've longed for Lucas to succeed. But I think that's because I've wanted to see him confident and believing in himself. Since it's me who's helped him get there, it's almost felt as if it's me he's been falling for. So it's a little jarring to be reminded that this whole plan was designed for Lucas to get with someone else.

I hear the first team race announced and wander away from the crowds. The start of the course is far out of sight, but a radio commentary is being broadcast over a Tannoy. I can picture Tristan sitting at the front of the boat, enjoying the number of eyes on him. The starting pistol is fired, and the commentator begins to narrate the action. Everyone was anticipating an Oxford versus Cambridge rematch, but it's actually Leander, a star-studded private rowing club stacked with Boat Race alumni, who squeezed past Oxford in their semifinal. Since they beat the Boat Race winners, the smart money is now on Leander to win. But from the start, Cambridge is in the lead. Henley has some dumb rule where the race commentator is only allowed to state facts, like which crew is leading and the distance between them. Leander never get close to catching up with Cambridge. Never get within three-quarters of a boat length, according to old Mr. Razzle Dazzle up in the commentary box. Soon, the boat comes into my sight line. I can't see Tristan's face from here, but Fran is screaming at him, forcing him to keep up the intensity right to the end. As the boat glides in front of me, Tristan collapses backward, his chest heaving. It's taken everything out of him, but he's passed the test with flying colors. He's turned Cambridge into winners.

. . .

I don't have the strength to congratulate my teammates. This one stings. There's not that long until my race, so I go off and change into my Lycra. As soon as I return to the public area, I attract looks. That's the funny thing about Henley—on the one hand, you have the prim and proper dress code of the steward's enclosure, and on the other hand, there are people walking around like I am now, with everything on show.

Back when I was posing for those photos a moment ago, there was nothing I wanted less than to be gawked at. But right now, it feels like the only thing I have to offer. I help myself to a glass of Pimm's. One glass can't hurt. Before long, I get talking to Fenella, the mother of a boy at some boarding school who's rowing in the junior final, who is suitably impressed when I tell her I rowed in the Boat Race. She doesn't need to know I'm no longer in the first boat.

Fenella wastes no time in telling me she's here without her husband. She doesn't try to hide her regular glances at my crotch. I'm not in the mood for flirting, but maybe another glass of Pimm's will help. I'm sure Fenella's husband won't mind. God knows what he's off doing. Maybe I should go the whole hog with Fenella, given that she's already more or less seen the whole hog with the way I'm dressed. If I'm quick, we can have a romp in a field, then I can get to the starting line in time for—

"George?"

I turn on my heel to see Lucas.

"Oh, hey, Lucas. This is Fenella."

Fenella looks annoyed at the interruption. Lucas frowns at my glass of Pimm's.

"We need to go and get ready for our race."

"I'm ready."

"Can you come now please?"

I make my excuses to Fenella, who treats herself to one last look at my crotch as I walk away. Lucas leads me across a field and stands underneath a large oak tree.

"Have you been drinking?"

I take a defiant sip of my Pimm's.

"What's going on, George? We have a race."

"It's the second stream. No one cares."

I slump down against the tree. Lucas takes the glass of Pimm's from my hand and pours it onto the grass, then sits quietly next to me. I feel a sudden urge to rest my head on his shoulder. Instead, I turn away and pick at some grass.

"Rick Toledo looked at me like I was garbage."

"Rick Toledo's here? Damn." Lucas sees my reaction and looks guilty. "You're still rowing for Cambridge. It's not the end of the world."

"That's easy for you to say. You have Amir."

Lucas looks surprised at this comment. Perhaps I am too.

"George, what's got into you? I've never seen you like this."

This time, as I catch his gaze, I can't help it. I collapse my head onto his shoulder.

"I'm in my flop era."

I feel Lucas tense at the unexpected physical contact, but he manages to give me an awkward little pat. "No you're not."

"I am! Nothing's going to plan this term."

"Yes it is. I'm going to help you pass your exams, and then we're going to fight our way back into the first boat."

I sit up and look at Lucas. "You could at least say it like you mean it."

"That's just how I speak! I'm not great at pep talks." Lucas sighs in frustration. He's trying, bless him. It's me who won't budge.

"I just feel like I've let everyone down."

"Like who?"

"Deb. My agent. Rick Toledo. My parents, if they even care."

"Well do they?"

I shrug and look away.

"George, you can't live your life for other people's benefit. Especially if some of those people are never going to be impressed. What do *you* want?"

His gaze feels so penetrating that I have to look away. What *do* I want? My mind is blank. Aside from resting my head back on Lucas's shoulder and getting another one of those pats. I wouldn't say no to that.

"You don't have to answer that right now," says Lucas. "But I'm gonna need you to remember what it's like to really fight for something."

I got nothing.

"Come on, George, there must have been one time in high school. Did you never get dropped from the football team?"

I laugh at the idea.

"Didn't get cast in the school play? Didn't make prom king?"

I shake my head. Now that I think of it, everything did come easily to me back then. The only thing I ever had to fight for was my parents' approval. Then it hits me.

"My dad's a big golfer. There's this annual tournament at the country club where everyone takes a caddy. And every year, he'd take my brother. I was desperate for my dad to take me one year, but he said Chuck was bigger and stronger. There was no way for me to catch up to him. So one weekend, I put on my dad's golf bag and wore it round all day. To the store, to dinner, everywhere. I wouldn't take it off. And eventually my dad said I could be his caddy that year."

Lucas clasps his hands on my shoulders, his eyes ablaze.

"That is the George I need right now. Let's go strap on that golf bag."

. . .

It's true that ordinarily, no one would care about the second team race. But by some quirk of scheduling, it's happening after the first team race, setting it up as the finale. In addition, Oxford and Cambridge have satisfied the crowds by making it through to the final. It might not be a true rerun of the Boat Race, but given people's general fascination with that rivalry, plus Lucas's and my participation, the race is hotly anticipated.

Lucas and I get in the boat with the rest of our crew and row out to the starting line. All races at Henley begin at Temple Island, which is exactly what it sounds like—an island in the middle of the river containing a Greek-style temple, whose white columns and domed roof glint in the sunlight. In front of the temple, several dozen VIP guests sit on wooden chairs, as if they're the ruling emperors. They're close enough for me to be able to see their Italian leather shoes and designer shades. Time to put on a show.

The race starter calls us to get set, and I slide into my starting position. As I do, I notice something wrong with my seat. It's not sliding as smoothly as it should.

"Hang on," I say to Lucas.

Lucas frowns and raises his hand.

"Waiting on Cambridge," says the umpire.

"What's the problem?" Lucas asks me.

"I don't know. I think I need to tighten the screw."

"Are you ready, Cambridge?" says the umpire.

"NO WE ARE NOT!" I yell.

Lucas looks startled. I don't know where that came from either. But Lucas has got me all fired up, and I don't want to let him down now. These people can wait. I find the screw that's loose and tighten it, then give Lucas a nod.

"You sure?"

I burst into a smile. "I got this."

Lucas lowers his hand, and the starter fires his pistol. I spring into action. I'm determined to win, but it's not about beating Oxford.

I'm doing this for Lucas.

No one except him could have pulled me out of that hole I was in before the race. It's crazy to think who he and I were to each other the last time we rowed in a race together. I know we were technically teammates, but it's hard not to look back at the Boat Race and think that we were working against each other. Not anymore.

We've never felt like more of a team.

Each time I slide forward on my seat, my face is inches away from Lucas's. As our eyes lock together, something electric passes between us. Sure, technically his commands are passing into my ears and my brain is converting them into instructions for my body—not to mention the seven teammates behind me, all pulling their weight.

But I swear that what it comes down to, more than anything, is that magical sense of mutual understanding each time our eyes meet. It's almost what's motivating me to keep going, knowing that whenever I complete a stroke, I get to slide forward and re-enter Lucas's orbit.

I'm so locked in that I have no idea how close the Oxford boat is. Usually, I can get an idea based on Lucas's facial expressions, but today he isn't giving anything away.

He screams at me to take up the stroke rate.

Oxford must be in front.

With each pull on my oar, it gets harder. And each time, Lucas demands more.

I'm running out of steam, but we're almost at the finish line.

"I need more," Lucas says urgently.

"I can't," I gasp.

"You can. Ten more."

I'm filled with one last burst of adrenaline. 10, 9, 8, 7 ... I'm at 2 when I realize we've crossed the finish line, I feel the roar of the crowd. Who won? I turn to check and do a double take. Oxford are still about ten seconds away from finishing. What the hell?! That's an insane advantage on a course this short. We absolutely destroyed them.

I'm still in shock as we row into the bank and clamber onto shore. The spectators are losing their minds. Fran races up to me.

"Fucking hell, did you see that time? You killed it."

I glance up at the clock. We completed the course a whole five seconds faster than the Cambridge first boat. That's even wilder than the length we beat Oxford by.

"Sorry," I say to Fran. "We kind of stole your moment."

Fran scoffs. "George, if I cared about having my moment, I'd be a gymnast, not a cox." She glances behind her to check no one's listening. "All I can do is get the best out of my team, which

I did. But we both know that on a good day, you're better than Tristan."

The rest of the Cambridge squad comes down to the shore to help us in and congratulate us.

"Top effort," says Tristan. "Very impressive."

He looks sick. On the one hand, you can't compare the results from the two races. Conditions are different. Context is everything. But no one is thinking about context.

"Nice," says Deb.

That's wild praise by her standards.

"Did you ever doubt us?" I ask, grinning.

Deb says nothing. She has to play this carefully. It's not a great reflection on your judgment if your second team does better than your first. But maybe she can tell people she planned this all along, forcing me and Lucas to prove how good we are.

"George!" yells Jemima. "Bloody hell. I knew you could do it."

I turn to see an extremely drunk Jemima trailed by Rick Toledo.

"That was seriously impressive, man," says Rick. "Especially considering how the wind picked up at the end."

"It's a team effort," I say diplomatically.

"Yeah," says Rick, "but it all comes from the top. You were immense."

Jemima beams at me. "That's Olympic-level talent right there."

I guess we're not going to mention the fact that she sent me to the male model bargain bin under an hour ago. There's only one person I want to celebrate this with. I look around and spot Lucas. As our eyes meet, it hits me what we just achieved. I was too overwhelmed at the finish line, but we really did something back there. I want to throw my arms around Lucas, but as I catch up with him, we're accosted by a familiar face.

"Amazing effort, boys," says Landon.

He's had dental veneers since we last saw him, which look almost glow in the dark.

"No one cares about the second team," says Lucas.

"Bollocks. You've got everyone talking."

"Happy to entertain them," I say.

"You should never have been in that race," says Landon.

"Maybe we deserved it."

"No way. Deb tried to embarrass you, but you didn't let her."

I'm not saying anything to that.

"Listen, boys—you two are the dream team and you know it. If Deb can't see that . . . maybe you belong somewhere else."

. . .

Eventually, Lucas and I make it away from the crowds and back to the locker room. It feels good to be a winner again. Landon's right. A time like that is hard to deny. A time like that makes us the de facto first boat.

I strip off and get in the shower opposite Lucas. I face the wall, but can't resist glancing toward him. I meant what I told him about his butt. It looks great in a suit, but seeing it in the flesh is something else. I look down and realize I'm getting turned on. Goddamn it. I glance back to check that Lucas hasn't noticed, but catch his eye instead.

He holds my gaze for a split second. What's he thinking? Is there even a tiny part of him that would like it if I walked over there, pushed him up against the tiles, and kissed every part of him from top to bottom?

I jolt as someone enters the changing room. Lucas and I both flush red. I grab my towel and start getting changed. A couple of moments later, Lucas walks over and does likewise.

"Landon has no shame," I say.

I'm having to hold my towel very carefully.

"He's pretty successful," says Lucas.

"Really? His second team just lost, and his first team didn't even make the final."

Lucas is doing the towel dance too. Does that mean he was also turned on? I can't remember the last time anyone in the rowing squad was this modest.

"You're not actually thinking about defecting, are you?" I ask Lucas.

He hesitates before responding. "I just hope Deb appreciates us."

"She does," I say. "She will now."

"She better."

We've both got as far as putting on our underwear. I feel like I've made it to the other side of a minefield.

"Lucas, can we enjoy what we just did? We were incredible."

Lucas smiles. "You see how far a little childhood trauma goes?"

I frown in confusion.

"That story about your dad. Isn't that what got you so fired up?"

I shake my head earnestly. "No, Lucas. You did."

. . .

The next day, Rick Toledo emails me to repeat how impressed he was with my victory. He attaches his analysis of the wind conditions to prove his point. I forward it to Jemima, who forwards it to the CEO of the sports agency. By the end of the week, Jemima is having "conversations" with major sponsors. But maximizing my media profile is going to have to wait. Training is on hold while everyone focuses on exams.

The mood around college is tense. The library is open 24/7, and you can't move without hearing someone boast about how late they stayed up studying, or how annoyed they are with themselves for dropping three marks on their latest practice essay.

Even a couple of weeks ago, this would have freaked me out. But since Henley, I've been feeling different. There's nothing I can't achieve if I put my mind to it, and that includes in the classroom. Lucas has drafted some model essays based on the questions he thinks are going to come up in our exams. He's still planning to steal the actual questions when they're printed out a week before the exams, but he says it's a good idea to memorize his answers in the meantime.

However, as I sit down to study, I find myself reviewing the topics more widely. Between *Economics for Dummies*, the lectures I've been attending and everything Lucas has helped me with, I'm really starting to master the subject. It's amazing to realize how many concepts have gone over my head in the past three years because they've been needlessly overcomplicated. Cambridge might want to think about that.

Or maybe it's deliberate. Maybe the intellectualism that everything is dressed up in is a way of keeping certain people out. But Professor Mishri isn't that type. She's clearly slightly amazed to see me committing to some good old-fashioned studying, but she's also delighted. She gives me as many extra supervisions as she can schedule. Lucas thinks this new approach can't do any harm and lets me study with him in between. We get into a routine where he comes over to mine every evening. I leave every session fizzing with newfound knowledge and counting down the hours until the next one.

After all that effort, my first practice paper is a big disappointment. Professor Mishri is honest with me about what I got wrong, and the answer is a lot. The second practice paper is not much better. But Professor Mishri urges me not to lose hope, and I throw everything at the third one. I'm thrilled when she reveals that I scored forty. That's a pass! This requires some explanation from Professor Mishri, since I still don't understand the dumbass Cambridge marking system. Apparently, forty is the lowest mark you can get and still pass, translating to a third-class degree, whatever that is. I get the impression that for most Cambridge students, a third-class degree is basically failing, but I don't care—I've passed. I've passed!

Well, obviously I haven't passed yet, but I've shown that I'm capable of passing. Now that I've done it, what reason is there to think that I can't do it again? There's still several weeks to go until exams. Lucas stealing the exam topics has meant I've only had to review about a quarter of the syllabus. If I can scrape together a passing mark, why would I cheat? It's never sat right with me—it just always felt like the only option.

But Lucas didn't cheat his way to Amir. He did the hard work, took the risks, dug deep within himself, and now he's got the real thing. I want that. I've wanted it ever since I was a freshman in high school and did my presentation on Hercule Poy Rot. I've wanted to prove to the world that I'm smart. I've wanted to prove it to myself.

I'm aware that everyone would tell me not to risk it. Jemima would be horrified. Deb would never say it in so many words, but I know she'd think I was crazy. And Lucas . . . he's always been clear what he thinks of my chances. One practice paper won't change that.

But didn't he also tell me to figure out what I want? It's this. I'm sure of it.

When Lucas comes over to mine the next evening for our study session, he's barely through the door before I brandish my practice paper at him.

"What's that?" Lucas looks at the mark on the paper. "Oh my god, you hero!"

He gives me a high five, then looks at me solemnly.

"George, I owe you an apology. I really underestimated you."

I can't believe what I'm hearing. This is Lucas we're talking about.

"Thanks, Lucas. That means a lot."

Lucas blushes. "Well, you earned it. Imagine how well you're going to do once we get hold of the questions."

I give him a coy look. "What if we don't?"

Lucas frowns. "Why wouldn't we?"

I take a deep breath.

"I don't want to cheat. I want to sit my exams for real."

11

LUCAS

IT'S 8:00 P.M. THE NIGHT BEFORE my first exam and Amir and I are going at it in his room. I'm talking about studying, obviously. Can you imagine anything more romantic than studying together? Possibly yes, but I've spent much of the past few weeks studying with Amir and I had no idea I was going to like it this much. We do it in his room because then Amir has access to the tea bags and biscuits that he likes. We listen to Bach as we study. Amir offered to listen with headphones, but I find it calming. I like how it connects us. We don't talk at all once we're studying. Amir sits at his desk, poring over his textbooks of Renaissance paintings, and I sit on the floor cross-legged, making notes in my illegible handwriting. Amir always looks completely focused, but I have to admit I spend a lot of my time daydreaming.

I can't believe how well this has turned out. Admittedly, when I pictured myself with Amir, I didn't see us studying together while listening to Bach. But it's hard to explain how blissful it feels. It's better than sex.

Not that the sex hasn't been good. It started slowly, doing what I've always done with boys—kissing and fumbling and getting each other off. I was probably rushing things in the past, but Amir likes to take his time, and I followed his lead, observing what he did to me and copying what felt good. That's the great thing about both being men. To put it bluntly, you've got the same parts, and it makes it very easy to know what works and what doesn't. At least, as far as third base. I'd like to go all the way, but I don't know how to bring it up.

Amir is too polite to talk about these things, and I'm scared to tell him I've never done it. Maybe we don't have to talk about it. Maybe I can make it happen without saying a word. I get up and cross over to Amir at his desk. He's got a book open in front of him depicting frescoes on the walls of a chapel in Italy. He told me the name of the artist, but I've forgotten. I slide my hands down his torso and nuzzle into his neck. Amir tenses.

"I need a study break," I whisper.

"I need to finish this section."

I kiss his ears. "Can't it wait?"

"No. I'm doing the Pomodoro method."

I spin Amir's chair around and straddle him. He looks startled, but closes his textbook, then kisses me back. I could have waited for him to finish his section, but there's something thrilling about interrupting his rhythm. We move to the bed, our clothes come off, and we slip into our usual routine. Except that this time, after a while, I turn and back into Amir suggestively. It takes him a moment to pick up my intent.

"Do you want me to—"

"Yes," I say hurriedly. I'm not sure I'll cope if either of us says it out loud.

"I mean, if you're up for it," I add.

"Definitely," says Amir. "Let me just—"

He fumbles around in his bedside drawer, then maneuvers me onto my front. I'm not sure if that's because it's his favorite position or it's less awkward if we can't look each other in the eye. A few moments later, I feel Amir pressing into me. Honestly, I can't tell if he's in or out or some disastrous third option. Either way, I'm pretty sure this is not how it's meant to feel. Amir seems dissatisfied and I feel like I'm the problem, but I can't think of anything to say that won't make it worse. I'm relieved when, a few moments later, I hear my phone vibrating.

"Do you want to get that?" asks Amir.

I swear that's relief in his voice too.

"Er, I guess I should see who it is."

I grab my phone and see a missed call plus a stream of messages asking where I am.

"Fuck! Shit! George!"

Amir sits up in bed and frowns in confusion. I look guilty.

"I said I'd meet George at mine to study."

"Again?" Amir asks in surprise. "That's nice of you."

I shrug modestly. "I'm happy to help."

Amir peers at me with curiosity. "What's the deal with you guys?"

That word makes me flinch. "What do you mean?"

"It's just . . . Wilbur couldn't believe I'd seen you two kissing in the club. He thought you hated each other."

Why am I starting to sweat?

"The kiss was nothing, honestly. A joke that went too far. Look, George and I have had our differences, but we've been getting on better since I've been helping him with his exams. He's a good guy."

Amir holds my gaze. I really can't tell what he's thinking.

"Cool," he says. "You should go then."

. . .

"Better late than never," George says with a look of mock disapproval when I make it round to my room a few minutes later and let him in.

"Sorry," I say. "I got distracted."

"No worries," says George, "we've got plenty of time. Can we start with some econometrics?"

I hesitate. "Are you sure about this?"

"We can start with macroeconomics if you prefer."

"No, I mean sitting your exams yourself."

George frowns. "We discussed this. The first exam is tomorrow!"

"I know," I say, "but it's such a huge risk. There's still time to cheat."

George looks at me solemnly. "Do you remember that story I told you about Hercule Poy Rot?"

"How could I forget?"

"Yeah," says George, "same here. I've never stopped wanting to prove that I'm smart. It would honestly mean more to me than winning the Boat Race."

I sigh and nod. To me it's still not a risk worth taking, but I created this monster. George is standing up for what he wants and refusing to do what other people tell him. Good for him.

My phone buzzes, and I look down and see a message from Amir saying he misses me already and wants to walk me to my exam tomorrow. I can't help grinning.

"Look at you," says George.

"What?" I say, blushing.

"You're down bad."

I laugh bashfully. "I'm not hating it."

"Please," says George. "You two are like an old married couple."

"It's been less than a month! But we have started using the b word."

"Bitch?"

"Boyfriend."

George looks slightly taken aback. "That was fast."

"I mean . . . we waited long enough."

"Yeah, no, this is everything you wanted. I'm happy for you."

As George takes a seat on my bed, I swear he looks wistful. We've got into the habit of doing our study sessions there because it's easier to spread out all our papers and comfier than the floor. I sit opposite and look at him with interest.

"Have you had girlfriends?"

George looks up in surprise.

"I always used to have girlfriends. Like, in middle school. Nothing serious. I mean, we didn't do anything. Then in the first week of high school, I got together with Kyla Mount. She was in junior year, and everyone thought it was crazy that she wanted to date a freshman. But she pursued me so hard. Then six weeks later, she broke it off."

George looks like he's reliving the memory.

"She didn't give me any explanation. I went a bit insane demanding to know. I wasn't even that upset about the breakup, I just couldn't bear the idea that I'd done something wrong. After that, I guess I was wary of letting people get too close to me."

"Whereas your one-night stands never leave disappointed?"

George laughs. "Like I said, don't knock it till you've tried it."

That lands awkwardly. We feel like two different people since the last time George made that joke.

He looks at me thoughtfully. "The funny thing is, I totally get it. Kyla Mount, I mean. Sometimes you really can't explain why you don't want to see someone again." George averts his gaze. "That night at the gay club . . . I went home with Hot Spider-Man."

My eyes widen. "You kept that quiet."

"I guess I did."

"Was that . . . the first time you've been with a guy?"

"Second. And I liked it. I was going to see him again, but then . . . I stood him up so I could study."

"You stood him up?"

"Like a month ago. He could still be waiting for me at the bar for all I know. I'm terrified of bumping into him."

"Wait, are you telling me you ghosted him after arranging a date?"

George blushes. "I couldn't figure out the right wording."

"George, you are terrible! Get out your phone!"

He does as I tell him. I dictate a message from him to Hot Spider-Man, apologizing for the long delay and explaining that there was a last-minute change of heart that felt impossible to communicate. George can't bring himself to press send, so I do it myself.

"There," I say. "That wasn't that hard, was it?"

George looks up in surprise. "I guess not." He smiles at me gratefully. "Now do you see what a terrible boyfriend I'd be?"

. . .

Tomorrow's exam is on global capitalism. George gets out his notes and we rattle through the topics one by one. There's no denying that he's still a pretty weak candidate by Cambridge standards, but all we're aiming for is that magic forty-mark threshold. I can't deny that he's feeling capable of it. I'm embarrassed when I think how easily I wrote him off. There's something about his earnestness and his desire to please that makes him respond to things at face value in a way that can sound dumb. But once he turns off that switch and thinks for himself, he's really quite smart.

By the time we get to the end of our list of topics, it's past 2:00 a.m. George collapses his head onto my bed in exhaustion.

"Oh my god, Lucas, we did it. I really can't thank you enough."

"We had a deal, didn't we?" I'm incapable of accepting compliments.

"Yeah," says George, "but you've gone above and beyond."

"You haven't passed yet."

"But who thought I'd even be in with a chance?" George sits up, all excited.

"I want to thank you properly. Have you ever been to Trinity Ball?"

I burst out laughing.

"Do you know how much those tickets cost?"

The week after exams is known as May Week, even though it takes place in June. Just another of those nonsensical Cambridge traditions. Several of the larger colleges host black-tie balls, and Trinity's is known to be the most lavish. The St John's ball is also pretty spectacular, but I've not been in previous years. I tell people it's because of the price of the tickets, but really it's because I've had no one to go with.

"I know how much they cost," says George. "I bought a pair."

"Ooh, who are you going with?"

George smiles. "I never got around to finding a date. They're for you."

I'm momentarily lost for words.

"You can have both of them," says George. "You and Amir."

"George, that's really sweet, but we're going to the St John's ball the next night."

"Go to both! It's May Week!"

"I can ask him, but I don't think Amir would do a ball two nights in a row."

George looks surprised. "Oh. Well, the tickets are yours."

I feel a flood of affection toward George. "Let's go together."

George frowns. "Won't Amir mind?"

"No. He's not like that."

It's more that I think he won't object, but no need to get into fine distinctions. I blush as I recall what Amir and I were doing before I came here.

"Actually, George, can I ask your advice?"

"Go ahead."

I glance at my feet.

"Just now, Amir and I were trying to . . . you know . . ."

I can't bring myself to say it, so I make a gesture with my hands, which prompts George to burst out laughing.

"It's not funny!" I say, smarting.

"Sorry," says George, "but you can say it out loud."

"I can't. I'm too embarrassed."

George takes this in and pauses to think.

"Have you talked about it with Amir?"

I shake my head.

"You have to be able to talk about it," says George. "It's such a huge deal. Plus it doesn't have to be embarrassing. What could be hotter than telling someone what you want to do to them?"

I laugh uncomfortably and look away.

George smiles. "I get it. Honestly, I do. But if you can't talk about it with Amir, why don't you start with me?"

So I do. I explain that there's a part of me that's desperate to try it, but another part of me that finds the whole idea dirty and shameful. George tells me these are normal reactions, but it's a part of the body that can be washed perfectly clean just like any other body part. He even tells me the best way to do it.

"I've never been on the receiving end," admits George. "And I've only been with one girl who wanted to do it. From what she said, it's all about relaxing."

"Right," I say, "then I'm screwed."

George chuckles and turns toward me. "Lie down."

"What?"

"Lie on your side. It's a good position."

I'm not sure what George is planning, but I trust him. I do as I'm told, then he lies behind me and spoons me. I freeze.

"What are you doing?!" I exclaim.

"You're so tense, Lucas."

"No shit."

"How are you meant to feel pleasure in that state? I'm not letting go till you relax."

That's easier said than done. I'm terrified that we're about to have a repeat of Dr. Civeris's closet, until I realize that George is shrewdly not putting his crotch anywhere near me. It's my upper half he's holding on to, and it feels kind of tight until I realize it's me who's clenching every one of my muscles. I close my eyes and try to relax, but my heart is pounding. I can feel George's breath on my neck, but I have to admit that it's a nice sensation. I try to ignore the frenetic beat of my heart and focus on the calming rise and fall of George's breath. Let go, I tell myself. What's the worst than can happen?

. . .

"Lucas."

I blink my eyes open. I'm lying on my bed and I can feel George behind me. It's light outside. We must have fallen asleep. But that wasn't George's voice. I turn and see Amir standing over me, holding a coffee cup and a paper bag that I have no doubt contains my favorite almond croissant from the artisan bakery on Magdalen Street.

"What's going on, Lucas?" Amir trembles.

George's study notes are splayed all around us on the bed. George is fast sleep and has a very visible morning glory that Amir is now staring at.

"Oh my god, I didn't—"

I shake George awake.

"Lucas?" he murmurs.

"What happened?" asks Amir.

Now doesn't feel the moment to explain.

"Er, we were studying . . . I don't know how we . . . what are you doing here?"

"I said I'd walk you to your exam! It starts in thirty minutes."

I'm relieved to hear that we're in a rush. It means we have to focus on getting to the exam on time, and not . . . everything else.

As George puts on his shoes and I splash some water on my face, Amir waits calmly. I can tell he's not happy, but he doesn't want to upset me when I'm about to sit an exam, and that just makes me feel worse. It's no longer the romantic walk he'd envisaged, and I almost want to put him out of his misery and tell him to go home, but I can't make it sound like I want him to leave me and George alone.

Instead, the three of us hurry over to the lecture hall in silence as I guiltily gobble my croissant. Amir kisses me goodbye, and George and I race inside and take some seats near the back. As soon as the exam starts, I breathe a sigh of relief. I can answer these questions in my sleep.

But what about George? I can't see him without straining around the girl sitting in between us, but he has special dispensation to write his answers on a laptop, so I content myself with the sound of him tapping at his keyboard. Before I know it, the three hours are up. I race over to George and ask how it went.

"Really well!"

"Really?"

"Yeah! Loved that question on a certain Mr. Carlos Marx."

"Tell me you didn't write Carlos."

"Lucas, please."

I laugh in relief. "Just checking."

George beams proudly. "There wasn't a single question I couldn't answer. Bring on the next one."

We don't have long to wait. The very next day, we're scheduled to sit our second exam, on macroeconomic principles. This is much more theory-heavy than the first paper, and I would have liked to squeeze in another study session. But since George insists he doesn't need one and I don't want to upset Amir, I decide not to push it. On the morning of the exam, I'm twice as nervous as I was the previous day. This time, I manage to sit with a clear sight of George.

I quickly regret it. I can't take my eyes off him, convinced that every time he pauses, he's given up, and every time he types furiously, he's getting it wrong. I get so distracted that I have to pull myself together to complete my own answers in time.

Outside the exam hall, I ask George how he found it.

"Yeah," he says, "it was all right."

"Just all right?"

"That question about equity was weirdly phrased."

"No, it wasn't," says Eleanor, popping up behind us. "Not if you understood what it was asking."

"I understood," George says hotly.

"Great," I say, shooting a glare at Eleanor. "Two down, one to go."

But I can't stop thinking about George's comment. What if he did misunderstand the question? What if he misunderstood the whole paper? There are two days until our third and final exam, and I'm not prepared to take any chances. I practically lock George in my room.

Amir is disappointed I don't want to study with him, but I have one goal, and that's to pull up George's grade as high as I can. The two days pass in a blur. George and I barely remember to eat and drink. This is a situation room.

By the time we turn up to the exam, I'm so wired I feel as if I'm either going to produce a revolutionary new theory or forget my own name. As always, the exam goes by in a flash. As we file out of the exam hall, some people cheer, others burst into tears of relief. I look at George nervously.

"Nailed it!" he grins.

"Are you sure? Cos if you're not, the cheat book had a few ideas about how to—"

"Lucas, don't you dare. I'm so proud of myself for doing it the hard way. I'm never cheating at anything ever again."

As I smile back at him, George's expression turns melancholy.

"What's the matter?" I ask with a frown.

"Nothing," says George. "I just . . . I guess we're kind of done with our deal."

I feel my chest tighten. "I hadn't thought of that."

"Me neither," says George. "It's been fun."

"Not just fun," I say. "We both got what we wanted."

"Totally," says George.

We hold each other's gaze. Maybe it's a good thing that today spells the end of whatever George and I have been doing for the past few weeks. But the thought of it ending is surprisingly devastating.

"Right," I say, turning away in relief. "Let's go celebrate."

. . .

Amir has his last exam on the same day as me, so we meet up and head to a drinks party in college. Afterward, we go back to his room for a nap. I wake up before him, feeling horny, and decide there's no better time to put into practice what George taught me. I get up and take a shower, then come back and tell Amir what I want to do. He looks slightly startled to hear me state it so directly, but he's also relieved that I've taken the reins. I suggest that he tries the position I did with George, although not in so many words. He does as I ask, then eases in slowly.

I hold my breath. It's hard to describe the feeling. It doesn't hurt like I thought it might, but it's somehow too much and not enough, all at once. I'm certainly not relaxed.

I close my eyes and picture myself back on my bed, melting into George as he holds me. Like magic, something clicks. So that's what all the fuss is about! I find myself wanting it harder, faster, stronger. But Amir doesn't want to hurt me. I promise him it doesn't, but I'm not going to push him. Not when it already feels so good.

Afterward, I could happily fall asleep, but Amir has promised to attend a party with the rest of the History of Art crew. Once night falls, he takes me to a house on the far side of town. I'm nervous that it's going to be another Leonardo DiCaprio not knowing which cutlery to use on the *Titanic* situation, but this is a very different vibe. Everyone is dressed in thrift store clothes which fail to hide their tans from Easter holidays in Cannes and Portofino. The kitchen is a mess, but I spot a bottle of olive oil that I know for a fact costs £11.50 at Sainsbury's. People are drinking from plastic cups, but talking with cut-glass vowels that were honed at boarding school.

A girl in paint-splattered dungarees bounds up to us.

"Hey, boys," she says in an incredibly plummy tone.

Amir introduces me to her as his course mate Romily.

She observes Amir taking in the room. "You're judging us, aren't you?"

"It's not like you can't afford a cleaner." Amir turns to me. "Romily's parents would die if they saw how she lived."

"No they wouldn't. My parents are feral."

"Which is proof you're posh."

"We're not that posh."

"Your dad was master of Magdalen."

"He was acting master. For one term."

"I take it back. You're practically working class."

"At least my dad's not an oligarch."

Amir looks annoyed at the claim.

"My dad is not an oligarch."

"Amir."

"Fine, he owns a company, but he started from nothing. Aren't you like fourth cousins with Prince William?"

I can't believe what I'm hearing. All these years I've spent feeling inferior, and these people are competing to be less privileged.

"Guys, sorry, but you both lose."

Romily and Amir look at me in surprise.

"Single-parent family, state school education. We were on benefits for half of my childhood. That is trash you can't buy."

Amir is lost for words. Have I blown it? I've told him what my mum does for a living and he didn't seem at all judgmental. But

I'm not sure his social circle knows that he's dating a pleb. For what feels like ages, nobody says anything. Then Romily smiles.

"You win. I don't know what you're doing hanging out with us pricks."

Romily takes this as her cue to introduce me to everyone at the party, who all seem delighted to meet someone with a bit of a twang to their accent. I'm not sure how I feel about being adopted as their token poor friend, but I'm not going to worry about it tonight. The people on this side of the castle wall know how to have fun. Once it gets late, someone puts on some techno. Amir hastily retreats to the kitchen, but Romily drags me onto the dance floor.

"You're exactly what that boy needs," she grins. "A kick up the arse."

Romily reaches into her pocket and pulls out a tiny bag of what I think must be MDMA crystals.

"Want a dab?"

"I've never done it."

"Oh my god, you have to try. You might feel a bit anxious when you first come up, but ride that out, and you'll never look back."

Romily dips her finger in the bag then puts it in my mouth. The taste is horrible, sour and chemical, but I immediately feel a tingle. Romily says it will take a while to kick in properly, so we keep dancing. About half an hour later, I start to feel anxious.

I do my best not to panic. Romily said this would happen. I try to ignore the images scrolling through my mind: an undignified death, lurid headlines, and none of the mourners at my funeral believing that it was my first time. Then George sends me a selfie from the bar he's at with Johannes, and his goofy smiling face really sets me off.

What have I done? Why did I ever agree to let George sit his exams? That was never the plan. It's such a huge risk, no matter how much George has improved. It would be a disaster if he failed. I need him to be around next year.

We need each other.

We proved it at Henley. Rowing won't be any fun without George. He's the first real friend I've made in the squad apart from Fran. But I'm never going to be out on the river with Fran, and if George isn't in that stroke seat, who will it be—Tristan? Fuck that.

Except this isn't about me.

George was the one who chose to take the risk, and I have to respect that. He stood up for himself for the first time. But why did he do that? Why did he put everything that he's worked so hard for at risk? It's because he's convinced it will prove that he's smart. Will it? Does it work like that? Has getting with Amir proved anything to anyone? No—all it's proved is that it was a stupid way to look at things.

George is smart, but passing these exams will prove nothing. If he fails, on the other hand, he might never recover. He'll be Hercule Poy Rot for the rest of his life. But he also won't have rowing to fall back on. He'll have nothing—and it will be all my fault. I let him sit the exams. I gave him that self-belief. This is on me.

It's too late to stop him from sitting his exams, but it's not too late to do something about it. I tell Amir I'm feeling sick and need to go home.

I can feel a plan forming, but it only comes into focus once I'm back in my room and get out the cheat book. It describes the marking process, how exam scripts are taken back to the faculty then distributed among different lecturers to be marked. I have to act fast. Thank god George typed his answers. The book describes how scripts for those candidates are printed out then added to the handwritten ones. I get out my laptop and type out the answers to the questions in the paper I'm most worried George fucked up. I've always had a good memory. I can remember the style George writes in. I'm not even feeling nervous anymore. I feel amazing. This is an incredible idea. I'm a genius. The writing flows like a dream.

Once I've completed one paper, I decide I might as well do all three. In no time at all, I have three substitute exam scripts printed out. I don't even think of this as cheating. These are just the answers George would have written if he'd reached his full potential. But writing the answers is the easy part.

Around 2:00 a.m., I head out toward the economics department. The cheat book gives me all the information I need. I wonder how many people have used it over the years. Do any professors know about it? Is it the cause of dozens of unearned degrees? Or am I the only person daring enough to pull the moves that it makes possible?

As I arrive at the economics department, my heart is in my mouth. I catch sight of my reflection in the door.

That's weird—my pupils are like saucers.

I punch in the security code, and the door clicks open. As soon as I enter the building, an alarm sounds, loud and shrill. I race over to a closet underneath the stairs to find the alarm box, flip up the lid, and enter the code. Nothing happens. What the hell? Wait—I'm using the door entry code. I pull out my phone, find the alarm code, and enter it. The ringing stops. Or does it?

I'm convinced I can still hear it, but no, it's just ringing in my ears. I dash upstairs to the department office. There are piles of exam scripts on the head of department's desk, just as the cheat book said there would be. I sift through each pile of papers until I find George's manuscripts, then switch in the substitutes.

No one will ever know the difference.

12
GEORGE

WHEN I FIRST LEARNED THAT Cambridge University was divided into colleges, I assumed it would be like the houses in Harry Potter, where Slytherins and Gryffindors openly despise each other. In reality, it's not like that—no one takes the historic rivalries between certain colleges seriously until it comes to sport. The Bumps is an intercollege competition that has been running almost as long as the Boat Race. The university rowing squad might be accustomed to competing against each other for places, but the Bumps is the one occasion when we're officially on opposing teams.

The Bumps was conceived as a way to get around the fact that side-by-side racing is next to impossible on the thin and windy River Cam. Each boat starts a length and a half ahead of the boat behind, and the goal is to catch up with the boat in front of you and "bump" into it. The Bumps takes place twice a year over four consecutive days, with one race per day, meaning that the most you can hope to move up is four places in any given season.

Places are maintained from previous seasons, and whoever is at the front after four days' racing is crowned Head of the River. It's really quite simple.

"I'm not sure I understand, honey."

"Mom, you weren't listening."

"I was! We're just not in the best way to take it in."

My parents have dialed in from their sick bed. The restaurant had a salmonella outbreak, and it's had to close for a couple of weeks due to health and safety regulations. When my parents told me, I thought it was a great opportunity to speak to them while they were finally not running around and distracted. But given that they're still recovering from salmonella themselves, their brains can't take in information.

"Maybe you should go take a nap."

"We just took one," says my mom. "We're trying to stay entertained."

"Sorry for boring you."

"You're not. It's just a little hard to picture."

I have a sudden thought. "Why don't you come?"

"Where?"

"Cambridge."

"But you said you're racing tomorrow."

"Not for that. For my graduation."

My mom looks surprised.

"You don't have your result yet."

"I know, but I've got a good feeling."

I've been on a high since my exams. I can't remember the last time I felt this good about anything. It beats any of my sporting victories. I guess I'd have to say it was when Chuck bet me I couldn't bounce a Ping-Pong ball into a cup from the other side of the kitchen. I sat there for weeks practicing that shit. But when I finally did it, he was so annoyed, he beat me up. So yeah, this probably feels better.

"When is your graduation?" my mom asks.

"A week from tomorrow."

"Christ, George, that's soon."

"Yeah, but you'll be recovered by then, and the restaurant won't have reopened yet. It's perfect."

My dad mumbles something to my mom that I can't hear, and I assume they're preparing to break it to me gently.

"Let's do it," says my mom.

My mouth drops open. "Are you serious?"

"Why not? Right before we closed, we got a huge tip from a couple who got married here. You're right—the timing is perfect."

"Oh my god. This is amazing."

My parents chuckle, as if they too can't believe they've finally agreed to this.

"You'll have to tell us somewhere to book for lunch," says my mom. "Do you want to invite any of your rowing friends?"

My heart jumps at the thought.

"I'll see what their plans are. There's this one guy, Lucas . . . I think you'll really like him."

"We can't wait," says my mom. "We'd better go look up flights."

"Keep me posted. And wish me luck in the Bumps."

My mom looks blank. "The what?"

. . .

I'll wait a bit before inviting Lucas to lunch with my parents. We already have a ball to attend together. Maybe I'll ask him at the last minute. Or do it once we've had our results. This is my first day without either work or rowing hanging over my head for as long as I can remember. My first day not seeing Lucas. It feels strange, but that's only natural when we've been spending so much time together, especially given how intense those final study sessions were.

Except that I miss him so much today that it almost feels like a breakup.

That's an insane thing to think, but everyone goes a bit crazy during exam season. The first Sunday after exams in Cambridge is known as Suicide Sunday. The university has tried for years to stop people calling it that, but it gives you an idea of where people's heads are at while they wait for results. The typical response seems to be to drink until you forget all about it, and there are celebrations happening all around me.

As I open Instagram to check what's going on, the first thing I see is a photo that Lucas has posted of him and Amir at brunch. I feel a pang of envy. They both look so happy.

I want that feeling. I want someone to send me texts that make me burst into a grin. But it's a bad time to try and meet someone, right when the majority of my year group is about to leave Cambridge forever. I suppose I'll make do with a one-night stand as usual. I go to check my DMs, then find myself downloading Grindr.

I'm not sure what makes me do that. Maybe talking about sex with Lucas made me curious. I upload my usual photos, then decide to include one of me in a Lycra singlet which leaves almost nothing to the imagination. It always felt too slutty for Instagram, but if I'm putting myself out there, I might as well go for it. I hesitate over what to put in the box where you describe what you're looking for. In the end, I go for a peach emoji.

The photos are marked as awaiting approval, but as I go onto the home page, I see that I already have a stream of messages. That's weird. What interest can people have in a blank profile? As I read some of the messages, all becomes clear. Some men send photos of themselves, others write vivid descriptions of what's on offer. As soon as my photos are approved, the messages go into overdrive. I click on one to find that it's a video of a man being—yikes! I've done some pretty full-on sexting with girls in my time, but that was nothing compared to this.

I open another thread, and see that a guy has sent a message saying "you're hot," which feels chivalrous by comparison. I look at the guy's profile. He's pretty hot himself. I reply "you too." The guy responds with a photo of his ass. A crazy sequence of events when you think about it, but I can't help it—I'm turned on. I inform the guy. He replies "pics?"

I remember the first time I sent a dick pic. This girl Bella Rodriguez asked for one, and I couldn't decide which to send, so I asked Travis for his advice and he helped me pick one. Crazy that I thought that moment was about her, not him. For all the photos I have of myself, I'm not sure I have an up-to-date image of the prize exhibit. I ask the guy to wait, then drop my pants. I don't require any effort to get to full mast. After several attempts, I decide that photographing from above isn't the most flattering angle, and I'd be better off bearing down on the camera, or rather towering above it. The logistics of this are a little more complicated, and it takes a while to get the shot I'm envisioning. But eventually, I take a photo I'm proud of. Who could say no to this?

I do some quick color correction, then deliver my handiwork. The guy is on his way to see me within minutes.

When he arrives, he's shorter than I expected, and his face is more doughy than in his photos. He doesn't have a name. No, seriously—I ask, and he won't tell me. Before I have time to take him in, he's kissing me. Except that it's not kissing as I know it. Any aliens observing us from outer space would think he's trying to eat me. Which he is, in a way. On his profile he described himself as a bossy bottom, which I didn't read until he was already en route, but now I'm seeing what he means. He's got us both naked within seconds. I mean that—it's him who undresses both of us, with a speed that can only come from practice.

The urgency is a bit much, but it's also exciting. Because suddenly, without knowing how we got there, I'm fucking him.

I don't tell him it's the first time I've fucked a guy. I try out some different positions, but he wants to be on all fours so he can jerk himself off. That's fine, but I've never loved this position. I feel more of a connection with my bedroom wall opposite. I can't even picture the guy, because I barely remember what he looks like. I liked the anonymity at first, but now it's weird. And then I feel it happening. Everything's less tight. The mechanics are slipping. What's going on? This has never happened to me. The guy turns and looks at me, or rather, it.

"Sorry," I say. "I need a minute."

I think he's going to snap at me, but he looks sympathetic.

"Don't overthink it. It's a dick."

Such a good point. It takes almost nothing to get those things up and running. I recall that time in the closet with Lucas. My god, that was hot. Suddenly, I'm as hard as I was then. The guy grins with pleasure and just like that, I'm back in the saddle.

Man, I'd love to do this to Lucas. Just once. Just to see how it felt.

Who am I kidding—there's no way that getting my hands on that cute butt of his wouldn't feel amazing. No sooner have I had that thought than I feel the climax coming. The guy is right there with me. We finish together and he turns to me, breathless.

"Holy shit—where did *that* come from?"

After he leaves, I lie on my bed in a daze. I can't get Lucas off my mind. If I missed him earlier, I'm now full on longing for him. He's made this term the most enjoyable of my life. And it's not just because we've become friends. I want him. I want to follow through on everything we've gestured toward ... the kiss, the closet, the showers at Henley. After all that build-up, how could the sex not be mind-blowing? But sex won't be enough.

I want him to be my boyfriend.

Crazy to even think those words. I always assumed I'd end up with a girl, no matter how much sex I did or didn't have with men beforehand. But I'm not thinking in hypotheticals anymore. I want Lucas to stand over me and force me to send the texts I'm scared of sending. I want him to explain complicated concepts in a way that doesn't make me feel dumb. I want to tell him how beautiful he is a hundred times until I'm sure he believes it. I want to do it every single day until we're both old and wrinkled. Because I don't just want him to be my boyfriend.

The truth is, if I'm really honest, I love him.

Strange as it sounds, I love Lucas. I love who he is underneath all the bluster, and I love the man he's made me become. Nobody else makes me smile at the mere thought of seeing them. Nobody else makes me long for them this much. It's a longing so intense that I can't keep it to myself. If I can tell Lucas I want to sit my exams, I can tell him the one thing I want even more than that. I'm going to tell Lucas that I love him.

. . .

In some ways, now is a good time to do it, with exams behind us and training on pause. In other ways, I couldn't have picked a worse week. For the duration of the Bumps, we're rivals—I'm rowing for Trinity, and Lucas for St John's. I decide that the only thing for it is to tell Lucas how I feel straight away, as soon as I see him, before we get distracted by any racing. On the first day of the Bumps, I arrive at the boat house early. I haven't planned what I'm going to say, but I'm sure it will come to me.

I find Lucas seated on a bench outside, looking over his race plan. He looks up casually and I freeze. My mouth is dry.

"Are you OK?" Lucas asks.

"Just a bit nervous."

Lucas laughs. "You, nervous? Yeah right. You're trying to put me off."

I can only stare at him. What's happening? Just come out and say it.

"Have you seen that clip of Rafael Nadal doing a banana shot?"

"What?"

I don't know where that came from. "My mom does an amazing banana cream pie."

"George, are you sure you're OK?"

"Yeah, it's just—"

I'm literally short-circuiting. This is bizarre. Just then, a short stocky guy walks up to me. It's Marcus Pollard, the Trinity cox. He gives me a high five.

"George! So excited to work with you, man."

"Uh, sure," I say, flustered. "Hey, listen, you're actually a bit early. I need to have a word with Lucas."

"Why? He's the enemy!"

"Can you give us a minute?"

"No man, we need to talk tactics! Bye, Lucas."

It's actually a relief to forget about Lucas and talk about the competition. Marcus is convinced this is Trinity's time, having been stuck in second place for almost a year now. Last term, during the Lent Bumps, we had four consecutive attempts to get into first position and fell short each time. But university rowers are only allowed to compete in the Summer Bumps, once we're free from Boat Race duties. It's a huge advantage for any college to have a university rower on their team, but it also creates pressure and expectations. My arrival in the Trinity team is our big chance to win. To add to the appeal of victory, Tristan's college, Peterhouse, is the boat currently leading.

After Henley, any race is going to feel unglamorous, but the Bumps are uniquely chaotic. Since it's only exciting if you witness a collision, and there's no way of knowing at which point on the course it might occur, a majority of spectators watch on bicycles, following their chosen pairing. The tow path is carnage, and there are often more crashes involving bikes than boats.

As we row into our starting position, I'm not feeling very motivated. Whatever happens in the race feels irrelevant in the face of my secret mission. Why couldn't I tell Lucas how I feel? It's usually only bad news that I shy away from—unless that's what I fear it will be to Lucas. Before I can focus and get in the zone, the starting pistol sounds. We're off! I start pulling. But while I make sure to do enough not to get bumped by the boat behind, I don't have the drive to make a push for victory. As I settle into a rhythm, I sense a lack of noise from the tow path and deduce that this isn't a thrilling contest.

"Are we safe?" asks Marcus.

I glance down the river. The boat behind is nowhere near us. "Yeah."

"Then let's go for it. Come on, man. Go, go, go!"

I do the best I'm capable of. But the first three teams all come home in the positions they started in. That's the problem with the Bumps—teams have their standings for a reason, and the most likely result of any given race is that each team gets slightly farther ahead of the team they're already ahead of. As I look at Marcus, I can tell I've disappointed him with my lack of effort but that he doesn't want to admit it.

"Well," says Marcus, "we held on to our place."

I manage to force out a smile. "Yay."

...

Overnight, I catch up on the other race results. Lucas and the St John's boat managed to bump their way up from fifth to fourth, which means that Lucas will be in a good mood. There's no reason not to tell him how I feel today. After how tongue-tied I got yesterday, I decide to write it down. It takes me ages to compose a few simple sentences. I can't think how to deliver it until I find an old greeting card with a picture of a lake on the front. I issue a later meeting time to the Trinity team, so I know Marcus won't bother me, then stroll down to the boat house.

The sun is shining. I'm filled with optimism. But as I arrive, the first person I see is Amir.

"You're early," I say, forcing a smile.

"I made Lucas his favorite sandwiches," Amir says, holding up a paper parcel.

"Aw. That's so nice of you."

It's a punch in the gut. Somehow, the sandwiches make Lucas and Amir's relationship feel even more real than the photo of them at brunch. I want to throw that stupid paper parcel in the river.

"Have you seen him?" asks Amir.

"I don't think he's here yet."

Amir glances down and sees the card in my hand.

"Is that for him?"

"This? No, no, no. This is for . . . my grandma."

Thank god I didn't write Lucas's name on the envelope. I clutch the card behind my back. Amir smiles at me genially.

"So you and Lucas are going to Trinity Ball together?"

"Yeah, Lucas was so helpful with my exam prep. I wanted to thank him."

Amir looks like he wants to say something but doesn't. I wonder what he said to Lucas about catching us asleep together. I'd almost like him more if he got mad about it, but I have a funny feeling he didn't.

"I heard you two are going to St John's Ball," I say.

"Yeah, if Lucas isn't too tired by then. Speak of the devil."

I turn to see Lucas. As I do, he swipes the card out of my hand.

"What's this?"

"HEY!" I snatch it back.

Lucas and Amir both stare at me.

"It's for his grandma," says Amir.

"Shit, is she OK?"

"She's fine."

Lucas hands me back the card and turns to Amir. "He's been trying to knock me off my game. I thought it might be Anthrax."

* * *

As I go to meet the Trinity crew, I'm feeling fired up. I don't know if it's adrenaline or seeing Lucas and Amir together, but I'm absolutely determined to win. I gather my teammates and tell them I refuse to do this three more times. Today's the day we're going to take the lead. That's easier said than done. But sometimes, deciding the result before you get in the boat makes all the difference.

From the moment the race begins, I'm in my own world. I don't need Marcus to tell me we're inching closer to Peterhouse with every stroke. A hundred yards from the finish line, I feel the bump.

We've caught them!

I clamber out of the boat and go to lap up the applause. Tristan comes striding up to me. He's seething.

"Congratulations," says Tristan, shaking my hand and attempting to crush it. I give him a generous smile.

"You had a good run at the top."

Tristan looks haunted. "No one's ever held on to first place as long as we have."

"Yeah, well, we'll give it a good shot."

"You'd better do," says Tristan. "I'll be coming for my crown tomorrow."

. . .

That's the problem with taking the lead with two races to go. Nothing would be more embarrassing than immediately ceding it back to Tristan. I decide that I need to focus, and I'll speak to Lucas after the next race, not before. I'm not going to mess around with cards this time. That whole process helped me figure out what I want to say.

Lucas and the St John's boys have scored a second consecutive victory, which means that I'm in first place, Tristan in second, and Lucas in third. Anything could happen on day 3. I arrive at the river feeling confident. I didn't appreciate it yesterday, but beating Tristan is a big deal. After this and Henley, I'm back to my winning ways. All I have to do is get through one more race and hold on to first place.

As I get to the boat house, I catch a glimpse of Tristan rallying his teammates. I know in that moment that he isn't going to beat us. He can say what he wants about coming for his crown, but it's obvious that losing yesterday has broken him. Sure enough, I barely break a sweat as I lead the Trinity boat across the finish line, ensuring that we'll start the final day in first place. I feel butterflies as I realize the time has come to speak to Lucas. I disembark from the boat, step behind the boat house, and rehearse what I'm going to say.

Then I notice a commotion brewing. Tristan is striding down the tow path, looking even more livid than yesterday.

"Bullshit," says Tristan. "Absolute bullshit. Where is he?"

Tristan storms past me. I race up to Ed and Ted, who were in the boat with Tristan.

"What happened?"

"We got bumped by fucking Lucas," says Ed.

"We didn't get bumped," says Ted, "we got steamrolled. Our boat is trashed. Lucas is going to pay for that. Literally."

I walk down to the water's edge and see what Ted means. In the race between second and third, the front of the St John's boat didn't just bump into the back of the Peterhouse boat—it thrust into it with so much force that it caused the entire back of the boat to snap off. It's a miracle the rower in the bow seat wasn't injured. The boat has started to sink, with some of the Peterhouse rowers up to their waists in the water, trying to salvage it. The tow path is mayhem. Several people have filmed the incident, and some are calling for St John's to be disqualified. I spot Fran watching in amusement.

"Did you see the crash?" I ask.

"Yeah," says Fran, "it was pretty brutal."

"Tristan's fuming."

"He's just mad he lost."

"So you don't think it was unfair?"

"Unfair? George, this whole competition is ridiculous. A race where the goal is to ram into each other from behind? Tell me which private school boy came up with that."

She gestures at the fight that's still raging on the river bank.

"Look at them. They're loving this. You can't call it the Bumps, then get mad when the bumps are too bumpy."

Can't argue with that.

"Where's Lucas?"

"He ran away."

"He what?"

"He got the fuck out of here. Tristan looked like he wanted to kill him."

As I walk back to campus, I can't help feeling relieved at missing Lucas again. It's only then that I realize it's me who's been avoiding him all week. I could have texted him at any point over the past few days to arrange a time to talk. I could have confessed everything in a text if I really wanted to. I've been putting it off so I don't have to admit how petrified I am. But I can't keep doing that. I message Lucas asking if we can meet before tomorrow's race to talk about something important.

That night, I barely sleep, staying up late reading rowing group chats I'd muted. Opinion is split on whether Trinity will hold on to first place, or Lucas and the St John's boys will make it four wins in a row and snatch the win. I fire off some bullish replies, acting as if that's the outcome I care about. But the magnitude of my task in the morning and its potential fallout is starting to overwhelm me.

How have I convinced myself this is something I need to tell Lucas? Is it really better to get it off my chest if Lucas doesn't respond positively? Do I have any reason to think he will?

I don't doubt that Lucas has grown very fond of me. I'm pretty sure he's got a crush on me too. But he's always been clear that what he's most attracted to in Amir is his intelligence. How can I compete with that?

Except, Lucas did agree to let me sit my exams. He knows what the stakes are. He knows how hard I'd take it if I failed. Doesn't that show he thinks I'm smart?

The truth is, I have no way of knowing if I don't tell Lucas how I feel. I have to take the risk. Even if he turns me down, these feelings are too big to keep inside me.

The next morning, I get dressed and head to the boat house where I've arranged to meet Lucas in the club room. I arrive early and pace around, knocking a few billiard balls into their pockets. A few minutes later, Lucas enters, dressed in his St John's hoodie. Even the smallest size is still too large for him.

Damn him for looking this cute.

"Come on then," says Lucas. "What's all this about?"

I can barely look him in the eye. "Um, I'm sorry about the timing of this, but I just . . . I had to do it."

"Is everything all right?" Lucas looks concerned.

"Yeah," I say. "Everything's good."

"You promise this isn't another one of your tactics? You've got me paranoid."

"No, I swear to god. This is serious." My hands are shaking. The words won't come.

"What, George?"

"I think . . . I think I've fallen for you."

Lucas double takes, as if he can't have heard me correctly.

"I know you're with Amir, and I know you probably don't feel the same, but . . . I had to tell you."

I hold my breath and wait for Lucas to respond. As the corners of a smile creep onto his mouth, I'm filled with hope.

Then he bursts out laughing.

"Good one, George. You had me for a minute. That was some good acting."

"But—"

"You are fucking dirty, you Trinity lot. I'm not falling for it. We'll beat you where it matters—on the river."

Lucas walks out chuckling to himself.

I feel my chest cave in.

It's not just that he didn't respond as I hoped. It's the way he thought, without hesitation, that the idea of me liking him was a joke.

His heart didn't leap at the prospect. He instantly dismissed it. How did I let myself think that any other outcome was possible? I'm such an idiot.

Somehow, I make it to the starting line. The boats get into position. Word has spread about this year's dramatic competition and the tow path is clogged with people who've come to watch. The starting horn sounds. I kick into gear. But my arms have nothing to give.

I can hear the crowd willing St John's to catch us. I try not to look, but it's impossible to miss the fact that they're already advancing on us. I see Marcus staring back at me in confusion, wondering where my fight has gone. How can I possibly explain? My heart is broken in two.

I know what's coming, but it's still a shock when I feel the St John's boat crash into ours. The crowd cheers. I gasp for breath and clutch my stomach in pain. As the St John's boat pulls into the bank, Lucas leaps out and into Amir's arms. I think I'm going to be sick.

13
LUCAS

"THERE," SAYS AMIR. "You look lovely."

"What do I do if it comes undone?"

"Call me. I'll talk you through it."

Amir has insisted on lending me his spare black tie for Trinity Ball. He had the one he wore as a teenager sent up from London. (How do you get things sent up from London? Did a butler bring it in a horse and cart?)

I think I prefer a clip-on bow tie, plus this suit is kind of starchy and doesn't fit as well as the one George rented for me. But it's so sweet of Amir to go to all that effort.

"Send me photos," says Amir.

"I will. I can't wait to go to our first ball together tomorrow."

Amir tucks a rogue strand of hair behind my ear.

"You sure you can manage two in two nights?"

"I'll behave."

Amir kisses me on the forehead. "I know you will."

It's so cool how relaxed Amir is about me going with George. I'm not sure he'd be quite so cool if I told him what George confessed in the boat house. It's occurred to me since then that he might have been telling the truth. Actually it occurred to me in the moment, which is partly why I laughed it off. But that's ridiculous. I get that it all got a bit confusing between us at the end there, but declaring your love to someone who has a boyfriend? That's something else. That's serious.

George has never even been open about being into guys. There's no way he actually wants to date a man, not when he's spent a lifetime as this wholesome jock who has women throwing themselves at his feet. And even if he did, he wouldn't want to date me. I'm just too different. Too sarcastic. Too pessimistic. Not to mention the fact that he looks like a supermodel and I don't. People like George just don't fall for people like me. He *must* have been joking.

As I head over to Trinity, the college is buzzing. Trinity May Ball is legendary, in Cambridge and beyond. Vanity Fair once described it as the third greatest party in the world. Every element of the ball is designed to convince its attendees that it's worth the £250 price of the ticket. Even the queue is glamorous. People are lining up around the edge of Great Court in their ball gowns and tuxedos, sipping champagne as they wait to be permitted entry. A few weeks ago, I would have been panicking that everyone was looking at me and knowing my black tie was borrowed. But after that house party with Amir and his friends, I've realized they're just as likely to be worried I'm judging them. Which I totally am.

"Come in," calls George as I knock on his door.

I walk in to see him topless with a towel round his waist.

"Sorry," he says, "I'm a bit behind."

He tells me to take a seat and strolls into his bedroom. As he shuts the door, he tugs his towel loose and I catch a glimpse of him naked.

I feel a surge of lust that almost floors me. What's wrong with me? It's the confession in the boat house. It's changed things, whatever I try to tell myself. That and knowing George sleeps with men. Suddenly all sorts of things are easier to imagine.

I walk over to the window and try to distract myself by observing people in the queue. A few minutes later, George emerges in his tux, struggling to clip his bow tie on.

"Can you help me?"

I look at him, blushing.

"If you can reach," George adds with a grin.

"Fuck off," I say, swiping him playfully. As I stand behind him to fix the tie, I'm hit by the scent of his aftershave.

This is disorienting.

"We should get in line," says George.

He turns and notices my distracted gaze.

"Are you OK?"

"Yeah," I say. "Why wouldn't I be?"

We join the queue and are admitted into the ball soon afterward. Trinity's ancient courtyards have been lit with flickering lanterns and multicolored spotlights. I grab a glass of champagne, feeling a bit overawed. The mood is weirdly restrained, with everyone acting like they've been here, done that—but then, lots of them have. The first people we bump into are Tristan and Eleanor. Tristan is wearing an enormous silk cummerbund, while Eleanor has a fur stole around her shoulders. They don't look a day under fifty-five. I've only ever had one proper conversation with Eleanor at a boat club dinner, but I feel like I know her intimately. I got so annoyed by her attempts to prove she was better than me at economics that I kept changing the subject, and we covered everything from the relative merits of the various Bake Off presenters to her preferred method of cooking monkfish.

"Trinity Ball, eh?" says Tristan. "You two are inseparable these days."

I smile at Tristan. "They're calling us the dream team."

Tristan scoffs. "Officially you're still the second team."

"Only cos training's on pause. You wait."

Tristan laughs. "Don't you still have to pass your exams, George?"

"Yeah," says George. "What about it?"

Tristan smirks at Eleanor. "How do you fancy his chances, Ellie?"

Eleanor glares at him. I'm sure she's spent hours of her life bitching about George to Tristan, but presumably she wants to keep up appearances in public.

"I wish him all the best," Eleanor says tartly.

"As do I," says Tristan. "But I think I'll wait until results day before I get too worried about this 'dream team.'"

Thank god I swapped George's papers. It's given me the odd moment of panic, but George really believes he's going to pass, and spoiler alert—he is.

As we start to sample the ball's entertainments, George bounces around like a kid at a playground. We play a few rounds of blackjack at a makeshift casino, where I lose, so George gives me his winning lollipop. In the main marquee, some American indie band is playing a load of songs no one knows. George feels sorry for them and insists on dancing like a goofball right at the front. A wandering magician performs a card trick that George finds so mind-blowing that he asks if he can post it on TikTok. We head to the food tent and gorge on Wagyu beef sliders and Thames oysters, followed by profiteroles, mini mille-feuilles, and suspiciously colored macaroons. Just when I think I can't eat any more, we discover a chocolate fountain.

"This is incredible!" George exclaims.

"Isn't this your third time at Trinity Ball?"

"Yeah! It gets better every time."

He dunks a strawberry under the chocolate fountain and hands it to me, but I decline. George gives me a chastening look.

"What's going on, Lucas?"

"I'm full."

"No, something's up."

I let out a sigh. "I just feel like I should save some of my energy for tomorrow."

George swallows hard. "What if there's an apocalypse tomorrow? You have to live in the moment."

"The world would fall apart if we all did that."

"I'm not talking about everyone. You, Lucas. You need to stop worrying."

I don't say anything, but I'm listening.

"It's cute that you want to save yourself for Amir. But we're young. You'll be fine."

"I guess."

George smiles and hands me a napkin. "So what are you going to do with this?"

Just then, I spot some chocolate on George's upper lip. I lean in and wipe it off. George is startled, but holds my gaze. There's an invisible force pulling me toward him. It's making me want to—no, I can't think like that. I screw up the napkin and chuck it in the bin.

"Done," I say with a flood of relief. "Let's party."

· · ·

The lawn on the other side of the river has been turned into a fairground. Our stomachs are in no state for such hijinks, which is unfortunate—for our stomachs. We bounce on the bouncy castle, whiz down the helter-skelter, and go round and round on the carousel. As we get on the bumper cars and crash into each other repeatedly, I can't remember the last time I had this much fun.

A Ferris wheel has been installed next to the river, casting a shimmering reflection with its neon lights. The queue snakes all the way up to the bridge, but eventually we make it to the front. George and I are shepherded into a seat, a safety barrier comes down, and the wheel starts to rotate. It didn't look all that tall from down on the ground, but once we get up to the highest point, my stomach lurches and I wish I hadn't eaten and drank quite so much.

From up here, we have a stunning view over Trinity toward St John's. But as I turn to George, he looks melancholy.

"What's wrong?"

George turns to me. "Nothing's wrong, it's just—" He looks into my eyes, but can't bring himself to say it.

I think again about his confession before the Bumps. Maybe I should bring it up. Just in a casual way, to see where it leads. If he really did mean it, it would be good to get it out there.

"George?"

Before I can continue, I hear a thud, then feel a big judder. The Ferris wheel has ground to a halt. I stare at George.

"What the fuck?"

I look down and I'm almost sick. The wheel has stopped turning with us right at the top. Beneath us, I hear nervous shouts and screams.

"Probably just a mechanical issue," says George.

"Just?!"

"It will get moving any second. We'll be fine."

"How can you say that?!"

"I just know we will."

"Give me one good reason."

George rests a hand on my arm. As he looks at me, all my fear melts away. What's about to happen flashes before me, and I know that if I give in to it, there's no turning back. But I don't pull away. I close my eyes and lean in to it.

14
GEORGE

I KNEW IT FROM THE moment we locked eyes. It couldn't have been more different from the time we kissed at the club. That time was pure impulse. This time felt inevitable.

I could taste the chocolate fountain on Lucas's lips, feel the wind in my hair.

I could have gone on kissing for hours, but after a minute or two, we were jolted out of it by the Ferris wheel starting to work. Once we got down on the ground, I thought we'd at least talk about what just happened. I felt bad about Amir, and I'm sure Lucas felt worse. But I couldn't bring myself to say anything, and neither could he.

We just kept on going around the ball like we had before. Except that everything was different. I can't speak for Lucas, but that kiss changed me. I can never go back to how I was before. There was a part of me that wondered if I could really go through with this. Now it's not even a question.

It's not about male or female. It's Lucas. He's the one.

As we stood and watched the fireworks, I saw him shiver and was desperate to put my arms around him and keep him warm. It was only at 6:00 a.m., after the survivor's photo, that we finally touched again, sharing a hug before we went our separate ways.

I didn't want to let go.

Now I'm lying in bed as the morning sunlight streams through my window and wishing Lucas was here. It's not a painful feeling—or maybe it is, but in a way that feels exquisite.

I can't think of anything I'd like more than to be cuddling in bed with Lucas. Not that we'd cuddle for long. The things I'd do to him. I can't bear to think about it. I thought about it enough when I got home after the ball, climbed into bed, and relieved all that built-up tension. What happens now?

Lucas has a boyfriend. He seems to really like Amir. But he must see that there's something special between us. More special than what he has with Amir? That's a question for him.

Maybe we can talk later, after we've received our exam results. I want to message Lucas and make a plan, but I don't know what to say.

I feel my phone vibrate and my pulse quickens at the thought that it might be him. But no, it's an email from Professor Mishri with a single line of text: Please come and see me at your earliest convenience.

I dress in a hurry and sprint across Great Court. It has to be good news. If I'd failed, she wouldn't want to see me in person. Maybe I've done so well that the economics department want to offer me a place on their master's course. Yes, that feels like something Professor Mishri would want to tell me face-to-face. I charge up the steps to Professor Mishri's study and burst in without knocking. She's standing talking to a smart-looking middle-aged woman who's cradling—is that a chinchilla?!

"George!" says Professor Mishri. "You scared me."

"You did say my earliest convenience."

Professor Mishri gives a pointed look to the woman, who lowers the chinchilla into a travel cage.

"Let me know what the vet says," says Professor Mishri.

The woman nods and walks out with the chinchilla. Professor Mishri turns to me.

"Well, at least you finally got to meet Tilly."

I can only stand and stare.

"Why don't you have a seat, George?"

I stay standing. I don't like the look on Professor Mishri's face.

"Look, George, it's bad news. You've failed."

It doesn't register for a moment.

"What?"

"You've failed your degree."

"No, how is that . . . what mark did I get?"

"You didn't."

I can't compute what I'm hearing. "But . . . I got loads of answers right."

"Yes, no, you got plenty."

Professor Mishri coughs and averts her gaze.

"You've been failed for plagiarism."

I freeze. Professor Mishri is silent.

"Is this . . . are you talking about my dissertation?"

"Please, George, have a seat."

I manage to stumble into the armchair that Professor Mishri is gesturing at. I feel hollow. This is like a bad dream.

"Let me explain," she says. "The person marking your work noticed that your exam answers were printed on a different type of paper to the kind we use. Which means that your papers were swapped."

I feel sick. I can't bring myself to respond. But I'm no longer confused. Lucas must have swapped my exam papers. That's the only explanation.

"Do you have anything to say?" asks Professor Mishri.

"No! I didn't swap anything! It must have been someone else."

Professor Mishri looks surprised, as if she can tell I'm being honest.

"Right, well, unfortunately that doesn't matter."

"What?! How can it not matter if someone swapped my exam papers without me knowing?"

Professor Mishri fiddles with her sleeves.

"Because, after realizing this, we submitted all your work to a plagiarism check. Including the dissertation. We have AI programs that can detect these things, compare them to previous essays and so on. It concluded that none of it was your own work, even though you'd made a good effort to hide it. At this point, I was asked my opinion and I'm afraid I did have to say that . . . I'd had my suspicions."

I'm too shocked to respond.

"Now there may be some complicating factors as you say—"

"Complicating factors? Someone's fucked me over!"

"That may be true, but the university isn't interested. There's clear evidence you cheated, and given the attention there's been on you specifically, everyone's keen for this not to get any more awkward than it needs to be. I'm so sorry, George."

As I leave Professor Mishri's office, my head is spinning. It can't be true. It just can't. I can't get my head around it. It's one thing for Lucas to swap my papers, another for him to let me believe I'm capable of passing on my own. To think I took that as proof that Lucas wanted to be with me. Then it hits me.

He doesn't believe in me.

He doesn't think I'm smart.

And if he doesn't think I'm smart, why would he want to be with such an idiot?

Why would he ever love someone like me?

This is even worse than failing my degree. I'm not good enough for Lucas. Thank god we didn't talk about what happened last night. How did I let myself get sucked in? I must have been blinded by love. I feel a burst of pure anger at what Lucas has done. I call him up and ask where he is. He sounds surprised, but says he's at a tea party at the orchard in Grantchester.

I jump in a cab and make my way over there.

The orchard is full of customers sitting in dark green chairs set among the dappled shade of the apple trees, but I can't see Lucas. Then I spot a private gathering in the far corner. A table has been set up, and an absurdly luxurious afternoon tea is being served. Amir stands at the head of the table, pouring tea into painted china cups. Eight or so guests sit on wicker chairs, eating cucumber sandwiches and scones with jam and cream. The women are dressed up like they're Alice in Wonderland. There's a man in a straw hat. Lucas is sitting next to Amir in a buttoned-up shirt. He looks up in shock as he spots me.

"Hello, George," Amir says tightly. "Did Lucas invite you?"

Lucas blushes. "No, I—"

"We're celebrating Lucas coming top of the year again. It's too late to include you in the seating plan, but you're welcome to have a scone."

"I just need to talk to Lucas."

I drag him away from the group before he can object.

"I know what you did," I say, eyes blazing.

Lucas gulps. "What are you talking about?"

"You don't have anything to confess?"

Lucas shoots a panicked look at Amir and his friends, who are watching in fascination while trying to maintain a sense of decorum.

"Would you like to explain why I've failed my exams because someone swapped the papers?"

Lucas turns pale. "What?"

"Don't fuck with me, Lucas, I know everything."

Lucas stares back at me. "Shit. Fuck. How did they find out?"

I feel a rush of indignation at his implicit admission. "Because, you dumbass, you printed them on the wrong type of paper."

Lucas is reeling. "And they failed you because of that?"

"Yes. It's called cheating."

"But . . . did you tell them it was me who did it?"

"Is that what you're worried about?"

"No! I'll go and confess right now if it will help. Fuck, George. Fuck!"

Amir walks up to us, clutching a teacup. "Is everything all right?"

"Obviously not," I snap.

Amir glances at his guests. "Lucas. All my friends are here."

"I'll be back over in a minute," Lucas whimpers.

Lucas waits for Amir to leave, then turns to me.

"Let me see what I can do, George."

"No. Stop. You've done enough."

He's genuinely distraught, but that only makes it worse. How did he think he'd get away with this? I can't look at him any longer. I go to walk away, then turn back, fuming.

"Just do me one favor. Don't ever speak to me again."

LUCAS

What have I done? What the hell was I thinking? George's life is ruined and it's all my fault. I can't let this stand. I know what I have to do. Fuck the consequences. And I'm not going to hang around and wait for an appointment. I tell Amir there's been a mistake with George's exams that might be my fault, then abandon the tea party. I can see that he's annoyed, and his friends think this is what comes from dating a commoner, but I really don't care about that right now.

As I head back to town, it takes a bit of googling to find the information I need, but eventually I establish that the man I want to see is called Edwin Dunn. He's the guy who spoke to me and George in the boat house at the start of term. Turns out he's the director of Strategic Impact for Cambridge University, whatever that means. His office is in a grand old building next to the Senate House. I walk in and tell a secretary I need to speak to Edwin Dunn urgently. She says he's unavailable. I say he knows who I am and he won't want to miss me.

She disappears, and a few minutes later, he's magically free to see me. He shepherds me into his room.

"I take it you know what happened," I say.

The man looks at me. Even though I now know his name, he's still so blank and nondescript that it doesn't seem to bear any relation to him.

"I'm not sure what you're referring to."

"George Holst."

He doesn't betray a reaction.

"He failed his degree because someone swapped his papers. It was me. I did it."

Still no reaction.

"If anyone should be failed, it's me."

"Have you received your exam results?" the man asks.

"Yes. I got a distinction."

"Then you have your result."

"But don't I need to be punished for cheating?"

The man looks at me coolly. "Do we have any evidence you did what you're claiming?"

"I'm confessing it."

"That doesn't mean you did it."

"Why would I confess if I didn't do it?"

The man shrugs. "Maybe you think you can both get off that way. You might get some punishment, but you'll still have your degree result. And George will get to stay."

I have to laugh at his gall. "Who would risk that?"

"It's conceivable."

"Only because you just conceived it."

"It's irrelevant, in any case," says the man. "He cheated on his dissertation."

"His tutor's known that all along! She never said anything."

The man narrows his eyes at me. "What did I say to you at the start of term?"

I'm momentarily silenced.

"Don't embarrass the university. We do not want a scandal."

"Oh, I can make a scandal. I can go public."

"I assure you that won't end well for you."

I don't flinch. "Do I look like I care?"

He wasn't expecting that. I can see his mind whirring, wondering how he's going to keep me quiet and stop this from blowing up. I need to keep pushing.

"I'm the number one student in my year. I grew up on a council estate. This university needs people like me. Trust me, you don't want this to get ugly."

As I say it, I'm trying not to let my nerves show. What am I even threatening? Is there really a scenario where this all works out for me and George if we go up against him? Then I remember I have one last trump card. I reach into my bag.

"These are George's real exam papers," I announce. "I kept them."

The man glances down at them in surprise.

"I didn't read them properly before I swapped them, but I've had a look and they're really good. Even if you fail him on his dissertation, he might have done enough to pass."

I thrust the papers into the man's hands.

"Mark them fairly," I plead. "George tried so hard you wouldn't believe. Punish me if you really have to. But please don't take it out on him."

GEORGE

The email is unsigned. It's sent by a secretary, but there's no name attached, other than the university. I have no idea who was behind the decision, but I've got it in writing:

> On reflection, the university has decided to award you a degree. However, you will not be permitted to attend graduation or continue your studies at Cambridge.

My first thought is relief. Leaving Cambridge without a degree after three years would have been hard to come back from. But once the dust settles, there's not much to be happy about. Lucas already offered me a degree on a plate. I decided I'd rather sit the exams and get the result I deserved. That chance has gone, and so has the thing this was all originally aimed toward—rowing for Cambridge next year. I'm not even allowed to graduate. That feels like an unnecessary kick in the teeth.

Are they worried about publicity? Maybe that's why I'm getting the degree after all—give me enough to stop me complaining, but ensure that I slip off into the shadows and never return.

They've got their wish. I start packing immediately.

I have to get out of here. Leave Cambridge today. There's nothing left for me here. I already regret confronting Lucas. What was the point? It doesn't change anything. I need to get away from Cambridge, away from the boat club, away from Lucas. Everything that has given my life meaning over the past term.

I check my phone and see a message from my parents. They're heading to the airport to fly over for my graduation. Oh god, what am I going to say to them? Do I tell them the whole story? Of course not—they don't want to know their son's a cheat. That's what I can't forget here: I may have eventually changed my mind about cheating, but not for ethical reasons, and not when it came to my dissertation. I don't deserve a thing.

I log on to my computer and find a flight to Madison, Wisconsin. Maybe I can stay in the city with my cousins for a few days. I'm not ready to face my parents. I'll call them in a minute. Make up some excuse. As I fill in my details on the airline's website, it asks for my passport number. My bags are in a jumble all over the room. There's no knowing where my passport has ended up. I find a binder full of documents and tip them onto the carpet. Most of it's junk—a ticket to last year's ball, a lanyard for the steward's enclosure at Henley.

Then there it is: the business card of Landon Hughes, the Oxford rowing coach.

AUTUMN TERM

OCTOBER–DECEMBER

15
LUCAS

IS THERE ANYTHING WORSE THAN being up and about before the sun has risen? It's 5:45 a.m. and I'm walking down King's Parade in pitch darkness. I pass the Corpus Clock—a bizarre metallic sculpture displayed outside one of the colleges that features a giant grasshopper with glowing red eyes and feet that tick-tock back and forth.

It's weird to be back in Cambridge, where curiosities like this are par for the course. I was only half an hour away at my mum's house for most of the summer, but it felt like a different world. I have to admit it was nice not having to think about rowing. Unlike the rest of the squad, who spent the long summer break nursing their endorphin addictions in the gym, I could afford to basically forget about rowing for two whole months. I can't say I missed it. But now that I'm back in Cambridge, I'm glad it's going to be taking up all my free time. It's all planned out for me, twice a day, six days a week, with barely a moment in between.

It's going to be so weird rowing without George. I haven't seen him since that day at the orchard in Grantchester. Edwin Dunn took the exam papers but showed no sign of giving in to my threats, so I left his office without knowing what his next move was.

I called George to let him know that I'd tried my best, only to find that he'd blocked me. Shortly after that, he vanished from Cambridge and stopped replying to the entire rowing squad. There's no way I was going to go public without speaking to George first. In the end, I was forced to drop it.

It's seared in my memory how angry George was the last time he looked at me. But that wasn't the worst part. The worst part was how I saw straight through his anger. Behind it was a devastation that had nothing to do with him not having a degree. It was how I'd betrayed him. Ignored the one time he stood up for what he wanted.

Maybe it's no surprise that he still hasn't forgiven me.

The day after it all went down, I told Amir about kissing George at the ball. He blinked twice, then asked if I thought it would happen again. I said no. Amir said that in that case, there wasn't a problem. One week later, he took me on holiday to Tuscany. The first week was just me and him. He'd planned everything meticulously. We stayed in the most amazing boutique hotel in Florence. Amir had a long list of galleries he wanted to visit but was worried about queues, so we got up very early every morning, which meant we also went to bed early, and didn't drink in the evenings. We saw so much, and even though I had an app that told me all about the paintings, Amir gave me his own mini lecture on every single one, right down to the smallest details.

For the second week of the holiday, we went to stay with Amir's friend Wilbur and his family in a villa outside Siena. Ridiculous place with an infinity pool and a personal chef. It was the kind of holiday I never could have imagined growing up. I sort of know Wilbur from the boat club, though we've never really talked. For the first few days, I was uncomfortable. Then I remembered my mum's philosophy: if they're nice, I'm nice. I couldn't deny that everyone was being welcoming. No one cared that I'd gone to a state school. I felt like we were all really bonding. But on my last day there, Wilbur's mother took me aside and asked if I could put in a good word with Deb about Wilbur being picked for the Boat Race. Hard not to think that was the main reason I was invited.

After that, I was glad to go home to my mum's house and dial the glamour down to a zero. That was until I told her what happened with George. She was livid. Don't get me wrong, I'd spent weeks being mad at myself, but I hoped my mum might understand the misguided logic that led me to do what I did. Nope. She couldn't see how I could have convinced myself to take someone else's fate into my hands like that. She was in a mood with me for days. She only came round when she saw how much I was suffering. I think I was in shock at first. Then in Italy, there were too many distractions. But once I had no one for company but my mum and her manky old budgerigar Leslie, it came down to one simple and devastating fact: I miss him.

I miss him so much. I wake up thinking about that night at Trinity Ball. And not just the moment on the Ferris wheel. Sometimes at night I lie awake, wondering what would have happened if I hadn't got caught swapping the papers and George was going to be in Cambridge next year. Amir has a job at Christie's, so I'm only going to see him on weekends. If I'd been in the boat opposite George six days a week, would we really have been able to go back to how it was before?

I certainly wouldn't have found it easy to be in close physical proximity. Maybe something would have happened between us. Maybe even more than last time. But that's the problem with George, he's too damn hot. Take that away, and what are you left with? We were great friends, yes. He's incredibly sweet and fun. He brings out a side of me that I adore. He's way smarter than you think when you first meet him.

Hang on, what were the negatives? Oh yeah—he hates me.

I don't blame him. I deserve that reaction. I don't know where he is, what he's doing, or who he's with. He's moved on from Cambridge. I don't doubt that he's moved on from whatever weird crush he developed from spending too much time with me. Hard to think what he can be doing without a degree. He's probably back in Wisconsin, working at his parents' country club and taking the hottest girl in town for corn dogs at Big Bertha's Barn Dance. I'm sure I'll move on soon too. I'm so lucky to have Amir. My biggest dream came true.

Sure, I never dreamed that my first boyfriend would spend hours of his free time trying to track down the perfect fountain pen ink. But everyone has their quirks. He's kind. He loves taking care of me. He's even promised I can move into his flat in Mayfair at the end of this year when I finish my master's. By then, George will barely be a memory.

. . .

Six a.m. at the train station isn't the best time for catchups. Deb informed the squad over the summer that George wouldn't be returning, and everyone assumed he failed his exams and moved back to America. There are a few new faces, while Dakani has joined the civil service fast stream and Sprout has gone off to be a management consultant, but most of last year's squad have chosen to stick around and finish what we started. As I get on the train and hear Ed and Ted moaning about the price of Pret breakfast baps, it feels weirdly good to be back. I save a seat for Fran, but Johannes swoops in next to me.

"Hey, man," I say in surprise. Johannes and I have never been seat buddies.

"I've got a proposition for you," Johannes says urgently.

I perk up in intrigue.

"Tristan is running to be boat club president."

"Yes, I saw the announcement."

Until recently, everyone assumed that George would be president again this year. He was so perfect for the role that no one would have dreamed of running against him. I hadn't thought about the fact that the position was now vacant until Tristan sent a grandiose email to the squad last week announcing his candidacy as if he was running to be president of the free world. He'll make a terrible boat club president, but I can't bring myself to care.

"We need you to run against him," says Johannes.

I laugh in surprise. "Why me?"

"You're the only one who can beat him."

I feel exhausted just at the thought of it.

"I really don't have time to be boat club president."

"Lucas, you have to. Tristan's parents got divorced over the summer. He's in such a bad mood. Think how shit it will be if he's our leader."

"Yeah, it will suck, but that doesn't mean I should have to do it. Why can't you?"

Johannes looks baffled. The thought of being in a leadership role and having to constantly take a position on things is completely unfathomable to him. Even what he's doing right now is a big step.

"I can't be president. It's Tristan or you."

He's right. Anyone else, and Tristan would get in their ear and turn them into a puppet leader. It's not like I have anything else to fill my winter evenings with.

"OK, yes, fine—I'll do it."

. . .

When we arrive in Ely, I bump into Wilbur. We have nothing in common, but now that we've been on holiday together, we have to act like we're friends. I'm only now realizing how much it's going to suck not having George here. I'm chatting to Wilbur about how great it's going for Amir at Christie's when Tristan marches up to me, brimming with rage.

"I heard you're running against me for president."

Jesus, that got around fast.

"I haven't committed to it."

"Why would you do that?"

"I don't know, Tristan, maybe because no one likes you."

Tristan glares at me as if he wants to crack my skull open, then reaches up and flicks my earlobe.

"Ow!" I yell, recoiling. "What the fuck was that?"

"You asked for it."

"You're such a fucking gimp, Tristan. At least punch me in the face."

Tristan starts sizing up to me, which is hilarious, because he's so much taller than me that it only makes him look dumb, like he's picking a fight with a child.

"Boys," shouts Deb.

"He started it!" screams Tristan. "He's running for boat club president purely so he—"

"Enough!" says Deb.

She claps her hands and divides us into crews. Everyone falls quiet. After what just happened, Wilbur is suddenly looking like a desirable option, but Deb puts me in a boat with Tristan as stroke. I look at her in disbelief.

"You're gonna make me sit in a boat with him after that?"

Deb shrugs. I have no choice but to slouch over to the boat. I'm planning on ignoring Tristan, but as he gets in his seat, he's buzzing.

"Hey, I didn't mean it back there."

I don't respond.

"Look who she picked. This is definitely the first boat."

I hold Tristan's gaze. "It better fucking not be."

"It blatantly is. We need to lay down a marker."

"Oh, now you want to be best friends. Which is it, Tristan?"

Tristan quivers with rage and leans in close to me. "Listen, I know I'm not George, but I'm the best you're going to get, so you might as well get over it. Should have sucked his dick while you had the chance."

Tristan has succeeded in firing me up. Just not in the way he intended. Once we've completed our warm up, Deb orders a sprint, and Tristan nods at me. But as Deb blows her whistle, I start counting the stroke rate deliberately slowly. Tristan frowns.

Usually, it's his job to set the pace. The cox only intervenes when something's gone wrong. Tristan slides forward on his seat.

"What are you doing?"

"You're out of time," I hiss.

"No I'm not."

"Yes you are. Follow me."

I continue to count, and Tristan has no choice but to follow. He can feel in his bones that we aren't going as fast as we could be, but there's nothing he can do about it. He just keeps getting redder and redder, more and more frustrated. By the time we cross the finish line, he's ready to explode.

I ignore him and look over at Deb. Her expression is impervious as usual. But as we row into the bank and carry the boat up to the van, Deb approaches me with a stern look.

"A word, Lucas?"

"Go for it."

"Not here. Boat house, this afternoon."

. . .

Private meetings away from the squad are never a good thing. What the hell was I thinking out there on the river? Of course Deb saw what I was doing. There's nothing she hates more than people trying to game the system. In my eagerness to piss off Tristan, I've signed my own death warrant. On the train back to Cambridge, I sit with Fran.

"It could be about anything," Fran insists.

"No it couldn't. It's obvious. Me and George found a way to make it work, but I'm never going to get there with Tristan."

"What, and you think I am?"

"I think you'll handle him better than me."

Fran looks doubtful.

"I'm glad it's worked out this way," I say. "When you joined the men's squad, a part of me thought I should just step aside and let you have your chance."

Fran looks at me with disdain.

"When are you guys going to get over the fact that I've got a pair of tits?"

I'm rendered momentarily speechless.

"I didn't come here to be patronized," Fran declares. "My dream is to cox at the Olympics. I don't want anything handed to me on a plate. I want to earn it."

. . .

That afternoon, I walk down to the boat house and find Deb already waiting.

"Balcony?" she says.

She leads me to two wooden deck chairs on the first-floor balcony that look onto the river. Beneath us people are strolling along the tow path, but the river is quiet aside from a man in a kayak.

"It's really not a great river to row on," I say.

"No."

I turn to Deb. "You don't have to beat around the bush. I can take it."

Deb doesn't follow.

"I know you're going to drop me."

"What?"

"I lost it out there today. I was mad at Tristan, and I wanted to punish him." I look away, shamefaced. "I shouldn't have done it."

"Did you see how Tristan reacted?" asks Deb.

"Er, yeah. He was furious."

"But what did he do about it?"

"Nothing. There was nothing he could do."

"You think he would have reacted that way with Fran?"

I look at Deb in surprise. And not because she just spoke three sentences in a row.

"Because I don't," says Deb. "I think he would have ignored her and gone at the speed he wanted."

I really don't know where she's going with this.

"It's going to be you, Lucas. You and Tristan. I've made my decision."

"Wait, because Tristan's a misogynist?"

Deb is silent.

"But . . . me and Tristan hate each other. Do you really think this is a good idea? Look at what happened with me and George in last year's Boat Race."

"That was different."

"But—"

"Forget about George," says Deb. "I know what I'm doing. Oh, and one other thing . . . don't run for president."

I stare at her. "I . . . why?"

"Tristan needs it."

"That's not how it works! You can't reward him for being a monster."

Deb grits her teeth. There's nothing she wants less than to explain herself, but I've backed her into a corner.

"Look," she says, "we've lost our best rower. Our next best rower has some . . . issues, but we need him on the team. We need him to win. And we *are* going to win this year. Understood?"

16
GEORGE

I LOVE THE HOLIDAY SEASON in Wisconsin. Everything is covered in a blanket of white, there's a snow-sculpting contest on the hill above town, and some years the lake freezes over and gets turned into an ice rink. My parents always have to work, but Chuck decides to be nice to me for a week and we get into the Christmas spirit. We drive down Candy Cane Lane to see the lights, buy roasted almonds at the German market, then go home and stuff ourselves on cinnamon rolls and deep-fried cheese curds. There's nowhere more magical at this time of year. Which is why it's a shame that this year, I'm on a rowing camp with the Oxford crew in the middle of the French Alps.

My alarm goes off and I fumble around to put it on snooze. I see a Happy New Year text from my friend in New Zealand. How is it New Year's Eve already? I shudder as I feel the cold and pull the comforter up to my neck. My feet poke out of the bottom. We're staying in a seventeenth-century chateau that has been converted into a sports camp. That might sound glamorous, but the dorms here give little sign that this was once a chateau. They're as bare as they probably need to be when they have to accommodate a new set of athletes and their bulky bags of equipment each week. The twin beds are tiny, and my roommate Daley is fast asleep. The only benefit of getting up early is that I don't have to witness his morning jerk-off. My five-minute snooze is over before I know it. I force myself out of bed, pull on a tracksuit, and shuffle downstairs. I don't want to keep Landon waiting.

I didn't think twice when I called up Landon impulsively last summer. Lucas had always been open about the fact that he'd happily switch to Oxford if he didn't get the chance to row for Cambridge. Since he was responsible for me not being able to row for Cambridge, I didn't feel bad about doing likewise. I was never planning on keeping it a secret. But when I spoke to Landon, he couldn't have been more excited. He'd just signed a deal with a streaming network to have the cameras follow the Oxford crew for a year. The idea of having someone like me on the team, with my social media following and dramatic narrative arc, sent everyone into a frenzy. The whole squad were made to sign NDAs. We're not planning to reveal my presence on the Oxford team until the last possible minute, creating a suitably shocking "moment" for the documentary season finale.

I'm not sure how I feel about that. But I've been terrified about what the Cambridge crew will say when they find out, Lucas in particular. I'm happy to postpone that news for as long as possible. Mostly I'm just happy that, rather than having an embarrassing end to my British rowing career, I'm going to get a second shot at winning the Boat Race. True, my priorities had started to shift by the end of my time in Cambridge, but this year I'm signed up for a master's in business administration, which is not going to challenge me academically. Instead, I'm going to focus on what I'm good at.

"Morning, George!" says Landon as I arrive at the gym.

It takes a moment for me to adjust to the bright lights and realize there's a crew filming.

"You're cool with the cameras?" asks Landon.

"Sure!"

I'm contractually obliged to say that. When Landon told me last night he wanted to have a one-on-one early-morning gym session, I felt special. But then again, he could have picked someone else for this scene.

"We're loving the buddy arc that's forming between you guys," says the producer. "Viewers love a bromance."

I wasn't aware that Landon and I were buddies, but I'm not the one who's been watching the footage.

"Ignore the cameras," says Landon. "Let's do some weights, and let the chat flow naturally."

"You've got our conversation points, right?" says a producer.

"Oh yeah," says Landon. "Memorized them."

We do some warm-ups in front of a mirror. Landon makes sure to pick the same weights as me. It's hard not to stare at the chin implant he got right before we started filming. After a bit, he sits down on the bench to wipe his brow.

"So how do you like the camp, George?"

"It's awesome."

"Pretty special place to train."

"Totally."

"Are you bonding with the guys?"

"Yeah. I feel like I've known them forever."

"Maybe a bit more tentative," says the producer. "This is only episode three."

I blink and try to snap back into the conversation.

"Are you bonding with the guys?" says Landon.

"I'm getting to know them better every day," I say. "Still a long way to go."

Out of the corner of my eye, I see the producer give a thumbs-up.

"Nice," says Landon. "So you're not regretting the move to Oxford?"

I smile. We've already discussed this. In fact, we've filmed several confessionals to make sure the viewer is fully on board with my decision and doesn't see me as the villain. I have to convince people I didn't have a choice other than moving to Oxford. But I can't say anything that makes it sound like I'm going to go easy on Cambridge. The producer has assured me it will all come out perfectly in the edit.

"No," I say to Landon. "Best decision ever."

Landon gets up and walks over to me. "Put it there, bro."

He pulls me into the classic bro embrace. Maybe we are buddies.

"Cut!" says the producer.

Landon pulls back immediately.

"Thanks, George—you're a pro."

. . .

Officially, the Oxford rowing squad comes to the Alps for the new year to mimic the conditions of spring in England. But there's something about the light out here that's from another world.

Temple-sur-Lot is only an hour from the airport in Bordeaux, but it feels like the middle of nowhere. The village is perched on the edge of a wide, slow-flowing river. I'm sure Landon timed this morning's training session to coincide perfectly with dawn. The mist is rising off the river's placid surface, as streaks of orange and gold light the sky behind it. This scene is going to look so good in the TV show.

As we complete our warm-up, I see the silhouette of Landon standing on the river bank with his megaphone, the camera crew behind him.

"Right boys," says Landon, "this is the last scene we're shooting before the crew gets the night off. Let's go out with a bang. We're gonna be seat racing."

Everyone grumbles, or at least does as much grumbling as they can permit themselves in front of the cameras. Landon announces the first four to go out, and it's me, along with Tobias, Rodrigo, and Steve. It was weird having to learn the names of a whole new crew, but I've done my best to bond with these guys. Everyone's been so nice. I'm sure it helped that the producers made clear I was to get a positive reception, but I have no reason to think it's not genuine.

I get in the boat with the other rowers Landon has requested and share a look with Felix, who's going to be coxing us. Spending considerable amounts of time seated opposite Felix was a factor I didn't consider until I arrived in Oxford. I haven't forgotten what Lucas thought of the guy. Felix is the joker of the series, and some of his jokes have been aimed at me, but it's all good fun. As I slide into my starting position and get ready to pull, Felix leans into me and whispers.

"Don't go out hard."

"Why?"

"To make Tobias look bad. We don't want him to make the team."

Tobias is a German guy, very serious and not a popular figure among the English toffs who make up the bulk of the Oxford squad and seem to think it's still 1939.

"Who's we?"

Felix gives me a warning look. I glance around. The cameras aren't anywhere near us, but I'm wearing a microphone that picks up everything.

"Just do it," says Felix.

I try to think fast. They're not going to feature me engaging in any cheating. Felix isn't stupid, he knows that too. Which means it's him, not the producers, who wants this to happen.

Am I meant to object? Is that what the hero would do?

"I'm going to row my own race, Felix."

"They're not going to use this," says Felix, guessing my train of thought. "We'll get away with it, trust me."

"That's not the point."

As we set off, I give it everything I've got. But no matter how hard I pull, there's no escaping Felix, sitting right in front of me, giving me a death stare. I can just hear him, telling the whole squad I refused to obey his orders and turning them against me. I've put in so much effort to make them like me. I'm not sure I can stand becoming the enemy.

And so, without saying a word, I slow down my pace. Felix senses it immediately. He doesn't say anything either, but once we finish, he gives me a little nod of approval.

"Thanks, George," says Felix. "You're the best."

Tobias swings his leg over the bench and sits down next to me with his food tray. The meals here are served in a noisy cafeteria that does little to uphold the French reputation for haute cuisine. Usually I'm happy to sit with anyone at lunch, but right now Tobias is the last person I want to see. I can barely look him in the eye.

"Great effort out there," says Tobias.

"Thanks."

"Did you think our boat felt fast?" Tobias asks, fiddling with his juice box.

"Yeah," I lie. "We were solid."

"I don't know," says Tobias. "I felt like you got quicker once I was swapped out."

Does he know? Needless to say, I want Tobias to like me too.

"Don't go on how you feel," I say. "Only Landon knows our splits."

"Actually, the guys were timing too, and I heard one of them say I was slower."

"Tobias, don't listen to them, seriously."

"Guys, are we capturing this?" says the producer.

I glance up and see that a crew has swooped in on the fly to film my conversation with Tobias. I look at them in a panic.

"I thought you'd wrapped."

"Ignore us," says the producer. "This is great. Nice little pep talk."

That's the problem with trying to keep everyone happy. You can so easily tie yourself in knots. The producer has enough in the can to destroy my reputation at this point, but all I can think about is giving her and Tobias what they're asking of me. The producer waves her hands for us to continue.

"So you think there's a chance Landon will pick both of us?" asks Tobias.

"I, er, yeah, sure, of course there's a chance. You're a great rower."

Tobias's face is flooded with gratitude. "Thanks, George. I needed that."

He puts an arm around me and pats my back manfully. Behind him, the producer does a chef's kiss.

. . .

After lunch, I pull on a coat and go for a walk through town. I can imagine my mom liking a town like Temple-sur-Lot. It's not so different from where we live in Wisconsin. I wander along the main street, even though almost all the shops are closed. I've heard that the French know how to take a holiday. If only I'd taken their lead. There's one store open, so I go in and buy a postcard and some stamps to send to my folks back home.

I never made it back to Wisconsin last summer. My parents were so mad about wasting all that money on their flights to my graduation that I couldn't face seeing them, and I'm still not convinced a trip home would go well. But it's easy to get lonely in the week between Christmas and New Year's.

It's great how nice everyone has been on the Oxford crew, but it does get exhausting. I'd just started to get good at standing up for what I want, but I know why I've slipped back. It's because

I don't have Lucas hyping me up. I've worked so hard to forgive him, but I still get a flash of anger every time I remember what he did with my exam papers. And I hate feeling like that, so I try not to think about it.

But that just means the anger keeps coming back.

I haven't spoken to Lucas since that day in the orchard. I'm not even sure he knows they gave me a degree in the end, but I don't feel he deserves to know that. It's not like he had anything to do with it. Some days, I'm desperate to get in touch and tell him everything. That's why it's great I signed that NDA.

After all, what good can come from speaking to Lucas? He's still with Amir. I blocked Lucas on all my accounts, but one night I cracked and created a secret Instagram account so I could stalk him. He posts photos occasionally of him and Amir at private views or on foreign holidays. They look happier than ever. I know Lucas reacted as if my confession to him was a joke, but he must have realized it wasn't, after the kiss and everything else. He knows how I feel. And he never once suggested he feels that way about me.

So really, it all worked out, in the sense that it never would have worked out between me and him. It's actually better for everyone that I moved to Oxford. It's just a bit hard to appreciate on cold winter days in the middle of nowhere.

As I head back toward the chateau, my phone starts to ring. It's Jemima. I take back what I said about everyone taking a break between Christmas and New Year. There's no way this woman hasn't been hustling.

"Hi, Jemima. Where are you?"

"I'm on a sober retreat in Wales."

"Wow. That's so—"

"Just kidding. I'm drinking champagne on top of a mountain in Val-d'Isère."

"Ha. Sounds fun. How is it?"

"It's awesome, George, because guess who I just bumped into. Tamara Foyle."

Am I meant to know who that is? As far as I'm concerned, every British woman in Val-d'Isère for New Year's is called Tamara Foyle.

"She's features editor for *Vogue*. And she's agreed to a shoot."

"With who?"

"You!"

Jemima cackles. Then burps.

"Oh, but you know I can't do any press at the moment."

"It's not for now. We'd time it to the week of the Boat Race. Landon's already signed off on it."

At first, Jemima wasn't down with the whole year of secrecy thing. But she quickly saw what an opportunity it was to raise my profile. I should have guessed she'd be planning something like this.

"What kind of shoot?"

"It's going to be very classy."

"Will I be clothed?"

"Tamara wants you in your kit. We can place a strategic oar if you're worried about shrinkage."

"That's not—"

"I need a quick answer, George. I'm about to jump off a ski lift."

"What?! Do you mean jump on a ski lift?!"

"Potato, po-tah-to."

I hear someone shriek with laughter in the background.

"Can I get back to you, Jemima?"

"I'm going to take that as a yes."

"What? No, wait."

I don't need Lucas to help me stand up to people. I can say no. It's not that hard.

"I've got to go, George—I'll send over the contract. Tamara, you slag!"

. . .

Tonight's New Year's Eve party kicks off with a hallowed tradition: the eighty-fifth annual Oxford Boat Club Pantomime. As far as I can tell, a pantomime is a fairy tale combined with a drag show and a load of audience participation, which I'm finding hard to picture. But presumably tonight's performance will enlighten me. Felix has taken on directing duties. The cast have conceived a version of *Jack and the Beanstalk*—at least, that's the title they're using. It bears little resemblance to the original fairy tale. I've been told that the main purpose of this annual tradition is to make fun of Cambridge. People still talk about the version of Cinderella where two Cambridge-based Ugly Sisters tried and failed to deny Cinderella her prince. But no matter how hard I try, I can't follow the target of the satire. This is just *Jack and the Beanstalk* with all the key details changed to something rowing-related. Jack goes to market to sell his mom's boat, and comes back with five metal screws. When his mom throws the screws in the flower bed, they grow into an oar, which Jack uses to climb up into Giant Land. That makes no sense. Screws don't grow into oars in the way beans grow into beanstalks. But maybe it makes sense if you're British.

"Fee fi fo fum," Felix declares in the role of the Giant, which I have to admit is hilarious casting. He's attempting an American accent, for some reason.

"I smell the blood of an Oxford man."

The guy playing Jack gasps in mock horror.

"Who are you?"

"I'm George Holst," Felix thunders.

Everyone bursts out laughing.

"And why are you so massive?" asks Jack.

"Because I rowed for Cambridge but I got too big for my boots."

Everyone laughs again.

"But, George," says Jack, "we're on the same team."

"I don't care. This is my TV show. It's all about meeeeeeeee!"

I don't believe this. They've made me the villain. All that effort I've put in to befriend them, and the minute the cameras stop rolling, they reveal what they really think of me. I even did what Felix asked in the seat racing, and still I'm the enemy. Still he mocks me.

I can't win. And I don't know why I thought I could.

"Ooh, he's not happy," someone shouts from the audience.

Everyone turns to look at me. I've let my mask slip. It would be so easy for me to smile through this, force a laugh, convince everyone I'm a good sport. But what would be the point? I don't want to waste another minute trying to get these boneheads to like me. I stand up, swipe a bottle of vodka from the table, and walk out.

. . .

Up in my room, I've drunk half the bottle of vodka before I know it. I start firing off Happy New Year messages to random people. I don't bother sending one to my parents. They've got some big party at the country club and will be rushed off their feet getting ready. I start to compose a message to Chuck instead, getting nostalgic about Candy Cane Lane and cinnamon rolls. But after so much vodka, I'm struggling to type, so I video call him.

"Dude, what's the matter?" Chuck asks as he picks up. He's in the living room at home, sipping from a mug and wearing a Christmas sweater Mom knitted for him.

"Nothing. I just wanted to say hi."

"It's New Year's Eve. You should be partying."

"Says who? You're not."

"It's 3:00 p.m. I'm heading out later. Gonna go watch the Big Cheese Drop with Mom and Dad."

I feel it like a blow to the chest. "They said they were working tonight."

"They were, originally. I convinced them to take the night off."

My face turns sour. "Of course you did."

Chuck looks puzzled.

"You were always the favorite."

Chuck bursts out laughing. "What are you talking about?"

"Admit it."

"Are you drunk?"

"We both know it's true."

"George. Don't do this."

"Why don't Mom and Dad like me?"

"Jesus, George!"

I stare him down.

"Of course they like you," says Chuck.

"They never have time for me." I'm trying really hard not to cry in front of him.

"You never come home."

"'Cause they're always so busy."

"Yeah, George, they work goddamn hard."

"Except when you tell them to stop."

Suddenly I look at Chuck and wonder what the hell I'm doing. It's Chuck. We're not going to have a heart-to-heart. That's not what we do.

"Don't tell them we talked, OK?"

Chuck scoffs, but I can't tell if that's because it's the first or the last thing he'd do.

"I have to go, Chuck."

"Dude—"

I look at him desperately.

"Do me a favor and pour the rest of that bottle down the sink."

. . .

I always was good at doing what I'm told. But now I have no liquor left, and it's still only 10:00 p.m. I feel weirdly obliged to stay up until midnight, but I can't bear the thought of being alone in my room for another two hours. No more drunk texting. Definitely no more calls. I log onto Instagram and see that Lucas has posted a story. It's a shot of a rowing oar dipping into a river not dissimilar to the one at Temple-sur-Lot. "New year, same old" reads the caption.

He must be at Cambridge's rowing camp in Spain. I wonder what he's doing right now. Probably having the time of his life at whatever party they're throwing.

But what if he isn't? What if he's still as hung up on the events of last term as I am? What if he's sitting alone in his room, filled with desire and regret? What if he thinks back to that night at Trinity Ball and realizes he's never been so happy?

What we had was one of a kind. There's no way I'm the only one who sees that. There's no way Lucas doesn't miss it too. He's going to find out what I've done eventually. Much better that it comes from me. I unblock his number, then remember the NDA. I'll be in serious trouble if the news gets out. It's not like Lucas is someone I can trust anymore. He'll just have to find out when everyone else does. Then my eyes fall on the postcard I bought to send my parents.

Lucas definitely knows that Temple-sur-Lot is where Oxford has its training camp. All I need is a way to let him know it's me.

Then it hits me. I already came up with the perfect words when I wrote that card for him during the Bumps. I can still remember those three sentences by heart. I write them out on the postcard. I've covered the cost of stamps to Wisconsin—it will easily reach Cambridge. I don't know where Lucas is living this year, but if I address it to his college, it should get to him.

I layer up and head outside to find that it's started to snow. The rest of the squad have come out and are doing naked snow angels. The producers really missed out on some great content by wrapping early.

Nobody notices me as I traipse into town and find the post office. My hand hovers over the mailbox.

THE BOAT RACE

APRIL

17

LUCAS

"**I'M TELLING YOU GUYS,** it's based on science."

"Bullshit."

"I'm serious. There's a physical benefit to holding it in."

"Wait, is he talking about holding in your pee?"

"No, no, no," Johannes laughs. "Tell them, Lucas."

I turn to my captive audience.

"I'm reading this article which says . . . you shouldn't ejaculate before a race."

The whole team bursts into hysterics. Standards are low with this crowd. We're on the coach to London and we've been stuck in traffic for almost an hour. Somehow, we've made it through the winter and there are only five days until the Boat Race. We're traveling down today to give us plenty of time to get used to the river and, more importantly, the media frenzy. Most of the squad have become hyperactive in the face of their nerves. Given that I'm more nervous than anyone, I'm happy to entertain them.

"That's not even the best part," I say, reading from the article. "For optimum results, you have to hold it in for several days, then just beforehand, get as close as possible."

"You mean edging?" Rotter exclaims.

"Basically, yes."

"Like when? On the start line?"

Everyone is beside themselves with laughter.

"Gents!" barks Tristan. "That's enough."

He marches down the gangway like a sergeant major.

"Come on then," says Tristan. "What's the joke?"

Our smiles are wiped from our faces.

"Spit it out, Rotter."

"It's nothing. Lucas read an article which said we shouldn't wank before the race."

Everyone snickers.

Tristan shoots me a glare. "Is that true?"

"That's what it said."

"Let me see." Tristan snatches my phone and skims the article before handing it back to me. "Right. This seems legit. Share it on the group chat."

I stare at him in disbelief. "I was joking!"

"Well I'm not. I'm the fucking president."

Tristan's reign as boat club president hasn't been as bad as we were expecting. It's been worse. Reign of terror might be pushing it, but not by much.

"I want everyone to participate," says Tristan. "I'll be checking."

"How?" says Rotter.

I turn to him dryly. "Do not question the wank police."

"LUCAS!" screams Tristan. "I am deadly serious. We must do everything in our power to win on Sunday. Including this."

• • •

Our base for the week is a large rented house in Putney, a leafy neighborhood on the south bank of the Thames full of semi-detached houses and riverside pubs and the starting point of the four-mile Boat Race course. The idea of staying in a house is to create as homely an atmosphere as possible, but the team isn't accustomed to living in such close quarters, and I'm worried I won't last five days without being driven to murder at least one of them.

And by one of them, I mean Tristan.

Deb doesn't want us to exert ourselves too much, which means we only do a short training session each morning on the Thames. There are a couple of evening events, including an alumni dinner with the usual suspects in their regulation blazers, but most of the time, we're either watching some dumb action movie or arguing about which dumb action movie to watch next. The second team are staying in the house next door. I visit as much as possible to hang out with Fran. I feel a bit bad about this. Fran only joined the mens' team for one reason, and it wasn't to cox the second boat. It's not like I even beat her fairly. But Fran hasn't let it get to her.

Today we're sitting in our regular spot on her porch, chatting aimlessly.

"Do you think he's going to drag Eleanor into it?"

"How do you mean?"

"The night before the race. Do you think Tristan will ask her to edge him?"

Fran looks at me irritably. "I don't know, Lucas."

I pull back in surprise. What did I do?

"I'm sorry," says Fran, "but you've been coming round here every day complaining about how your teammates are taking this all too seriously. I'd love to have that problem."

I'm so unaccustomed to being called out like this that I can only listen in shock.

"Deb never even gave me a chance," says Fran. "Don't ask me why, but you know she didn't. I really don't hold it against you for beating me to it. But please don't make me feel bad for caring."

. . .

Two nights before the race, we're given the evening off. I go to meet Amir and his parents at a bar in Mayfair. I should never have let it come to this. Things haven't been great between me and Amir for a while now—at least, not on my end. Amir seems as happy as ever, which makes me feel worse that I'm not.

On paper, he's everything I could ever want, but there's something missing. It's hard to put my finger on what. I've long been aware of our differences, but I've never thought that was an issue in itself. Some couples complement each other perfectly. I see them at restaurants or at parties, chatting for hours and laughing themselves silly. I'm not even sure Amir thinks of me as funny.

A few times recently, I've been close to saying something. But I've been so busy with Boat Race preparations that somehow the plan to meet Amir's parents got put in place before I could say no to it. Since they stay at the Mayfair flat when they're in the UK, and the plan is for me to move in once I finish my master's, Amir wants us all to meet before we become occasional flatmates. As I get out at the tube stop, Amir is waiting where we agreed.

"Do you not have a jacket?" he says, brushing some fluff off my shirt.

"Why, are your parents going to be offended?"

"No—I just don't want you to get cold."

Amir leads me to the bar where his parents are waiting. It's oozing wealth from every corner, a gleaming mahogany bar and miniature brass lamps that look like they're polished daily. The maître d' takes Amir's coat, then shows us to our table. The clientele is mostly either businessmen or couples on dates, scrubbed to the nines, enormous smartphones resting on the table in case of a lull in conversation.

Amir's parents stand as we reach them. His mum's hair is freshly coiffed, her perfume fruity and overpowering. His dad is wearing a three-piece suit. He steps forward and shakes my hand.

"Lucas, we are so glad to meet you."

"You too!"

His mum goes for a hug, but instead of feeling comforted, I'm overwhelmed. We take our seats, and a waiter appears to take our order.

"I'm not drinking," I say. "Tap water's fine."

Amir laughs affectionately. "We'll get a bottle of mineral water for the table."

We stumble through the kind of small talk I was prepared for. Amir took pains to assure me his parents have no issue with his sexuality. His mother's own mother was a cleaner, so apparently they're fine with that too. I have to admit that I don't detect anything other than warmth.

"We're very happy about Amir's job at Christie's," says his dad. "You know he was involved in the sale of a painting to our friend?"

"I heard."

"Do you know what you'll do after graduating?"

"He's going to move in with me," says Amir.

"Yes, but for work."

"I've got a couple of interviews lined up," I say. "One at McKinsey."

Amir's dad looks concerned. "There's a lot of downsizing going on in that sector. If you want, I can put you in touch with my friend at Apple. They're hiring economists."

I know he's trying to help, but I can't bear the idea of being in debt to Amir's parents.

"That's so kind of you," I say. "I'm going to focus on job applications as soon as the race is over."

Amir's parents clasp their hands together in excitement.

"We can't wait!" says his dad. "We're just disappointed Wilbur didn't make the team."

"Wilbur came out to Tunisia when the boys were teenagers," says Amir's mum. "He's such a nice boy. We were hoping Amir would take up rowing."

"Mama."

"It's OK, habibi," she says, clasping my hands in hers. "We have Lucas now."

The words hit me in the gut. Amir's mum beams at me, but I can't smile back.

She glances at her husband. "Can I tell them?"

Amir's father nods.

Amir and I share a puzzled look.

"Boys," says Amir's mum, "we don't want to get in your hair once Lucas moves in. We've decided to buy you your own flat."

Amir gasps in delight. "That's so kind of you. Where?"

"Wherever you want," says Amir's dad.

Amir turns to me and sees that I'm frozen in shock.

"How amazing is that?"

"Uh, yeah," I manage to stutter.

Amir frowns and gives me an urgent look. I know I'm meant to be expressing my gratitude. But I can't get the words out. Amir's parents have clocked my reaction and both look slightly stricken.

"Anyway," says Amir's dad, "we just wanted to let you know. Tell us, Lucas—where should we stand on Sunday to get the best view?"

. . .

I manage to stumble through the rest of the meeting, but we're all relieved for it to end. After we've said our goodbyes to his parents, Amir walks me to the tube station in silence. Neither of us wants to initiate the conversation, but once the station comes into view, we stop in the middle of the street and Amir turns to me.

"My parents just offered to buy us a house and you didn't even thank them."

"I did! I thanked them right before we left."

"Yeah. About half an hour too late."

"I was in shock. Buying a house together is a huge step. Whoever's paying."

"Not for them. My parents have tons of investment properties."

"That's not why they're doing this."

Amir chews his lip and doesn't respond.

"We've been together less than a year, Amir."

"So? We're committed, aren't we?"

"We've never even said 'I love you.'"

Amir flinches at the words. "Maybe we should have this discussion after the race," he says.

"No, Amir. I've been putting it off for way too long."

I've rehearsed it a dozen times in my head, but now that it's here, I don't know where to start. Just be honest with him. No sugarcoating.

"We don't make each other happy," I say quietly.

Amir looks astonished at the notion. "I make you packed lunches. Tuna sandwiches. I hate tuna!"

I feel a jolt of injustice on his behalf. I'd assumed he felt somewhat similarly to me, but maybe tuna sandwiches is what happiness is to him. I hold his gaze, even though it pains me to do so.

"I'm grateful for everything. But it's not me."

Amir is hit with a flash of indignation.

"What am I meant to say to my parents?"

"Honestly, if that's your biggest worry right now, it kind of proves my point."

Amir wants to object, but he can't. Maybe I'm poking at things he had no interest in examining closely. Or maybe none of this is a surprise to him, but he'd made his peace with it. As I turn to leave, he looks panic-stricken.

"Lucas, if you walk out of here . . ."

What? No more tuna sandwiches? Then there's our very own flat and the job at Apple. There's a whole life laid out for me.

I look at Amir and think of how desperately I longed for all this a year ago. But who even was that Lucas? That Lucas didn't have a clue what he wanted.

That's something I've learned the hard way. Amir hasn't been a bad boyfriend. But he doesn't make me laugh. He doesn't make my heart race. He doesn't push me out of my comfort zone. Lord knows where I'm ever going to find someone who does all that, but that's no reason to hang around in a situation that I know isn't right.

I give Amir one last, lingering look, trying to communicate all the things I can't bring myself to say. Then I turn and walk away.

. . .

Miraculously, I sleep through the night. When I wake up, my first thought isn't sadness. It's relief. I'm sure it will hit me after the race. Or maybe I've done my grieving already. In any case, as I head downstairs for breakfast, there's more than enough to distract me. All the rowers are piling on the carbs, plus gallons of water. Today is the weigh-in, a tradition almost as anticipated as the race itself, mainly because it's the first time the Oxford and Cambridge crews come face-to-face. This year, anticipation is at fever pitch. Oxford have been behind closed doors all year because of this stupid documentary series. It's given them an air of mystique, but I can't imagine they've got anything up their sleeve except Landon's usual bullshit.

The actual weight of the crew doesn't matter when it comes to the rules, but the goal is to establish yourself as the heavier team, and by extension, the most powerful. Taking on water is a tactic well-known by both sides, but there's still a psychological advantage to winning the contest, so everyone drinks until they're ready to burst. Afterward, we file into a minibus and drive the short distance across the Thames to Fulham, a neighborhood more or less identical to Putney except for the fact that it sits on the more prestigious north side of the river, so its residents feel appropriately superior.

The Hurlingham Club is one of the most ostentatiously exclusive sporting venues in London. Electronic gates glide open to reveal a perfectly manicured lawn where elderly members play bowls in front of a white Georgian clubhouse fronted by Doric columns. As the minibus drives up, none of us say anything, silenced by the sight of TV crews with their vans parked next to the clubhouse. We know we're going to be the bad guys of the Oxford series, but they've struck a deal with the regular broadcaster of the Boat Race, so we're going to be featured whether we like it or not.

"Shit, Deb," says Johannes, "I'm desperate to pee. What do I do?"

Deb looks at him. "Wait."

"What if I can't wait?"

"Pray."

Cambridge are being weighed first, so we make our way to the media room. According to tradition, you weigh the lightest crew member first, building up to your strongest titans. There's a minimum weight for coxes, otherwise men's boats would be exclusively coxed by women. But it's still seen as an advantage to have a light cox, rather than carrying what could be construed as dead weight. I'm never going to be as light as Felix, but I've been fasting since last night to avoid any unkind comments in the media. I step onto the scales—59 kilograms. Not the lightest, but enough to avoid becoming a talking point. I step off in relief and allow each rower to take their turn. Tristan has been bulking up for months and tips the scales at 89 kilograms, befitting his status as stroke.

The media look impressed, and I'm feeling increasingly confident. Maybe this really is our year.

"Lucas?" says a familiar voice.

I turn and see Helen Wheeler from *The Daily Telegraph*.

"Can I ask a few questions?"

"No."

"Lucas," says Deb.

I look back at Helen Wheeler and sigh. Deb's right. Even refusing to comment could be spun into a story.

"Helen," I say insincerely. "Hit me."

Helen Wheeler beams and presses record on her Dictaphone. "So, here we are ... back where it all went so wrong."

I hold Helen's gaze and wait for the question.

"Are you worried about history repeating itself?"

"No."

"What's different this time?"

"Everything. Different attitude. Different team."

"So you still blame George Holst for last year?"

"I didn't say anything about George. Only half this year's boat were in the team last year."

"That includes Tristan Barnes. Does this year's lineup suggest things might have been different last year with him as stroke?"

"Helen, you are the only person who's still obsessed with last year. We moved on a long time ago."

The media round continues along these lines for another twenty minutes. Once I lock into the talking points Deb has drilled into us, it's easy. Just as we're wrapping up, a hush falls over the room.

That can only mean one thing—Oxford are here.

I take a deep breath. I'm not looking forward to seeing Felix, but I can stare him out, no problem. At least staring is all that's expected of me. My teammates are puffing themselves up and trying to look as big and scary as possible. As the first Oxford rower walks into the room, a journalist chuckles. He's wearing a hoodie emblazoned with the letters F.T.T. Everyone who was at the formal dinner knows immediately that it stands for "Fuck the Tabs."

"Fucking idiots," says Tristan.

Deb hisses at him. She doesn't want us to lower ourselves to their level, and flatly vetoed Tristan's suggestions of doing something similar. That doesn't change the fact that standing here and sucking up a display like this is humiliating. I watch as the team walks in, each rower more bulked up than the last. Then I freeze.

A guy near the back has exactly the same hair as George.

I laugh. Imagine. I can't see any more than his hair, since his teammates are blocking the view, but then I see a shoulder, and can't help noticing it's just like George's too. I must really be nervous for my mind to be sending me there. I wait to get a proper look at this imposter. As the guy makes it into the room, I turn pale. That's uncanny. They look identical. Wait, surely it can't be? Yes. Fuck. It is George.

"What the hell?" says Tristan.

I stare at George. How is this real? How is George standing right there in front of me? George, on the Oxford team. Is this a joke? But George looks deadly serious. His eyes are lowered, his expression blank.

"Fucking traitor!" screams Tristan. "Are you actually fucking kidding me?"

The media has cottoned on to what's happened, and are now taking photos, tweeting breathlessly and racing up to Landon for comment. I've never seen anyone look so smug. Helen Wheeler is delirious with excitement. But the president of the Hurlingham Club, a punctilious man in a cream suit, is beside himself.

"Gentlemen," he protests, "can we please have our first Oxford crew member up for weighing."

Somehow, Felix makes it over to the scales. Our crew regroups on the other side of the room. Though I'm holding it together, I'm in pieces. Now George's silence and Oxford's secrecy makes sense. Still, I can't believe that George has gone and done it. All those times I suggested defecting, I was never serious. I don't care that he's rowing for Oxford. I care that he hid this from me. He's been in England this whole time and he never said anything. I want to march up to him and demand an explanation. His expression has remained implacable, his eyes fixed on some imaginary spot as if he wants to pretend he's not in the room.

"I cannot fucking believe this," splutters Tristan. "You do NOT switch from Cambridge to Oxford. You do not row for the enemy!"

"Tristan," says Deb, shooting her eyes at the TV cameras.

They're filming us from all angles. I don't know why I expected any less from Landon. He's creaming himself over Tristan's reaction. Johannes pulls Tristan away from the cameras and tries to calm him down. The Oxford crew continue weighing in one by one. They're loving every minute of this.

George is the last one to go up. Why won't he look at me? I need him to look at me, just once. I need to know what he's thinking. But as George steps down off the scales, he avoids my gaze studiously. The president of the Hurlingham Club declares Oxford the heavier crew. They burst into furious cheers.

· · ·

On the minibus back to Putney, the mood is bleak. It's not just the fact that Oxford won the weigh-in. George being on their team is a body blow. Partly, it's how good he is at rowing. When he's on his game, there's no one better. But mostly, it's psychological. They've been plotting and planning and caught us off guard. The script has literally been written, backed by a multimillion-dollar production crew. How are we going to write a different ending? When we arrive back at the house, I'm ready to plod upstairs, but Tristan gathers us in the living room. There's an anger in his eyes that chills me.

"Two hundred years," he declares. "That's nearly four thousand men who've rowed in the Boat Race. Way more if you count all the different categories. How many have switched sides? Four. George just entered the history books, and not in a good way."

Everyone jeers in disgust. I don't think anyone cares quite as much as Tristan, but he's giving them an outlet for their frustrations.

"This goes beyond the Boat Race. Oxford and Cambridge have been rivals for almost a thousand years. We respect each other immensely. But you're either one or the other."

Jesus. I'm not sure what's scarier—if he actually believes this stuff, or he's hyping himself up because that's how much he wants to win.

"So fuck George. Fuck him. Picture him winning. Think how bad you'll feel."

I picture Oxford on that podium. George being showered with champagne. What do I feel? Nothing. No, that's not quite true. I'm curious to know how George will feel in that scenario. Is that what he wants more than anything? Will it all have been worth it?

"We are not going to let that happen," says Tristan. "I refuse. We've got a plan and we're going to stick to it. Those losers won't know what's hit them."

. . .

I can't wait to get away from that raging ball of testosterone and shut myself in my room. Not long after I do, I hear Tristan barking orders at someone in the corridor and I'm reminded of what he meant about sticking to our plan. The wank police. You couldn't make it up. I can't say I'm feeling particularly horny, but I suppose it's one way to pass the time. Amir and I had joked about how he was going to come over and edge me, but I don't think either of us meant it seriously. That's another thing that was far from ideal about our relationship. Even after all that advice from George, our sex life never really took off.

Maybe that's inevitable when we only saw each other on weekends, but we did it on Sunday mornings, almost without fail, and I could tell you more or less the exact choreography of how it proceeded from start to finish. It doesn't give me a wealth of material to draw on for this exercise. I know where my mind is going before I start. The same place it goes all the time, sometimes even while I was having sex with Amir.

The time I was in Dr. Civeris's closet with George.

Sure, there were other moments. The showers after Henley. The kiss on the Ferris wheel. Looking back, the attraction was there from the start. It was probably why I took against George so strongly. Much better to find him annoying than admit I found him hot. Even the kiss in the club, so awkward and confusing at the time, now feels like it was sparked by an attraction we didn't understand and had even less control over. But nothing compares to that time in the closet. When you've pressed your boners up against each other like that, can you really say you haven't had sex? Of course we haven't. That's why it was so hot. So hot that I really can't think about it for very long or I'll fail this exercise.

But where does that leave me? The same place I've been stuck with George since last summer. What might have been. Why wouldn't he look me in the eye earlier? What's he going to do when we line up tomorrow at the start of the race? Will he look at me then? Or row the whole race without glancing my way? Then what?

He might be OK with that, but I'm not. I can't have him so close and still have everything so unresolved. I can't row against him tomorrow until he's looked me in the eye and explained himself. I get out my phone and send him a text: Hey, can we talk?

18
GEORGE

"HAS GEORGE EXPLAINED THE course to you?" Rick Toledo asks my parents.

"No," says my mom.

She does have a short memory.

"So the two sides of the Thames are called Surrey and Middlesex." Rick places salt-and-pepper grinders in the center of the table as he explains. "Those are both the names of English counties."

"Middlesex isn't a county," says Jemima. "Not anymore. Not unless your name is Geoffrey Chaucer."

"Let's not overcomplicate it," I say.

"Eek wel I woot, he seyde myn housbonde," says Jemima.

My mom looks bewildered.

"*Wife of Bath*," says Jemima. "Learned it at school. Absolute legend."

"Who's she talking about?" says my mom to my dad.

"Geoffrey," my dad says confidently.

"What about him?"

"Absolute legend. His wife is in the bath. Not sure what that has to do with anything."

I'm at a restaurant in Battersea with my parents, Jemima, and Rick Toledo. When Rick learned that my parents were flying over, he invited us all out to dinner. When I mentioned it to Jemima, she invited herself. Believe it or not, she's four months sober. Turns out she actually did jump off a ski lift at New Year's Eve, broke both her legs, and had an epiphany. You'd think that not drinking might make her less chaotic, but based on tonight's evidence, that's just her personality. I'm hoping everyone will settle down once we order.

"Ciao ciao ciao," says Landon, striding up to the table.

"Landon," I say, clocking his fresh fake tan. "What are you doing here?"

Jemima smiles at me. "We thought it would be great to touch base with the whole team."

"Is the whole team coming?" My mom looks around anxiously.

"I mean us," laughs Jemima. "George's team. Your son is on the verge of big, big things."

My mom looks awkward. "I wouldn't know about that."

"Let me run you through it," says Jemima. "The *Vogue* piece drops tomorrow. Then George is shooting a campaign for Reebok. Met Gala in the fall. Custom Balenciaga."

My parents look baffled.

"After that," says Rick, "we need to get George back in the US college system. We're thinking an MEd at Stanford."

He smiles at my dad.

"Wouldn't that be nice? Your son back stateside."

My dad frowns at the menu.

"Stanford's a long way from Wisconsin."

Thanks, Dad.

"And by then, the TV series will be live," says Landon. "And someone will be the internet's new boyfriend."

He grins at my mom, but she turns to my dad.

"Ron, do you think they put flour in the coq au vin?"

"Mom, Landon's talking to you!"

My mom shoots me a look and turns back to Landon.

"The network is delighted with the rushes from yesterday," says Landon. "All we need now is the money shot—George standing up in the boat, arms raised in victory. How do you like the sound of that?"

My mom frowns. "It sounds a bit dangerous."

"Nah, not for your boy. He can do anything."

"I wouldn't say that."

"You must be so proud of him," says Jemima.

My mom turns red and says nothing.

"Sure they are!" says Landon. "They produced this gorgeous specimen."

My mom looks at my dad. "Ron, maybe we can ask the waiter."

"MOM!"

Everyone is startled by how loudly I spoke. Me included.

"No need to raise your voice," says my dad.

"Yes there is! You haven't been interested in anything since you landed. Every time these guys talk about me, or rowing, or Oxford, you change the subject."

My parents don't know what to say. I've never spoken to them like this.

"We're here, aren't we?" says my dad.

"Only because the network paid."

"Well, we lost all that money on flights when we were planning to come to your graduation last year."

Jemima and Rick share an uneasy glance.

"Maybe there's a better time for this convo," Landon says tactfully.

"When?" I say. "I never see them."

The waiter comes to take our order, and my parents frantically engage him about the coq au vin recipe. I feel the moment slipping through my fingers.

"George," says Landon, "you've got a big day tomorrow. Let's put a pin in this."

. . .

I manage to hold myself together and make it through the meal. Everyone acts like the previous conversation didn't happen. Jemima spends most of the time trying to list the ceremonial counties of England while my parents sit in silence. Landon picks up the check, which means he's definitely going to expense it. When I tell my parents I'll see them after the race tomorrow, they don't respond. I just have to accept I'm never going to have the conversation I want to have with them. I'm never going to understand why they take so little interest in me. In that case, I might as well keep Landon, Rick, and Jemima happy. My team, I mean. They've invested a lot in me, as they keep reminding me. The least I can do in return is deliver tomorrow. Give them the money shot. I get out my phone to plot my journey back to Putney.

That's when I see the text from Lucas.

I stare at it. I feel like I must be imagining it. Is it a trick? What does he want? The thought of seeing him face-to-face, one-on-one, makes me sick. But that's no reason to avoid him. Not after what just happened at the table. The only question is when and where. We can't meet at either of our bases. Meeting in public is risky. I google hotels nearby and call the first one I find.

"Hi there, do you have a room free right now?"

I text Lucas the details, then head over to the Great Western Inn on Putney High Street. No one will suspect two men from rival squads of meeting here. In the hotel lobby, I stand in line behind a Polish family and a rowdy group of women from Liverpool.

Eventually, I get my key card and go up to the room. It's not too seedy, given the price tag. Outside the window, the river shimmers ominously beneath the moonlight. I turn on the TV and stare at an episode of *MasterChef Junior*. A few minutes later, Lucas texts to say he's downstairs. I'm struggling to control my breathing, but I'm also the most alive I've felt in months. Is this really happening? I pull myself together in time to turn off the TV and check my reflection in the mirror.

My heart is pounding so hard I can hear it. There's a knock at the door. I go over and open it. There he is. There's my Lucas.

Neither of us says anything. Every feeling I've tried to block out for the past nine months comes rushing back all at once. He looks the same. Just as small. Just as cute. Maybe cuter.

When he looks me in the eye, it's the best and worst thing ever to happen to me. Thank god I didn't look at him during the weigh-in. Neither of us knows how to proceed. Should we stand? Sit on the bed? Is that weird? Lucas walks over to the window and pretends to look at the view. I follow him halfway, then perch on the sideboard.

Eventually, Lucas turns to me. "It was a good twist. I'll give you that."

My throat is dry. "It wasn't my idea."

"Switching to Oxford?"

"No, keeping it a secret."

Lucas raises an eyebrow and says nothing.

"I signed an NDA," I insist. "I did try to tell you."

Lucas frowns.

"The postcard," I say.

"What? I didn't get a postcard."

"I sent it months ago. It was the only way I could think of to get around my NDA."

Lucas shakes his head, as if that's not good enough.

I'm hit with a flash of anger. "It's not like you've never done anything behind my back."

That one gets him. Lucas looks at me, heartfelt. "I'm really sorry."

"It's fine," I insist. "It all worked out. I got my own show. I'm going to Stanford in the fall."

Lucas looks surprised. "To do what?"

"An MEd."

"How can you do a master's when you don't even have a degree?"

"I do have a degree. They gave me one in the end."

Lucas's mouth drops open. "What?"

"They changed their mind. I just wasn't allowed to graduate or stay in Cambridge."

"Are you serious? So it worked."

Now it's me who's confused.

"I went to see that guy we met," says Lucas. "I threatened to go public."

"Wait, you got me my degree back?"

"No, George, you did. I gave him your exam papers. The real ones. I asked him to mark them fairly." Lucas places a hand on my arm. "Guess you passed after all."

I don't know how to describe what I feel in that moment. All this time, I've thought I must have failed or Lucas wouldn't have bothered to swap the papers. I assumed they gave me a degree out of sympathy. Now I learn that I actually earned a Cambridge degree. Me, George Holst. And all along, it was Lucas who helped make it happen.

"Why didn't you tell me they gave you a degree?" Lucas asks.

"There wasn't any point."

Lucas is unconvinced. I really don't want to explain, but we've got this far.

"Because you're with Amir."

Lucas averts his gaze. "Actually, we broke up."

I can't help it—my heart leaps at the news.

"What's that got to do with anything?" Lucas asks.

"I fell for you, Lucas. But I was never quite sure if I was your type. When you let me take my exams, I thought that meant you thought I was smart. Then when I found out what you'd done, I realized you never had."

Lucas looks astonished. "I didn't do it because I don't think you're smart!"

I'm taken aback by his conviction.

"Firstly, I don't think some stupid exams prove anything about anyone. But I realized you were smart as soon as I got to know you. I was scared of what failing would do to you."

He looks at me earnestly, willing me to believe it. I want to believe it. Then I see a thought flash across Lucas's mind.

"This one time, in school—"

I can't help smiling. "Is this a high school story?"

"Not what we call it, but sure. There was this talent show. My sister was down to perform. She was about fourteen. Loads of older kids performing. Loads of mean girls in the audience."

"Why are you telling me this?"

"I heard my sister rehearsing at home. She can sing, but she gets nervous. There were times when she couldn't hit the high notes. I kept picturing the mean girls laughing at her. Maybe even booing. And I got scared it was going to scar her for life. So I spoke to a few of her friends and most of mine. I told them they had to applaud really loudly. Give her a standing ovation. Maybe I went a bit overboard, but I needed her to see it as a success. When it came to the performance, she nailed it. She was so happy with the response. Then some idiot went and told her I'd instructed the whole school to applaud no matter what, and my sister was convinced that meant I didn't think she was any good. However hard I tried, I couldn't convince her it wasn't that at all. I believed in her. I knew what she was capable of. I went too far because I was desperate for her to see herself how I did. To understand how brilliant she was."

Lucas looks deep into my eyes. Before I know what I'm doing, I step forward and kiss him.

He freezes. For a moment, I think he's going to pull away.

But now he's kissing me back.

It's nothing like the kiss on the Ferris wheel. That was a stolen moment that didn't feel real. Here, we have all the time in the world—at least, it feels like we do. Except that every time our lips press together, I become more impatient. I'm ready to finally do the things I've been dreaming about all year.

We tumble onto the bed. First I'm on top of Lucas, then he's on top of me. Now I'm pulling his shirt over his head, my pants around my ankles, laughing as we remember our socks. I linger as I slide down his briefs.

Just like that, we're both naked. I'm naked in bed with Lucas. How did it take us this long? There's nothing like that feeling of shedding your clothes and feeling two bodies intertwine. I've never understood people who say it's like you've become one. For me, it's all about the fact that one of those bodies is not yours, but feels closer to you than you do to yourself.

Now Lucas is kissing his way down my stomach and liking what he finds. I lie back and close my eyes. He really knows what he's doing. He's not shy at all. I love how when you have sex with someone, you both turn into slightly different people.

I open my eyes and look at Lucas. He holds my gaze but doesn't stop. Damn, that's hot. So hot that if he doesn't stop soon, I'm going to get close. I'm not ready for that.

I sit up and push Lucas onto his back. I start slowly, but even the slightest touch produces a moan of pleasure. Pretty soon, I've got Lucas clutching the sheets and arching his back in ecstasy. Me when I'm in bed? I let my ego take over. I'm the only one who can make Lucas feel this good. I'm the best in the world. After a while, I flip him onto his front, kiss him on the back of his neck and ears, then slide down below his waist.

That butt looks even better up close. I tickle it with my breath, then my tongue. Now Lucas's moaning goes into overdrive. Something tells me no one's ever done this to him. I tease him into ever more intense exclamations. The louder he gets, the more turned on I am. Eventually, I climb back up, pressing into Lucas from behind, and tell him what I want to do to him.

Lucas turns to me. "Same."

"Really?" I look at him in surprise.

"If you're up for it."

"Yeah. It's just . . . I've never done it that way round."

Lucas grins. "You've been missing out."

I feel a rush of excitement at the thought of Lucas inside me. There's a brief interlude while we both take a shower and discuss logistics. Maybe I'm weird, but I like these pauses where you act like you're planning a long car journey. It makes me feel like the other person sees me as human and not some porn robot.

We get back into it slowly, lying on the bed, brushing each other with our fingertips and gazing into each other's eyes, getting drunk on the feeling.

At some point, Lucas climbs on top of me. I feel him kiss my cheeks. Yes, those ones. Then there's his tongue. Holy shit. He's a fast learner. Lucas can tell how much I'm loving it, which makes him go for it more, which makes me love it even more, and so on.

He comes back up to kiss me, and asks if I'm ready. As if it wasn't clear.

"You know what they call this?" Lucas says.

"Call what?"

"When the shorter guy's on top."

He grins at me.

"A jet pack."

That's another thing I love about great sex. Those moments of humor. Lucas turns me onto my side and curls behind me. A few seconds later, I feel him enter me. I try to follow my own advice and relax, but let's be real—I'm so turned on by this point that I can take anything. Lucas flips me into different positions, each one a revelation. By the looks of surprise and delight on his face, I'm guessing this is his first time too. After a while, I lean in and whisper.

"My turn."

Lucas lies on his back and I hoist his feet over my shoulders. As I ease my way in, we don't break eye contact, and I'm not sure I've ever known a better feeling. I've never been one to talk much during sex, but I'm struggling to keep my mouth shut. Because there's only one thing I want to say to Lucas, and I know it would be crazy to say it now. Instead, I close my eyes and embrace the feeling.

I love how this feels. I love how much Lucas is enjoying it too. I'm following his lead, not going any harder than he can take it, but he keeps asking for more. Time to show him what I've got. I'm not a porn robot—just a regular sex god. My only concern is that they can hear us in the room next door. Just kidding—that's their problem.

I could do this all night, but after a while, I feel myself starting to get close again. This time, Lucas works himself to the edge, so we can both finish together. Now I get it—that feeling that we're becoming one. I've never felt so satisfied.

I've never felt closer to anyone.

Afterward, we collapse onto the bed and lie there, catching our breath. I curl my arms around Lucas. I don't want to let go. But after a couple of minutes, he gets up and goes to the bathroom.

As I hear him take another shower, I feel weirdly upset. How can he move on from what just happened? Why can't we remain in this state of ecstasy forever?

But of course we can't. He needs to get back to his camp. We both do.

Still, when Lucas hurries out of the bathroom, drying his hair with a towel, he has an anxious look that I'm not prepared for.

"What happens now?" I ask him.

Lucas looks at me in surprise. "In case you'd forgotten, we have a race to row."

"Yeah, but then what?"

Lucas starts pulling his clothes on. "Can we talk about this after the race?"

"What is there to talk about?"

"I mean, for starters, the fact that you're moving to America."

I feel a rush of indignation. "So what was this? One last fuck?"

Lucas looks wounded. "Of course not. I just mean—I can't have the talk tonight. I shouldn't have done this."

"You asked to meet me!"

"I know, I didn't mean . . . George, it's not . . . it's just—"

It's what, Lucas? What is it? I know it's irrational, but I'm mad at him for puncturing the feeling I had five minutes ago.

What else matters apart from us?

"Can we please just have a conversation?" I plead. "Don't leave it like this."

"I'm really sorry," says Lucas. "We'll talk after the race, I promise."

"Don't walk away from me, Lucas."

Lucas gives me a look that says everything and nothing. Something catches his eye, and he brushes a finger along my cheek to remove a fallen eyelash. We both stare at it for a moment, silenced without knowing why. Then he turns and walks out.

19

LUCAS

TWO NIGHTS' GOOD SLEEP in a row was too much to hope for. My mind was a storm all night. Partly it's the sex. It knocked me sideways. It was the kind of sex that lingers in your body for hours afterward, like alcohol, only ten times more intoxicating. I don't think I expected it to be so much fun. I feel like we actually got to know each other through it. Not that the best part wasn't when George banged the hell out of me. But last night was about so much more than sex.

I've thought so much about George, missed him so deeply, lied to myself so repeatedly, and worked so hard to move on from him, that the prospect of finally being together was too much to take. Then there's the minor detail of him moving to America. Throw in the race and my breakup with Amir, and it's a miracle I got any sleep.

No one appears to have noticed my absence last night. If they did, they haven't said anything. As I sit down at breakfast and get myself a bowl of Weetabix, I'm convinced someone's about to call me out on it. Then Tristan sits in front of me and I do a double take. His eyes are bloodshot, his hands trembling. His anger from last night has been replaced with something far more wretched.

"Fucking hell, Tristan. Have some toast."

He casts me a haunted look.

"I just . . . can't believe he's done this to us. Why did he have to come back?"

As I look back at Tristan, I feel a moment of kinship I definitely wasn't expecting.

"You need to get a grip, man. If we all go out there thinking about what George has done to us in the last twenty-four hours . . . we won't stand a chance."

. . .

Half an hour later, everyone traipses to the front of the house where a bus is waiting to take us on the short journey to the King's College School boat house. I steel myself as we arrive. The club room is packed. There's Tristan's father with his new girlfriend, a sturdy woman his own age. Eleanor is clinging to Tristan's mother, who looks surprisingly buoyant. All the usual reporters are prowling, relishing this year's drama. Then I spot my mum and Casey. My mum has gone for a more casual outfit this year, while Casey has defiantly dressed up again.

"How are you doing, Lucas?" my mum asks.

"I've had better nights' sleep."

Does she know? Can she smell it on me? Is she going to call the wank police?

"I'm sorry, Lucas," says my mum.

"About what?"

"Amir."

Oh yeah. I forgot that I'd texted her and Casey to let them know. I don't think either of them were too surprised.

"Is everything OK between you two?" asks Casey.

"I think so. I mean, it will be."

"That's good," says Casey. "Cos he's over there."

I look to where she's pointing and turn pale. Amir catches my eye, and before I can decide any better, I cross over to him.

"What are you doing here?" I ask, trying not to sound accusatory.

Amir looks at me stiffly. "I'm here to support Wilbur."

I glance across and see Wilbur's mum chatting to Amir's parents. Amir's mum gives me a terse smile. God knows what Amir said to them.

"I heard about George," says Amir.

I tense up. "Yeah, can't believe he didn't tell me."

"Actually," says Amir, "I think he tried."

I frown in confusion. Amir looks sheepish.

"You were at training when the postcard arrived. It wasn't signed, but it wasn't hard to figure out who it was from. Took me until today to join the rest of the dots."

As I process what he's saying, I can only feel pity.

"I'm sorry, Amir. I really am."

Amir shrugs. "I shouldn't have tried to stand in the way." He flashes me a smile. "But I do hope you beat him."

. . .

Somehow I keep blocking out the fact that I'm about to race against George. Maybe it's because each time I think about it, I want to vomit. I excuse myself from Amir and go to find the rest of the crew. We gather at the base of the boat house and unload our boat from the trailer. A TV camera is thrust into my face. I'd managed to forget that every move I make today is going to be captured and broadcast to millions of people. But that's nothing compared to the thought of seeing George.

Unlike most years, Oxford's boat house is right next to ours. I'm pretty sure this was purposefully engineered by the documentary producers for maximum drama. As we carry our boat down to the water, I realize that the Oxford crew is right behind us. I can tell from the crowd's reaction, hooting and jeering and loving the spectacle. I glance behind me, and there they are in their dark blue kit.

George is right at the front. I barely catch a glimpse of him before looking away, but it's enough. How am I meant to get through this?

George's presence is firing up the Cambridge team. I can feel it. As Oxford carry their boat down to the river's edge, we're almost side by side. I glance at Tristan. I was hoping he'd have pulled himself together, but if anything, he's worse.

"Hey," I whisper. "You need to focus."

"Don't tell me what to do," hisses Tristan.

George glances across at us, and I see the moment he realizes the state Tristan is in. He doesn't look triumphant or anything, but it's enough to set off Tristan.

"What are you looking at?" Tristan shouts.

George smiles at him calmly. "Nothing."

"Fuck off."

One of George's teammates steps forward and holds out a protective arm. George veers away from Tristan, but as he does, he gives him one last look and winks at him.

"Amir."

Oh yeah. I forgot that I'd texted her and Casey to let them know. I don't think either of them were too surprised.

"Is everything OK between you two?" asks Casey.

"I think so. I mean, it will be."

"That's good," says Casey. "Cos he's over there."

I look to where she's pointing and turn pale. Amir catches my eye, and before I can decide any better, I cross over to him.

"What are you doing here?" I ask, trying not to sound accusatory.

Amir looks at me stiffly. "I'm here to support Wilbur."

I glance across and see Wilbur's mum chatting to Amir's parents. Amir's mum gives me a terse smile. God knows what Amir said to them.

"I heard about George," says Amir.

I tense up. "Yeah, can't believe he didn't tell me."

"Actually," says Amir, "I think he tried."

I frown in confusion. Amir looks sheepish.

"You were at training when the postcard arrived. It wasn't signed, but it wasn't hard to figure out who it was from. Took me until today to join the rest of the dots."

As I process what he's saying, I can only feel pity.

"I'm sorry, Amir. I really am."

Amir shrugs. "I shouldn't have tried to stand in the way." He flashes me a smile. "But I do hope you beat him."

. . .

Somehow I keep blocking out the fact that I'm about to race against George. Maybe it's because each time I think about it, I want to vomit. I excuse myself from Amir and go to find the rest of the crew. We gather at the base of the boat house and unload our boat from the trailer. A TV camera is thrust into my face. I'd managed to forget that every move I make today is going to be captured and broadcast to millions of people. But that's nothing compared to the thought of seeing George.

Unlike most years, Oxford's boat house is right next to ours. I'm pretty sure this was purposefully engineered by the documentary producers for maximum drama. As we carry our boat down to the water, I realize that the Oxford crew is right behind us. I can tell from the crowd's reaction, hooting and jeering and loving the spectacle. I glance behind me, and there they are in their dark blue kit.

George is right at the front. I barely catch a glimpse of him before looking away, but it's enough. How am I meant to get through this?

George's presence is firing up the Cambridge team. I can feel it. As Oxford carry their boat down to the river's edge, we're almost side by side. I glance at Tristan. I was hoping he'd have pulled himself together, but if anything, he's worse.

"Hey," I whisper. "You need to focus."

"Don't tell me what to do," hisses Tristan.

George glances across at us, and I see the moment he realizes the state Tristan is in. He doesn't look triumphant or anything, but it's enough to set off Tristan.

"What are you looking at?" Tristan shouts.

George smiles at him calmly. "Nothing."

"Fuck off."

One of George's teammates steps forward and holds out a protective arm. George veers away from Tristan, but as he does, he gives him one last look and winks at him.

Something inside Tristan snaps. He lunges across the concrete at George and launches a fist at him. It lands on George's temple.

I hear a terrible thud. Then a scream.

I look at George, but his mouth is shut. The scream came from Tristan.

He's crushed his knuckles, and is leaping up and down in pain.

George staggers but manages to stay on two feet. Both teams swarm toward each other. Everyone is shouting at once. The TV cameras whir.

Johannes leaps into the middle of it, doing his best to stop it from turning into a brawl. Amid all this, I keep my eyes on George. He's staring into the distance, trying to come back into focus. It's a miracle he's still standing, but I can tell the punch has knocked something out of him. I want to run over to him, but my feet are rooted to the spot. A race steward charges up to the chaos, demanding to know what happened. The Oxford rowers angrily inform him.

"That is completely unacceptable," the steward shouts. "The Cambridge stroke is disqualified."

By this point, Deb is standing right behind him. She looks at Tristan, who's still clutching his hand in pain. He gives Deb a pleading look. She holds his gaze.

"Idiot."

Tristan stares back, so crushed and pathetic that you almost feel sorry for him. I said almost. He looks up at the boat house, and there on the balcony are Eleanor, his mother, his father and girlfriend. And they thought they knew what bad publicity was.

The rest of us are still in shock. But Deb was made for moments like this. She walks up to our reserve crew and tells

Wilbur he's our new stroke. A few people are trying to argue we should be disqualified as a team, but not the Oxford rowers. They're pumped up by Tristan's disqualification—the last thing they want is a walkover.

Throughout all this, I can't take my eyes off George. A paramedic is examining him, while Landon pats him on the back. To be fair, I've never seen someone take a punch better. It's too early for a bruise to have formed, but it's clear the main casualty was Tristan's hand. Still, there's something vacant in George's eyes. Something that concerns me. I edge closer so I can hear the conversation between Landon and the paramedic.

"I'm a bit worried," says the paramedic.

"He's fine," says Landon. "He's a trooper."

He glances around, aware he's being filmed.

"George, mate, don't let Cambridge take away your dream. You've got this."

George nods vaguely, and that's when I see it for sure. He's not OK. He's trying to hide it. He doesn't want to let his team down. And now Landon's leading away the paramedic and George is preparing to get in the boat.

Without knowing what I'm doing, I stride up to George, ignoring the calls of my teammates. George looks at me in surprise.

"You don't have to do this," I say. "It's up to you, not them."

Landon races up and pushes me out of the way.

"Piss off, you little shit. Get in the boat, George."

George looks at him tremulously. "I don't feel good."

"Don't be a wimp." Landon leans in close and mutters under his breath, "Think of the money shot."

George's eyes flash with rage. His hand thrusts forward and shoves Landon in the chest. Landon stumbles backward and falls into the river with a splash.

The crowd gasps. The camera crew rushes forward.

George moves away from the water's edge. The paramedic snaps into action and guides him toward a waiting ambulance. The spectators are losing their minds. It's pandemonium. As Landon swims into the side, I feel a surge of optimism ripple through my crew. George is down. Serves him right, is the general feeling. The momentum is back with us. I look up at the boat house and see Amir with his parents and Wilbur's family, who are all beside themselves that Wilbur has made the team.

"We got this, Lucas," says Wilbur.

Do we? Got what exactly? I look at George as he's shepherded into the ambulance. He looks lost and bewildered. I cross over to him.

"Where are your parents?"

George's eyes darken. "I don't even know if they came." He gives me a stoic smile. "Don't worry about me. Go race."

I glance over at my crew, who are waiting for me to get in the boat, and suddenly I know what I have to do. I race up to Fran, and pull her into a huddle with Deb.

"Deb, do you remember telling me I only got my place in the boat because Tristan can't take orders from a woman? OK, maybe you never said that, but you implied it, and I always felt awful for Fran. We should never have given in to Tristan. But he's not racing anymore. And even if he was . . . I can't let George go to hospital on his own. I'm sorry, Deb. This matters more to me than any race."

Deb holds my gaze without the merest hint of emotion. "Fine."

Fran gives me a wry look. "You big old drama queen."

I race back over to George.

"What are you doing?" he says weakly.

"Room for one more?" I ask the paramedic.

"No, Lucas," says George. "One of us needs to win this."

"I don't care about winning. I'm coming with you."

"Why?"

I look at him and swallow the lump in my throat.

"Why do you think? I love you."

George looks so bowled over that I worry I've knocked him out cold. Then a smile fills his face. For a moment, I forget about the cameras and it's just us two. Behind me, my teammates are in uproar. They can't understand how I can throw away a whole year's training, right on the verge of victory. But that was never the real prize. He's lying right here on a stretcher, making me sick with worry. I get into the ambulance with George.

20
GEORGE

I OPEN MY EYES AND STARE at the ceiling. Where am I? I can hear a heart monitor beeping. I look around and see that I'm surrounded on three sides by a surgical curtain. Hospital. How did that happen? I have a vague memory of being driven across London. I notice a window behind me and try to peer out of it, but I can't see anything other than a concrete building, and wait—is that a river? Suddenly it all comes back to me. The race. The punch. Pushing Landon in the Thames. Lucas.

Did Lucas really come with me in the ambulance? He's not here now. Maybe I dreamed it. I glance at the clock and realize the race must be over by now. I wonder who won.

I hear a noise and look up to see someone enter. It's a nurse, a young Spanish woman who I think I met earlier, but it's all a blur.

"You're awake."

I attempt a smile.

"The doctor's given you the all-clear. Are you up to having visitors?"

"Sure."

The nurse turns and beckons. I'm expecting to see Lucas, but no—it's my parents. They race up to my bedside, their faces etched with concern.

"They've done a brain scan," says my mom. "They didn't find any damage."

I smile ruefully. "I'm sure if Chuck was here, he'd say they need to look harder."

My parents aren't ready to joke about it.

"It took us forever to get here," says my dad. "There were no taxis at Mortlake."

I look at them in amazement. "You were at the finish line?"

"Of course we were. We weren't going to come all this way and not watch. We just wanted to avoid the cameras."

My dad glances awkwardly at my mom, who turns to me.

"George, we were never not interested. It's just . . . such a different world. We feel so out of place."

"So do I, Mom! I could have explained that if you'd listened."

My mom fiddles with her necklace. "The past few years have been busy. But we'd make time. If you visited."

I frown and shake my head. "The last time I was home—"

"That was our fault. But . . ."

My mom turns to my dad. "Show him, Ron."

My dad looks uncomfortable.

"Show him!"

My dad holds up his phone. The background is a photo of me and him from that summer I worked in the restaurant. We're both grinning from ear to ear.

"That was a good summer," I say to my dad.

He can't look me in the eye. "It's not easy to gut a salmon. You learned fast."

My mom rests a hand on my arm. "You're always welcome, George. Any time."

I have a thought. "Did you meet Lucas?"

"Little guy?" says my dad.

"That's him."

"He was very kind to us," says my mom.

"Oh, he's special." I hold her gaze until she realizes. She does a little jolt of surprise, then sits with it for a moment. She looks at my dad, then back at me.

"You think Lucas might want to visit too?"

My stomach lurches. "That's up to him. Where is he?"

LUCAS

I know you're supposed to hate hospitals, but I've always quite liked them. I don't know what it is—maybe that feeling that people are working to make the world a little better. Not that I'm ever that sentimental.

Having said that, today hasn't been the easiest experience. Firstly, the doctor didn't want to let me see George. I had to wait outside while he had his scan. I kept myself distracted by following the chaos at the Boat Race. Casey has been texting me updates. They're only just lining up now. Apparently there was a big fuss over whether Fran was allowed to race again having just coxed the second boat, and everyone was arguing over the rules.

Then a moment ago, George's parents got here. That wasn't as bad as I was expecting. They were so grateful to me for accompanying George that we actually got on quite well. They're in there with him now. I hope it isn't upsetting George to see them. I want to protect him, but I couldn't object to them going in first.

I'm about to sneak up to the door and see if I can hear what's going on when it opens and there they are. George's mum walks up to me.

"He's all yours," she says. "We're going to go and see Buckingham Palace. You shout if you need us."

They shuffle off and I watch them go for a moment, before remembering I'm allowed to see George. I race in and see him lying in his bed. I was expecting him to look fragile, but even in this state, he looks like he could snap that thing in two.

"How did it go with your parents?"

"Good, actually. They really like you."

"We barely spoke."

"Then it must be your dashing good looks."

"What, not my cute butt?"

George smiles. "I still can't believe you ditched your team for me."

"Easiest decision ever."

"Good to know there's at least one person who doesn't hate me," says George.

I laugh dryly. "I'm pretty sure I'm even more hated."

"Please. They're currently re-editing an entire TV show to make me the villain."

"Then we'll just have to be hated together."

George smiles, then his expression turns serious.

"What are we actually going to do?"

I gulp as I realize what he means. "That depends."

"On what?"

"On how much you want to go to America."

George is overcome with a flood of emotion. "I want to be where you are." He bites his lip. "I love you, Lucas."

I feel like I must be dreaming. This gorgeous man is telling me he loves me. It can't be real. But the gorgeous man is George. My George. And nothing has ever made more sense. I want to hear him say it again.

"What was that?"

"I love you. So much."

Why did no one tell me how good this feels? It feels like the answer to everything.

Just then, my phone vibrates. It's a text from Casey. I look up at George.

"Do you want to go watch the race?"

"Surely it ended ages ago."

"No, they've been arguing over the rules. They're only just starting now."

George thinks it over. "Can we get there in time?"

"We can get to the finish line. If you're OK to leave."

George looks at me sincerely. "As long as you're with me."

With the doctor's permission, George is discharged. We catch a taxi to the finish line, but several of the roads close to the river are blocked off, so we get out and walk the last part.

Crowds are lining the river bank, and it's easy to slip in among them. A few people are wearing Oxford and Cambridge scarves or colors, but most of them are neutrals drawn by the spectacle. I wonder if anyone will recognize us. I ought to feel bad I'm not racing, but how can I feel anything but wonderful when I have

George by my side? We walk through the crowd, saying very little. When it gets too busy, George reaches down to hold my hand. Each time, I feel a surge of love that leaves me giddy.

As we get close to the finish line, the crowd is too dense to get any further. I stand on my tiptoes and try to see over them. George grins.

"You can go on my shoulders if you want."

"Thanks, but I'm trying to be incognito."

"Your call. I'll shout if I see anything."

"Great. We're rooting for Cambridge, right?"

As George smiles back at me, I'm overcome with a desire to kiss him. So I do. We could be anywhere in the world. George is here. George is mine. After a moment, a roar goes up from the crowd. I open my eyes.

"Wait, who won?"

George smiles and shrugs, and we go back to kissing.

EPILOGUE
LOS ANGELES, 2028

GEORGE

Lucas once showed me a clip where Sir Steve Redgrave, Britain's greatest ever Olympian, tells a reporter after winning his fourth Olympic gold medal that if anyone sees him near a rowing boat again, they have permission to shoot him. Four years later, he competed in his fifth Olympics and won another gold—avoiding any assassinations from people claiming an unusual defense. In the immediate aftermath of my second aborted attempt at winning the Boat Race, I decided I was done with rowing. Yet three years on, here I am in the LA Olympic Village.

"The security guard saw us," hisses Lucas.

"No he didn't. Just keep walking."

"What if he catches us?"

I grin at Lucas. "That's part of the fun."

We've busted into the Athlete's Village, despite neither of us having anything more than spectator's tickets. I haven't sat in a rowing boat since that day in London. We're here to support Fran. Only her race doesn't start for another hour, and Lucas has decided there's something he'd like to do between now and then.

Apparently, when he was younger, he read a report about how the Olympic Village was a hotbed of sex. Since then, it's been a major fantasy of his. All he needs is a bit of a push to get past his nerves. That's where I step in.

I spot a half-open door and pull Lucas inside. It's some kind of media room, with a desk and broadcasting equipment, but it's empty. I shut the door, then start kissing Lucas. But he's not ready to give in to it.

"What if someone comes in?"

I turn a lock on the door. "Happy now?"

Lucas notices the bulge in my shorts. "Someone is."

Lucas and I have been together for more than three years now, and he still turns me on as much as he always did. It didn't take us long to figure out a plan. Once the dust settled, I realized I really didn't want to go to Stanford. That meant I had to tell Jemima and Rick, which obviously scared the shit out of me, but Lucas gave me the courage to do it. He's great like that.

We moved to a tiny apartment in London, and Lucas got a job at a think tank while I figured out what to do next. The documentary series came out, and Landon was edited as the villain. He quit his job and moved back to Australia. Last time I googled him, he was the guest on a botched plastic surgery reality show.

The documentary got me a lot of attention, and Jemima kept encouraging me to capitalize on it. In the end, I sort of did. I'd been spending a lot of time in the gym while I was unemployed, and I decided to become a personal trainer. I used my social media following to get my business up and running. I love getting the best out of people, making them smile and be proud of themselves. Lucas makes sure I'm strict with them too. I have a few celebrity clients who pay double so I can give free lessons to people who can't afford it. That was Lucas's idea. I still post quite a lot of selfies. It's not a cry for help—I'm just giving the people what they want.

Most days I love my job, but it's not what I live for. Mainly it's the simple things. Lucas and I both missed the routine of rowing, so we decided to learn tennis together. Nothing makes me happier than playing on the weekend on a court in the middle of a beautiful old square in South London. Cooking each other meals from tomatoes we've bought at the farmer's market. Watching four episodes of *The Real Housewives of Orange County* in a row.

Every summer, we go to Wisconsin. Our first trip was sweet but a bit awkward. My parents tried so hard but couldn't relax. So the following year, we came up with a plan. Lucas and I ran a rowing camp for the local kids. We just did our second edition last week, and we're planning to make it a lifelong tradition. My parents do the cooking, and even Chuck drives the minibus. Lucas says half the kids have crushes on me, but trust me, they're obsessed with him too. It's bittersweet every time we leave, and I hate how much older my parents look each time I see them. But it does help me appreciate how young I am. How much time Lucas and I still have.

"Slow down," I say to Lucas as he frantically unzips me.

"We don't have that long until Fran's race."

I reach into his pants. "What do you want to do?"

Lucas gives me a cheeky smile.

"What we never got to do that time in Dr. Civeris's cupboard."

LUCAS

We emerge from the Athlete's Village looking flustered and head toward the rowing lake. That's one off the bucket list. I'd never have done it if George hadn't pushed me. I really don't know what I did to deserve him. And I'm not just talking about living out my sexual fantasies, although we did have a threesome last year with a very famous actor who slid into George's DMs.

The past three years have been happier than I ever thought possible. I can't tell you how good it feels when I get home from a long day of hating my colleagues and George is there to perk me up and give me some perspective. I don't actually hate my colleagues. Well, not most of them. I work for a think tank as a junior economist. It's demanding, which I like, but it's good to be reminded that it's just a job. Nobody's better at doing that than George. My god, I love that man.

In hindsight, I'm glad everything turned out the way it did. I'm not sure I would have appreciated how good I have it now if I hadn't had those nine months with Amir. Bless him, honestly. He's a good person, and he's living the life that he wants. According to Instagram, he's dating a Swedish art expert in his thirties. Their life looks unbelievably boring. I'm so happy for him.

I don't know what mine and George's future looks like. At the moment, we've got a routine that works, but I don't like the idea of it staying the same for the rest of our lives. I want to do something that scares me every few years, and I know George will hold my hand when the time comes. I see what it takes out of him every time we leave America, even if he smiles through it, and I'm well aware I could be earning more out there than I do in London. We don't have a ton of money, but life feels luxurious compared to how I grew up. George and I are both perfectly happy with cheddar cheese eaten straight from the fridge. If we did decide to move one day, we might have to get married, which I can't say is an idea that I hate. Can you imagine that man in a wedding suit?

"Boys?"

We look up to see Deb walking toward us. I grin at George, then we race over and bundle her into a hug despite her obvious reluctance.

"Oh my god, Deb," says George, "we talk about you all the time! The way you let Lucas follow his heart like that. You're kind of a gay icon among our friends."

Deb looks at George, deadpan. "Bollocks."

We both laugh.

"Who are you here to watch?" I ask.

Deb allows a proud smile to creep onto her face.

"Guess."

By all accounts, my impromptu speech at the Boat Race had a lasting effect on Deb. She not only installed Fran as her first choice cox, but became her mentor, and neither of them have ever looked back. Deb's seat is in a different part of the stands, so we promise to find her afterward and celebrate with Fran whatever the result. As we take our seats and the crews line up, I feel a pang of envy.

"Do you really not miss rowing?" I ask George.

He looks at me in surprise. "No. Do you?"

"Sometimes. People always joked about me doing nothing as cox, but there were so many things to think about."

"Maybe for you. I found it so dull by the end. I mean, compare this to if we were watching a match at Wimbledon. This is just a flat race. No twists and turns."

"But that's the beauty of it. It's so simple. So brutal."

George looks at me, amused by how fired up I am. "Do you honestly think we would have coped if we'd raced against each other in the Boat Race? Would we be here now if one of us had beaten the other?"

I ruffle his hair affectionately. "Speak for yourself. I know I would be."

I don't have to imagine it. George beats me at tennis most weekends. Sometimes I'm mad for a minute, but then he lets me sulk on the way home, buys me a treat at the bakery, and cuddles me on the sofa until I've forgotten all about it.

And that's how I know it was really me who won.

ACKNOWLEDGMENTS

Thank you to my editor TJ Ohler for seeing this story's potential and helping me shape it into something better. Your sharp editorial instincts and love of the genre have allowed me to tap into new pockets of emotion and romantic tension in all sorts of beautiful and unexpected corners, and I can't wait to do this with you all over again. Thank you to Mikayla Butchart and Sara Thwaite for a sensitive copyedit and proofread, and to Sierra Stovall, Molly Stern, and everyone else at Zando for showing faith in my writing and turning it into a book I can hold. Thank you to my agents: Ariele Fredman, Laurie-Maude Chenard, and Paloma Ortega for finding me the perfect home, engaging so closely with multiple drafts, and pushing me to produce my best ideas; Cathryn Summerhayes for sharing my ambition and always being so reassuring and responsive; Jess Molloy and Annabel White for your boundless enthusiasm, hard work, and thoughtful contributions at every stage of the process; and everyone at UTA and Curtis Brown, including Georgie Mellor, Aoife MacIntyre, and Cynthia Okoye, for dreaming big, caring deeply, and making it so much fun to be on the same team.

Thank you to Mark de Rond, author of *The Last Amateurs*, and Daniel Topolski and Patrick Robinson, authors of *True Blue*, which were both invaluable resources in filling in the gaps in my Boat Race knowledge. Any inaccuracies, intentional or otherwise, are on me. Thank you to the authors who inspired me to write in this genre, in particular Alison Cochrun, Jilly Cooper, Sophie Kinsella, and Eva Ibbotson. Thank you to my readers, who motivate me to never settle for shortcuts or clichés and write you the romances you deserve. I can't wait to hand Lucas and George over to you, and I hope you love them as much as I do.

Thank you to all my friends—including Alessandra, Amia, Amrou, Bea, Camilla, Dan, Emily, Farhana, Georgia, Georgie, Grace, Guido, Hatty, Hermione, Hynd, Jack, Jess C, Jess W, Max, Misha, Mursal, Oliver, Peter, Richard, Ricky, Ruth, and Simon—for reminding me what matters most in life, and especially to Sophie for encouragement and support when I really needed it. To my parents, Richard and Tricia; my siblings, Jonny, Chris, and Lizzy; honorary siblings, Emma and Jake; and nephews, Freddie and Jack, for time together that means everything and being so normal that I am forced to invent familial traumas for my characters. Thank you to Snufkin for filling my heart with more love than I thought possible.

Most of all, thank you to my partner, Vincent. Although it is true to say that this book wouldn't exist without you, that phrase somehow conceals rather than reveals the myriad ways in which you helped bring it into being. From having the initial idea in that hotel room in the Azores, to coming up with the title, conceiving fundamental aspects of plot and character, and reading multiple drafts, culminating in the most brutally honest and transformative set of notes I've ever received. But while you have a very real stake in the authorship of this book, your biggest gift was believing in me more than I did and leaving me with the tools to execute my vision. That and loving me with such care, joy, and imagination that nothing feels more instinctive for me to write than a happy ending.

ABOUT THE AUTHOR

ZAC HAMMETT grew up on the south coast of England and lives in London. *See You at the Finish Line* is his debut novel.